FOR JULIE GAIL BOBROWSKI,
IN LOVING MEMORY.

Caught between a single stone and a hard place.
No, that's not it.

A single stone gathers no moss.
Somehow, that's not right either.

You can't get water from a single stone.
Closer, but not yet.

You can't kill two birds with a single stone.
Now, who says so?

A SINGLE STONE

PART ONE

Friday

one

The difference between day and night would be imperceptible, a seamless sliding into deeper darkness. The air had grown heavy with the promise of rain as the first big storm of winter hovered beyond the sandstone cliffs of Pescadero, sixty miles south of San Francisco. Taunting the residents of the small town into hasty purchases of candles, bread, batteries, and milk, the dark clouds crept toward landfall.

At Brothers Market, prestorm shoppers were joined by knots of children in bright slickers. Linda Orett turned the corner into the bread aisle and stopped, transfixed by the three little girls at the check stand. How tender their dimpled wrists below the sleeves of their raincoats; how sweet their white socks, turned precisely along the tops of their identical sneakers. The oldest of the three, a round-cheeked child of about eight, flipped her ponytail off her shoulder and pointed to the jar of Gummi Bears.

Baby shampoo; she *couldn't* be smelling it, not really. *Your imagination is working overtime,* Linda told herself as she dropped a rye bread into the wire cart and continued on her way.

Alert now and on the edge of a carefully constructed happiness, she pushed ahead to the paper goods and stuffed a package of napkins into her shopping cart. It was a good sign that she had come to the market at a time when she knew the children—raucous, giggling, laden with books and rolled-up art projects—would be there. It was evidence of her growing strength that she had not avoided their eyes nor shut out the sounds of their whispers and giggles. She was healing—except for the headaches.

Scanning the shelves for the colors and patterns of familiar labels, Linda brushed a long hair away from her mouth and skimmed her list. A full pantry had always been one of her securities. Certainly she didn't have to change *that* in order to put the past behind her. She hefted a box of laundry detergent into the cart and pushed on toward the perimeter aisles—the real food, with scents that played in your head like music and shifted key as you walked by, food you could see and touch and recognize. The winey apple smells reached her first.

"Hey, Mizz Orett, this gonna be jest a baby blow—no need to buy us out." Nick Talaveros rubbed a Pippin apple on his crisp white sleeve and handed it to her. "A juicy one's good for whatever ails you. Too bad they started putting wax on the dang things. Don't even seem like it come off a tree no more."

Linda took the apple and dipped her head in thanks. What did he mean "Whatever ails you"? Did she seem to him to be ill?

The cilantro looked inviting—full, green, alive. And onions and garlic—she'd need those for dinner. She glanced over her shoulder. Talaveros was whistling and stacking apples. Maybe he'd only meant to say that even if someone were ailing, this good food would take care of them. *I'm fine,* she thought, straining to catch her reflection in the plate glass window as she emptied the groceries onto the check-out counter.

The clerk's Adam's apple bobbed as he rang up each item. Solemnly, he handed Linda her change. "Need any help out, Mrs. Orett?"

She glanced down: only two bags of groceries in her cart. "No. I can manage. Thanks, though," she said, forcing a smile. They ask everyone, as a courtesy, Linda reassured herself.

A long drive through the lush, newly green hills was out of the question right now. Too many perishables. She stowed the bags in the hatchback of her Honda. A quick walk on the beach would have to do.

Booming, the sea pounded the rocks and pushed on toward shore. Linda raised the binoculars, adjusted the focus. Dark specks resolved into the familiar forms of seabirds; darting above the waves, they wheeled away, leaving only water and sky. She turned to the right. A plume of spray; a seething roll of water: a humpback, perhaps, bringing up the rear of a months-long procession of whales to the warmer waters of Mexico.

A massive hulk rose from the sea. Linda held her breath and watched the arch of the animal's back lift out of the water and then slip gracefully from sight, its tail slapping the surface before it submerged. What do the giant mammals do before a storm? She tried to recall the lecture she'd heard three years earlier on the whale-watching expedition.

The day had been blustery and cold, much like today. Amy, her single braid bouncing against the hood of her sweat-shirt, had pushed to the front of the crowd, icy fingers clutching Linda's hand. One after another, the questions had tumbled out. Her round brown eyes opened wide, as though she might miss the answers if she blinked. Where did whales sleep? Were whales ever frightened? How did whale babies recognize their mothers? How did whale mothers know when their babies were sick? The guide, delighted that a six-year-old child provided him an opportunity to show off, invited Amy to come back and be his assistant on another outing. On the drive home, Amy had fought off sleep until she was sure that Linda had written down all her questions. "For next time, Mommy," she mumbled as her head settled onto Linda's lap and her eyes drifted closed.

Linda dropped a hand to her mouth; the binoculars tilted.

There had been no next time. *This is a good memory,* she thought. *Don't push this one away.* She let the binoculars dangle against her chest. A wave hissed at her feet; spangles of sand clung to her hiking boots. Cleansed and tired, Linda pushed a great breath out of her chest and stared at the sea and the lowering clouds until the gleam of an abalone shell caught her eye. She picked it up and ran her finger along the rough edge; it was only a fragment but the iridescent swirls of color traced lovely patterns.

"You gonna pay up or am I gonna have to carry your marker until next spring?"

Bea.

Where had she come from? Of course. You can't hear footsteps on the sand, Linda thought as she whirled around, her surprise already replaced by pleasure at the sight of the familiar blue windbreaker and baggy sweatpants. Bea's round features seemed sharper as she scowled at the wind and pulled a knitted cap down over her ears; only a wisp of gray hair poked out, flattened by a gust against her forehead.

Happy to be drawn into her game—Bea could always do that, right from the first—Linda groaned in mock concern. "I intend to win it all back. Can't be that much, anyway."

"It's written down in the camper, but best I can remember, it's gotta be at least eight hundred, maybe eight fifty. Gin rummy's a dangerous game, girl. I warned you I was *good.*" The wrinkles around Bea's eyes smoothed out as the wind died down; the two women fell into step, following the contours of the sand.

"What did you mean 'next spring'?" *Don't go away,* Linda thought. *I need someone who will talk to me without judging me or wanting to know more about my past.*

Bea shoved her hands into her jacket pockets and nodded. "This storm coming reminded me that Alfie and me bought the camper to be in the warm places when we retired from the fishing business. Even though he's gone, I figure it's my *duty* to go to New Orleans. Can't leave, though, until Smitty gets the damn carburetor fixed. Five, six days, I'd say." Her eyes narrowed and her lips pressed hard together. "You want a hot rum and a talk, honey? Camper's in the parking lot."

No, no talks and no hot rum. Linda had come so close last time to telling Bea everything. Now she didn't have to worry whether or not it was fair to infect Bea with her pain, whether telling her story would mean the end of their friendship. Bea was leaving anyway. The card games, sitting in the camper drinking rum-and-coke and smoking illicit Winstons: there would be no more of that.

"I have to get my groceries home, Bea. Drop me a card or something from New Orleans, okay?"

Bea closed the space between them. "I'm terrible for writing letters but you bone up on your card playing, hear, 'cause I'll be back. April. May. Somewhere in there." She tugged the cap over her ears again. "And I'll come looking to collect that eight hundred."

Linda felt her own smile flicker and then fade. She pushed off against the wet sand to give herself more speed and plodded up the path across the dunes, bucking a stubborn wind and listening to Bea's labored breath. She really *did* have to get back to the L-shaped cottage so that she could put the groceries away and start dinner before Matt got home.

Funny, even Matt had circled her warily this morning, staring intently at her face when he thought she wasn't looking, as though he could keep the darkness away by watching over her more carefully. Maybe he was afraid that she was about to slip back into the abyss she'd fought so hard to escape. Perhaps she wasn't aware of something that everyone else had noticed, some warning signal she was giving off.

When they reached the parking lot, they stopped, chests heaving from the exertion of the climb. The Volkswagen camper, its opaque louvered side windows cranked shut against the storm, huddled beside her Honda.

"Wait right there," Bea hollered, squinting to keep out the blowing sand.

Before Linda could protest, Bea was gone, rubber boots clomping on the asphalt. By the time Linda reached her car, unlocked it, and tossed the binocular case onto the seat, Bea had returned.

"You write down your address and phone number." Bea pointed at a blank space on the cover of a battered tide book and shoved a marbled green-and-black Parker fountain pen into Linda's hand. "I'll need to know when the sun's back in California. You watch out for the sun for Bea."

Linda unscrewed the pen cap, hesitated, then wrote. Maybe Bea would think up some excuse and call her before spring—and maybe she'd start to forget her as soon as she hit the Interstate. Linda returned the pen and the tide book, her fingers brushing the woman's rough hands. "And you drive carefully, okay?"

Bea grinned. "You just want a chance to win back that eight hundred." Her smile disappeared; for a second, Linda was afraid that Bea would grab her and hug her, but instead, she saluted, turned, and climbed into her camper.

Linda waited until the camper rumbled out of the parking lot; then she got into the Honda, snapped on her seat belt, and wished as she made the right turn onto the highway that she had something of Bea's—a deck of cards, one of her porcelain mugs, that blue-and-white crocheted pot holder—to keep over the long winter.

The road twisted back on itself in a hairpin. As the first drops of rain hit the windshield with a splat, she forced herself to concentrate on driving, and tried to bury the gloom of impending loneliness. All winter without Bea, without anyone

. . . except for Matt, and these days his silences were almost worse than being alone.

Unbidden, an image of the three little girls in the market rose before her.

None of them was blond, she told herself. *I'll be all right.* She fed the car more gas; suddenly, she was in a hurry to get home.

—and didn't your mother-in-law become so alarmed that she came to stay with you when your daughter was two weeks old?

(I must hide my hands. I cannot put her down. The chair is hard. The room is spinning.)

—A month after the birth of your daughter, your husband took you to see Dr. Gorchik. What did the doctor find on that visit?

(Find. Nothing to find. Nothing lost yet.)

—Please tell the court . . .

"The past is behind me. I can move forward," she muttered to herself. A single session with a therapist had yielded the suggestion that she use the same words to dispel the scenes every time they came up. She had been skeptical; now, after the millionth repetition, Linda still couldn't believe that she'd ever go one whole day without thinking about it.

As she approached her driveway, she slowed; a spray of pebbles scattered and she steered down the narrow drive, navigating between the rows of eucalyptus trees. The living-room light was on and Matt's van was parked under the bay tree. She coasted in to the spot beside the rickety potting shed.

Rain beat down steadily, a fine metallic pinging that threatened to revive her dying headache. Icy water stung her cheeks as she gathered the grocery bags and ran to the house, staggering into the kitchen with her bundles. Even with all the lights on, it felt oppressive, and she thought again that next week, soon anyway, she'd pull down all the old wallpaper. It was gray with a dark lattice pattern and even darker ivy climbing all over; sometimes, she felt pursued in that room, as though the ivy might leap from the walls and twine itself around her.

Matt's sonorous bass carried from under the spray of the shower. Linda slid the sacks out of her arms and onto the kitchen counter, listening to identify the song so that she could join in with the alto line. When they met fifteen years ago at tryouts for the Oakland Community Players production of *Oklahoma,* neither of them could have predicted where they'd be today.

He was singing the Lachrymosa. Mozart. Why the Requiem? Why today? She might go along for days, maybe even weeks, with the sense that she finally had everything in its proper place—and then suddenly she'd be flooded with new images, pictures so intense that she would hardly have time to recover her equilibrium before the next barrage that always began with the same question.

How could anyone think I murdered my own child?

two

Of course, she thought with a sigh. *I'm feeling this way because it's almost her birthday.*

Thanksgiving and Amy's birthday, all within two days of each other. It was too much. Even the year Amy was born, the excess had been apparent.

"If you go into labor tonight, dear, you're going to regret having so much in your digestive system." Matt's mother, Gladys, always talked like that: she had a digestive system, not a belly; she masticated her food instead of chewing it, as though bodies required clinical discussion and vernacular language was unseemly. But she had been right about one thing: when Linda's contractions started the next morning, it felt as though she would expel a large stuffed turkey instead of a baby.

Gladys was always generous with her advice.

—Linda, you have to face this. Having a baby changes every-thing—your career, your personal freedom, even your body. But motherhood is an honor. Now, pull yourself together and comb your hair.

(If you would just leave me alone, you'd be doing her a favor. Take the child with you. The walls are closing in on me.)

—I'll make coffee. You wouldn't want Matt to see you still in bed at three in the afternoon, now would you?

(Matt. Linda. Amy. So tired. Take the food away. Arms won't move. Legs won't hold me.)

And Gladys was still alive, while Amy . . . No, that wasn't fair, even though Gladys had been no comfort in those confused weeks after Amy's birth. If her own mother hadn't died two years before Amy was born, *she* would have known what to do. Even Bea, childless and brusque, would have done better. Gladys kept insisting, in her quiet, infuriating way, so controlled, so correct, that Linda would snap out of it as soon as she decided she *wanted* to. Dr. Gorchik suggested that Linda was *conflicted* about motherhood or *angry* over the loss of career momentum or *ambivalent* about her own sexuality. The worst of it was not understanding, the guilt, the worry that she wasn't trying hard enough.

Thank God Dr. Tress ordered the tests, to determine whether the problem had originated in Linda's body. She prescribed hormone therapy. And within eight weeks, motherhood became a mixed blessing instead of an undiluted curse.

And then later that bitch of an assistant DA, so eager to demonstrate that she wasn't going to be soft simply because the defendant was also a woman, had twisted the doctor's testimony and made it the linchpin of her case against Linda.

"That you, Linnie?" Matt's voice floated out of the bathroom on clouds of scented steam.

"You expected Greta Garbo, maybe?" Linda poured the coffee beans into a glass jar, stacked oranges in the straw basket, let go of the bad memories.

Suddenly, he was behind her, his wet hair brushing her ear as he kissed her neck and then buried his face in her hair. "Mmm. Tasty." His lips lingered on a spot below her ear, raising goose bumps on her arms.

It was so like him to pick a time when she was in the middle of something, a time when they hadn't spoken or touched each other in days. She would make the effort to meet him part way. But not until they'd had dinner and talked to each other like normal people, about the day, about their plans and their past. She took a half step forward, away from Matt's grasp, and turned to kiss him on the cheek. "That's the appetizer. Dessert later, after the fish soup."

A shadow crossed his face and he smiled and sniffed the air above the empty soup pot. "Fish soup. That's for peasants. *We're* having bouillabaisse." He pressed against her, his chest and thighs solid, protective as he drew her closer.

Not yet. She pulled back, frowning. "Later, Matt."

His body stiffened as tiny lines around his eyes deepened; then he shrugged and padded out of the kitchen. Linda reached for a large onion and peeled off the skin, scored the flesh, and started chopping it on the wooden board. Her eyes burned and teared. *Damn onion,* she thought, blotting the trickle on her cheek with the sleeve of her sweatshirt.

Outside, the eucalyptus tree shook ribbons of rain onto the muddy ground. Would they remember how to have a conversation? When they first moved here, nineteen months ago, they talked about the garden, about Matt's carpentry jobs or the books she had taken from the library. Lately, dinner had become a silent affair. After the dishes were done, she puttered with her plants in the little shed while Matt disappeared into the back room to work on his sculptures.

Those sculptures. Linda poured a stream of olive oil into the pot and wondered. He had put a padlock on the studio door, claiming that this tiny house made him feel crowded, that he needed privacy. To Linda, it seemed more like secrecy than privacy, but they had been through so much that she couldn't quite confront him with the distinction.

From the bedroom, muffled sounds of dresser drawers and closet doors stuttered through the silence. Uneasy, Linda reached a trembling hand to turn on the radio; the familiar sound of Bob Marley's voice drifted from the black box as the backup chorus sang about justice and God's love. She had heard enough about God's love to last her a lifetime. Amy is happy now in His love, they said. God gives you only what you can bear and His love keeps you strong, they told her. *Fuck off,* she wanted to scream at the radio, but she fiddled with the dial until she found the jazz station.

The onion pieces twitched and jumped when they landed in the hot oil. Linda examined the garlic head—cloves skinny and brown-spotted, but that was all you could expect this time of year. She broke off four, smashed her hand against the broad blade of the cleaver so that the skins split, peeled off the papery covering, and minced the meat.

The muscles across her shoulders bunched into knots when she heard Matt's footsteps behind her.

"You ought to go into Santa Cruz, buy yourself something nice to wear." He finished buttoning a blue workshirt and leaned against the sink. "Something pink or yellow. Bright."

Now it was her clothes. All summer it had been her hair. Maybe next he would tell her that her breasts were too small or her nose the wrong shape.

"I like my clothes," Linda said softly. "I've always liked pale colors, muted colors, earth tones. I like my hair. I like it long and blond and curly, just the way it grows out of my head." It felt good to build to a shout. "And you know what? I'm not going to change any of it."

As if to justify the shudder that passed through her, the wind howled and tossed needles of rain against the window. A husky, insistent saxophone solo filled the air. Linda lowered her voice so that Matt wouldn't hear the tremor of anxiety. "Pass me the anisette, would you?"

Matt pulled the bottle from the shelf and handed it to her. "Well, since you're so busy chopping and seasoning, maybe I should wait to tell you."

Another game. Why didn't he just say what was on his mind and be done with it? She shook her head, vaguely aware that she was coloring everything he said with a negative tint. It made her angry when he didn't talk to her but then when he did, she was annoyed at what he said or how he said it. She wasn't being fair.

"Maybe you *should* wait," she said, half-smiling. With the light behind him like that, the extra padding around his waist melted away, the work-hardened muscles of his arms and legs softened, the lines on his face disappeared, and he was twenty-two again and she ached with a memory of the time when their only burden was restraint. "Okay, what do you want to tell me? Do you have any idea how *smug* you look, Matthew Orett?"

"Tonight, you will be dining with the architect with a commission to design an extension for the Minetta house."

She ignored the tinny buzzing in her head; it wasn't fair to let her apprehensions mar his excitement. "Matt, that's wonderful. When do you start? How big a job is it? Tell me everything."

He began in a rush. "Carpentry was all right for a while but I don't need that kind of physical outlet any more. My brain is beginning to atrophy, definitely not good for the old self-esteem." He laughed, a bitter sound. Then he took her hand and fixed his gaze on her face. "I need to make things happen, to create spaces that are right for the people who use them. So when I heard Joey Minetta talking about enlarging his house, I drew up some plans. He phoned today and said let's do it."

Linda stirred the soup. *Be positive.* "You sound so happy. That's really terrific."

"Good," he said, the pulse on his temple throbbing, "because after I showed him some old sketches of yours, Joey asked if you'd do the landscape design."

She tried to catch her breath. He had no right . . . No, that wasn't it. She just wasn't ready. How could he not see that? She still couldn't trust herself to spend an hour in the Minetta house, never knowing when the sound of a child's voice would come rolling in from another room. Maybe she needed something besides her garden and the potting shed to occupy her, but not that. No, she wasn't ready.

"Sorry," she whispered. "I don't know if I can do it yet."

Matt gripped her shoulders. The tips of his fingers pressed hard through the layers of her clothing. "The first time's going to be the worst, but once you start you'll do fine. Besides, I have the feeling Minetta's counting on a package deal."

"Don't blackmail me, Matt. I need some time. . . ."

"Just consider it until Sunday and then if you're still not sure, I'll let it go."

Nothing's going to change between now and Sunday, she thought. Still, she nodded. Two days of peace. She could buy that much. Maybe she would even do the job. She simply needed more time to prepare than Matt thought she would.

"I want you to promise me, Linda. Promise you'll think about it."

How childish of him to make such a demand. She wasn't going to argue about what she would or wouldn't think about. "I already said that I would. Isn't that good enough for you?"

"I'll set the table." Matt grabbed up spoons and knives and shoved the silverware drawer closed with his hip.

There—he was doing it again, refusing to acknowledge that she'd said something. Linda scraped away a patch of dirt from a long, twisted carrot and then slammed it on the cutting board.

Matt didn't look at her when he came back into the kitchen.

She had to do something to defuse the hostility; she'd never be able to sit at the table and calmly eat her soup if this knot in her stomach didn't dissolve. "Things going okay with the Sharpe house?" she offered.

"Outer wall is sealed and the window's in. He thinks I

should work as fast as he talks. They're nice people, though. He used to run an ad agency in Orange County." Matt stuck his hands in his back pockets and tilted his head, an invitation for her to go on.

Maybe it would be all right, after all. "Half the people around here 'used to' something, you know? Maybe they're all seduced by the quiet. It's certainly more restful than Oakland was. And I like not having to look over my shoulder to see where the competition is. I like not worrying about whether my clothes and my car are right or if the doors are bolted."

"Are you saying that you like your current life so much that you don't want to do the Minetta job?"

If she had something to say, she'd say it. "It just seems like a saner way to live, that's all. I've made some discoveries in the past year and a half. It's okay for me not to want to push myself and make more money and have more responsibility."

"It's not okay for me. I'm an architect. I can't tread water forever."

And you wish we had our old life back. Before everything changed. It's not my fault, she screamed inside. *Don't make it my fault.*

She couldn't fight Matt any longer. Anything, everything else—the memories, the headaches—she could fight them. But not Matt. He was all she had. "I know it's different here. I just thought you were comfortable, too."

He glared. "Comfortable? You call giving up everything that made you happy—your work, your friends, volunteering at the museum, De Niro movies, the theater group, beating everyone at darts—you call that being comfortable? You call neglecting your appearance so that you look like a fisherman's wife comfortable? Living in this backwater—that's your idea of heaven?"

He had it all wrong. Maybe at first that's how it was. Not now. She simply felt better here, more in tune with the world.

"Truce." She held out her hand, waiting for him to grasp her fingers. He didn't move. "Matt," she whispered.

They stood facing off; they'd been here before, right up to the edge, almost ready to say the things they should. In the silence, Linda became aware that the music had stopped. News time. Automatically, she reached up to change the station again.

"Stop," Matt hissed. He grabbed her wrist too tightly.

The announcer's voice boomed in her head.

". . . the murder of seven-year-old Marianne Brandon. Lieutenant McNaughton added that the Oakland Police Department is warning parents to be on the alert for strangers behaving suspiciously around schools, parks, and playgrounds."

Her stomach heaved and she just made it to the sink in time. She vomited, then ran the water full force as she turned on the disposal.

If only she'd had some warning. If only there had been some sign—from the police, from God, from somewhere—then she could have watched over her child. As her trial dragged on, she had questioned whether she could have prevented Amy's death. She had felt somehow accountable. Then she'd even begun to wonder whether someone could do something so awful and not know about it.

". . . similarities in the case of little Amy Crell, whose mother, Linda, was acquitted of the child's murder for lack of sufficient evidence."

Linda picked up the wooden spoon, dipped it into the bubbling soup, stirred, lifted it out again. *The past is behind me. I can move forward,* she told herself as a teardrop of tomato broth fell onto the stove with a plop.

three

"Yeah, I got all my books and assignments from the teacher. She says even though it's only third grade, we have to have homework over the weekend. But it's dumb. It's not a real vacation without you, Papa. And what about Thanksgiving?" Julio sat on the edge of his bed, a brontosaurus poster making a green halo behind his dark head.

Thanksgiving: Sergeant Carlos Cruz felt his stomach twist. The only holiday he cared about, the day families came from all over the goddam country to be together—he hated the thought of missing Thanksgiving.

"So you think I should go to Santa Cruz with you and Carlito and Mama even if the lieutenant asks me to stay and help find out who killed Marianne Brandon?" Cruz spoke softly as he studied his son's round face.

The boy fixed his eyes on a speck of lint on the tan corduroy bedspread and said nothing.

Rumors had been flying all day: The mayor was leaning on the chief; the chief was putting pressure on McNaughton to prove to the public that the Oakland Police Department wouldn't let a child-killer walk the streets; McNaughton was canceling all time off. Carlos Cruz knew that everyone in Homicide was as anxious to wrap up this case as the mayor and the chief and the public were. So was he—but Carlito and Julio and

Elenya felt bad that he would be missing this vacation. When he got really honest, he didn't like the idea much, either.

Julio squirmed and sucked his lips, tried to hide the signs of his vulnerability—a quivering mouth, the tears that brightened his lower lashes.

"Hijo, I asked you a question."

"No, Papa. I think you should stay. But I don't want to go without you." The boy's sagging shoulders rose and his eyes snapped open with sudden understanding. "The killer won't be able to get me or Carlito if we're in Santa Cruz, right?"

Cruz hugged his son's small-boned body. "Julio, that's not why you and Mama and Carlito are going. Mama's classes are over and she's about to start a new computer project at work. She won't get any more time off until way after the summer."

They'd made reservations at the Seaspray Motel, two hours south of San Francisco: eight cabins, each with an ocean view, a fireplace, and a private hot tub on a fenced deck. Rain wouldn't stop them; they'd bundle up in coats and hats, tramp on the beach, sit by a crackling fire—except that he wouldn't be there at all unless there was a quick break in the Brandon case.

"I'll drive down as soon as I can. Meanwhile, you guys'll be good to Mama, help her have fun, right?"

"You think she'll want to climb those cliffs we saw last year?" Julio liked to have plans; he'd always been happiest with a schedule, even as an infant. No demand feedings for him.

Cruz laughed. "She might."

"Papa, will you help me pack? I could do it myself, but if you help, then we can talk about . . . stuff."

Cruz felt his chest tighten; he was missing his family already and they weren't even gone yet. "I have to go to that special meeting now. You ask Carlito to help you. One suitcase each—that's the limit."

Julio nodded, his black-brown eyes staring intently, as though he were trying to store up a memory of his father's face.

Cruz turned away from his child's disappointment and walked toward the light at the other end of the short hallway.

Elenya sat in the corner of the curve-backed sofa, both feet resting on the marble coffee table they'd bought at a San Jose garage sale when they were first married. Wisps of her thick hair escaped from the clips holding it off her face as she bent toward the needle and thread.

"Julio says he'll make sure you have a good time." Cruz leaned down to kiss the top of his wife's head.

"Not the same," Elenya said, stabbing the needle into the cloth and pulling it through the tiny button hole. "I've gotten used to the idea. It'll be kind of nice having them all to myself."

A pang of jealousy stabbed at Cruz. Couldn't she say something about missing him?

"I hate it that you're missing your vacation, *quierido*. If you can't get away for Thanksgiving, we'll come home. A couple of hours is all we need if you can get away."

First I want to be able to give thanks that we nailed the bastard, Cruz thought as he looked at his watch. "I got to go. The briefing starts in twenty minutes."

"Wake me if I'm asleep and you want to talk when you get back. Maybe if you talk about it . . ." Elenya pushed the needle down again.

"Talking won't change anything," Cruz muttered.

"Mama, can I take my Dungeons and Dragons stuff?" Carlito's voice, hoarse with fatigue, carried from the back of the apartment.

"Don't answer him," Cruz said. "He's ten years old and he's got to stop shouting like that."

Elenya nodded, then pulled the needle through the fabric.

Cruz trudged down the hall and stood in the doorway watching his sons as they lay on their stomachs reading comic books.

He'd seen that look on Elenya's face so many times, telling

him that he mustn't expect his sons to be perfect. They were good boys and he'd never hit them—except for that time last April when Carlito took a five-dollar bill from the dresser where Cruz emptied his pockets every night. Cruz found the bill hidden in a stack of Monopoly money. The boy denied it at first; finally, he admitted taking the money, but before all the words were out, Cruz slapped Carlito's face hard enough to leave a red imprint of his hand on the tender skin of his oldest son.

That was all, but for a second he saw how it *might* have been: So easy to lose control and pummel the small body until his anger was exhausted. Cruz felt a sick horror in his gut that he recognized as shame.

"How's the injury?" He touched the soft skin surrounding the bandage on Carlito's knee.

Carlito shrugged. "Fine." He buried his head in the Batman comic again.

"Better than the bike. Mama says it won't be fixed until next week." The repairs would cost almost as much as a new bike. If Carlito hadn't been wearing his helmet when he hit the asphalt . . . but he had. There was no point in making such a fuss about something that hadn't happened.

Julio untangled himself from the covers and hopped out of bed. "I'm gonna stay here with you, Papa." He grabbed a sweatshirt from the pile of clothes in the open suitcase, as though he were going to unpack everything he'd just so diligently packed.

"Whoa. Listen up, guys. Both of you are going with Mama. If I have to stay and work, then that's what I'll do, and if I can, I'll come spend some time with you. End of discussion."

Cruz flashed a thumbs up sign and a smile to his sons and turned toward the door before they could see the patches of red that flamed on his cheeks.

. . .

The Homicide room was dead silent. Morella tapped a pencil in the air above his desk; he slumped in his chair as though he were carrying the fifty pounds he'd lost last year in an invisible sack on his shoulders. Webster pointed to the thick report. Morella leaned closer, shook his head, and went back to his pencil-tapping. All done in silence, without expression.

Nodding to his partner, Carlos Cruz slid quickly into his chair. Jay Goldstein looked up, his eyes reflecting the deep blue of his sweater. It looked expensive but then Goldstein could probably make a Fruit of the Loom undershirt look like a luxury item.

"Hey, man, any word?" Cruz swiveled to face Goldstein.

Goldstein slipped the papers into a folder. "The bastard was careful—no prints on the doll, no witnesses, no nothing."

Cruz tried to hide his embarrassment. He'd been asking about whether time off was being canceled. Christ, how could he think about vacation now?

Erikson looked up from his report. "Hey, Professor, your shrink pal have any ideas about this case?"

"She's out of town." Goldstein flipped through a date book, then returned it to his jacket pocket. "She'll be back on Monday. I've got a call in to her."

"Maybe we'll have it wrapped up by then. You hear anything about your vacation, Cruz?" Sergeant Tina Cavessena's pink fingernails tapped a steady rhythm on the green felt blotter on her desk.

Cruz shook his head; it was harder than he'd figured, getting used to having Cavessena around. In the two months since McNaughton added the new team to the Homicide squad, Cruz had caught himself tiptoeing around at least a hundred times because Cavessena was a woman. Pain in the ass, really.

"Cruz."

She *was* pissed. Oh, jeez, this was turning into a drag.

"What, Cavessena?" He still couldn't decide whether to call her Tina or Cavessena.

"They never found the slimeball, right, who killed that other little kid . . . what was her name?" When she concentrated like that, her mouth made a funny circle, like she was going to blow a smoke ring.

"Crell. Amy Crell. Still in the open file. Also blond, also seven years old, and also in Oakland."

A grimace twisted Cavessena's face. "And the dolls. Shit, that's creepy, thinking of some slime going into a toy store and buying how many of these identical dolls and cutting these neat little Xs in their chests. . . ."

She'd come from Robbery and Assault—lots of blood and bruises but not as much out-and-out weirdness. She'd get used to it, they all did. "Stab wound's about the same. One knife thrust. Only one," Cruz said, his swinging foot banging against the leg of his desk.

"What about the mother? Didn't she walk on a technicality?" Cavessena made a neat pile of paper clips on her desk.

"Acquitted. Jury found reasonable doubt."

"What do you think?"

"Price and Erikson—it was their case. The mother sure looked like a good bust to me. You ask me, the mother *and* the father acted weird, but the mother—her prints on the knife, her strangeness when the kid was born . . . Maybe Herron got too eager and pushed it without enough preparation. I don't know."

"Anyone talk to her lately?"

"Which her, Tina?" Cruz let himself relax; they were cops and Tina Cavessena was a good one. Before she could answer, Morella hauled himself out of his chair, cursing as a splinter snagged the one pair of pants that he'd bought after his weight loss.

"All right, you guys. Pay attention. We got some things to go over before the lieutenant comes in."

Cruz shifted his chair so that he couldn't see Cavessena; this was her first departmental crisis and she didn't need him checking her out every second. He focused on the front of the room. Morella's sagging face looked even worse than usual and his hands were shaking as though he hadn't slept last night. He probably hadn't.

"Webster and me want you to know that we appreciate your good work. Toll-free number is activated and the press is getting the word out. And we got two exclusive fax lines. We gotta keep the information moving, you know? The city is freaked out, the mayor is freaked out, and I'm freaked out. This is a righteous case, guys, and we all wanna make it before Thanksgiving."

"Hey, Morella, why do me and Price have to spend so much time checking the park for witnesses? That's a bunch of crap and a waste. We already talked to the four people who—"

"Zip it, Erikson." Lieutenant McNaughton, with his usual perfect timing, appeared in the doorway, his pipe smoking furiously as he puffed away. Not a good sign. "Morella and Webster are in charge—they were catching and it's their case and they've made their assignments. You have a suggestion, write it up. Meanwhile, we've got a lot to cover. What we don't need is prima donnas, you understand?"

Cruz groaned inwardly; McNaughton was going to deliver his number about being team players, and that could only lead to one thing.

"Okay, here's the story." Morella ran a hand over his drooping mouth and stared at the wall behind their heads. "Unless you got a line on who owned that necklace—"

"It's called a *cameo,* Morella," Cavessena corrected.

"Okay, that *cameo,* then we got squat right now for leads, and Oakland is going apeshit. They want something and they want it yesterday. Drive-by shootings and barroom beatings, okay. Two assholes cutting each other on a street corner, no big deal. But kids . . . We just got the lab report back. At least we know that there was no sexual violation."

Silence covered all the small sounds; Cruz felt the knot in his stomach go a little slack.

"The autopsy showed pretty much what we expected—kid died as a result of a stab wound, right through the heart. Single knife thrust," Morella said, his voice falling off.

"Time of death?" Jay Goldstein's blue eyes narrowed the way they did when he was putting together pieces of a puzzle. It was an expression that, after five years as his partner, Cruz finally recognized. It had to do with concentration, not snobbishness.

"Coroner says between three, three-thirty, and five, but we already knew that."

Marianne Brandon was last seen leaving school at 2:40 P.M. yesterday. Two kids found the doll, practically tripped over the body, and raced to a pay phone and called 911 at 5:07. That was all in the first bulletin—and they still didn't have much more.

"What about the doll?" Jim Quinn, his freckles reddening, looked up from his notes.

"The doll's a key," Webster said. "Torso's been slashed in a crude X, exactly like the doll found beside the Crell child. Dolls are identical. Except for the cameo on this one. Laffco's Smiling Suzy. They sell a thousand pieces a month, six, seven thousand between now and Christmas. Have for six years."

Cavessena's nose wrinkled. "Didn't Linda Crell claim that she never saw the doll before?"

Morella nodded. "Irene Brandon says Marianne didn't have one like it, either. If they're both telling the truth, it's the killer's signature, like. But it's possible one of the parents is lying, you know?"

"I hope we nail Crell *good* this time." Erikson laced his

fingers behind his head and tipped back on his chair. "Yeah, beautiful."

Morella passed around a stack of papers. "We got these old photos. We're trying to locate them, but so far they seem to have pulled some sort of disappearing act. So Cavessena, Quinn, that's your main priority. But we all have to stay alert on all the angles, right?"

No one bothered to answer; they knew Morella didn't expect a response.

Cruz glanced over at Cavessena, who was scribbling in a small red leather notepad. *Amazing,* he thought. *Her fingernails hardly get in the way.*

"Goldstein and Cruz, you guys are gonna be our liaisons with this volunteer center over on Claremont. Mostly teachers and lawyers, like that—all hyped about the community helping to protect their kids, you know?"

"Obviously," McNaughton said, "that means that your vacation is canceled, Cruz. I'm sorry, but it can't be helped."

Carlos Cruz nodded and swallowed hard. "Can't be helped, sir," he said. "I agree."

four

Community councils: the Greeks, the Sioux, a lot of societies dealt with their problems that way, Jay Goldstein thought. But judging from tonight's meager turnout, most of Oakland's residents wanted no part of such responsibility.

A dozen people milled around the cold, poorly lit storefront, dispirited little groups dissolving and reforming in different combinations. Cruz, talking to a worried-looking couple, might have been just another concerned parent himself. Two men and a woman were unfolding the legs of an aluminum table; two teenage girls were stacking flyers on a black metal desk. A grandmotherly type was making coffee. At least all this activity made the participants feel better, Goldstein thought.

He studied the photo of the Brandon girl on the flyer that was taped to the wall. When he first saw her picture in the Homicide room, she was generic, an idea of a little girl. He had stared at the picture, not hearing what Webster and Morella were saying about the progress of the investigation. Finally, the tilt of her mouth, the extra wide space between her nose and her upper lip, the way her honey-colored hair swung away from her face, the solemn eyes that seemed to be preparing for the burdens of adulthood—these merged to form Marianne Brandon. Unexpectedly, Goldstein had felt a profound sorrow.

He imagined her watching a younger child being teased at

school. She would defend the victim; she had the eyes of a warrior, an upholder of principles.

This case would surely affect the objective/subjective balance he'd been struggling to achieve since he studied philosophy at Stanford. Lately, he'd begun to suspect that balance wasn't the desirable commodity he'd once sought. This time, for example, he had the sense that he should encourage his *feelings,* not his ideas, to lead him.

He approached the long table; a man in his late thirties, fine platinum hair combed straight back, sat hunched toward a pile of paper. An ethereal paleness emanated from the ivory of his skin, his amber eyes, and his cream-colored sweater; he stared up at Goldstein.

"I'm Sergeant Jay Goldstein. Oakland Police Department."

"I'm Dexter Williams." His index finger pressed down on the top sheet of paper; it was a neatly labeled drawing of a human eye. A childish signature sprawled across the bottom of the page.

Teachers and cops, Goldstein thought. *Always taking their work home.* "I'm looking for Charlotte Wertz. Could you point her out to me?"

Williams jerked his head back and then leaned, squinting, toward the circle of people in the center of the room. "Charlotte should stand right out, small group like this. She'd be the tall, dark-haired one, about thirty, thirty-two. What has to happen around here before people get mad enough to do something?" He waved his own question away and pointed to a lean, athletic-looking man in an Eisenhower jacket, slouched against the other long table set up along the rear wall. "Maybe you can talk to Albert Toller. He always makes it his business to know what's going on."

Goldstein nodded and threaded his way between empty chairs to the other side of the room. "Mr. Toller?"

Forehead wrinkled in concentration, the man wrote rapidly

on a yellow legal pad. The emblem sewn onto the shoulder of his jacket sported a lion and a flag. The jacket itself resembled an old seventies SWAT team affair: short, zippered, with a plush collar, slash pockets, and knit cuffs. "Mr. Toller, I'm Jay Goldstein from the Oakland Police Department. Have a minute?"

Toller's eyebrows raised as he tilted his head toward Goldstein. His hazel eyes, magnified by tortoise shell glasses, lit up. "Sure. But can we make it quick? I have to write up these calls and get the list of volunteers in order. Got a lot to do."

"I appreciate that. I'll try to keep it brief." Goldstein nodded. "You're in charge here?"

"Oh, no. That's Charlotte." Toller glanced at his watch, a digital affair busy with displays and buttons. "But if I can help you—show you around, tell you about our little group, whatever —I'll make the time. What do you need, Sergeant?"

"Actually, it's Miss Wertz I need to see right now. If you could find her for me . . ."

"There she is, talking to Mrs. Silcock and Mr. Hall." Toller pointed with his head to the middle of the room, then pushed his glasses up on his nose.

There was no question that the woman in the dark skirt and purple silk blouse was Charlotte Wertz. The pair beside her maintained their distance, as though she'd marked a boundary they didn't dare cross. Charlotte Wertz tracked his approach with her gray-green eyes, obviously doing some mental assessment of her own.

"Miss Wertz? I'm Sergeant Jay Goldstein, Oakland Police Department." He was beginning to sound like a broken record, but he had to say it. How many times until this one was over? How many introductions until they found Marianne Brandon's murderer?

"What can I do for you, Sergeant Goldstein?" Her voice was rich with a practiced but distant cordiality, a pure patrician

"Screw you" tone that people like his father acquired after years of getting their own way.

Goldstein was glad that he was wearing his wing tips and not the loafers he'd first put on this morning. "My partner and I have been assigned to work with the volunteers, to be the liaisons between OPD and this group. For now, we want to get familiar with your procedures. We want your people to get used to us."

Moving as though she were completely comfortable in her own skin, Charlotte Wertz reached up to touch a clip that held her dark hair at the nape of her neck. "Is there something specific I can do for you right now?"

Meaning, let's skip the small stuff so I can get back to work? He was in for a bit of a battle, he could see. "I'm interested in the way you're handling phone calls. I'd like you to show me your system for gathering and reporting information. That sort of thing."

"Put it over there near the window," she directed a bewildered white-haired man who was standing with a typewriter in his hands. "Over here," she called to the young man struggling with a large, wet cardboard box. "Good people. They really care. Fine. Our system is just fine."

Goldstein lowered his voice and took a step back, giving Charlotte Wertz more territory, allowing the illusion that she'd achieved a victory. "I do have some questions, but first I'd like you to show me your reporting protocol."

Charlotte Wertz's aristocratic face remained impassive. "I've already got the forms worked out. If this is to be a true community effort, the community has to run the show. I've seen this kind of thing disintegrate when people felt they were being coopted." From deep in her briefcase, she pulled out a letter opener and, with a single deft stroke, slit the tape on the box. She tossed yellow legal pads onto the table, then stopped to neaten the pile.

Goldstein lay his hand across the stack. "What procedures have you established, Miss Wertz, for your phone people?"

Charlotte cocked an eyebrow and straightened; back erect, she marched to the only desk with a functioning phone. Goldstein followed her. A paper taped to the corner of the desk asked for date, time, name, gender, phone number, and address of the caller. Several lines were left blank; the heading INFO preceded the empty space.

"Everyone who takes calls records all this information. Charlotte led the training sessions this morning." Dexter Williams appeared behind them; his eerily pale face shone with pride as he beamed down at Charlotte. "She said we should get callers to slow down, to give details about everything. She told us to keep the caller talking for at least five minutes, to get as much information as possible."

"And it's been working, so far. I'll show you today's reports. All quite detailed." Charlotte cast a sweeping glance around the room. "We may be a small group but we're extremely motivated, Sergeant Goldstein."

Charlotte Wertz's involvement in this volunteer effort went beyond simple neighborly concern; what *else* was she doing here? Goldstein put the question aside for the moment. "Miss Wertz, what you've set up is fine, but we need the name of the volunteer taking each call. Sometimes we need additional information and—"

"That was an oversight on my part." Charlotte colored under her makeup. "I'll see that Al Toller tells the others. You said you had questions." Her features again composed, she faced Goldstein; only her eyes flitted around the room, unable to settle into stillness.

"Well, first I'd like to know if you're related to the Brandon child."

"No. We live on the same block. Marianne—" She hesitated. "Marianne used to come visit me when she felt lonely."

"Lonely? What do you mean?"

"She was a latchkey kid, you know. No father. Her mother worked until five, didn't get home until six, and Marianne went to after-school programs three days a week. Even those programs are over by four-thirty. She had nowhere to go the other two days, except maybe the library or other kids' houses, if that was arranged in advance. Irene Brandon used to talk about being worried that she couldn't be around for Marianne, but she had to support both of them so—"

"So you befriended Marianne."

Charlotte's voice dropped to a whisper. "Marianne said she wanted to be like me when she grew up. She thought it was neat that I didn't have boring things to keep me busy all the time."

"What does that mean? What boring things?"

"I'm not married, I have no kids, no pets, no commitments. Except to my work."

"Which is?" Why would this woman be at home in the middle of the day when a schoolgirl was looking for company and a place to go?

"I'm a stockbroker. I used to teach high-school biology, if you can believe that. Now I work East Coast hours at the Pacific Stock Exchange and I'm usually home by three. Just like a teacher, right? But I have more—more time, more money, more respect. Anyway, I read, play the piano, study corporate reports. So I'm around." She fixed her stare on his face. "Any other questions?"

We'll see, Goldstein thought. "I'd like to check out the reports, the ones from earlier today."

The contours beneath Charlotte Wertz's skirt shifted as she leaned over and pulled a folder out of a cardboard box. "This is everything since we started taking calls."

Fewer than thirty sheets were fastened by a paper clip to

the inside cover of the folder she handed him. Business had been slow.

"I'm going to read these over there." Goldstein pointed his head toward an isolated corner. "Thanks for the information." Her handshake, as he expected, was firm—and quickly withdrawn as she went off, neat and self-contained, to deal with the next problem.

He settled himself into a cold metal chair and flipped quickly through the papers. Many of the reports described the five characters who had been hauled in for questioning this morning. All five were homeless, jobless, hopeless. And all of them had been six miles away at the Eastside Baptist Church food giveaway program from three to four-thirty on Thursday afternoon.

One caller reported seeing a nervous-looking man lift a bundle into a van—no color, no year, no model—two blocks from Lake Merritt.

Another said that three teenagers wearing red bandanas were displaying switchblade knives on the perimeter path of the lake. What else was new?

A man with a long ponytail and blue knit cap was spotted in a dented convertible, speeding away from the lake. Another unremarkable piece of information.

A caller saw a woman stumbling around the lake. When asked to describe her, he'd hung up.

All useless. So far.

A minor bustle of activity distracted him; two volunteers were pushing metal chairs into a line. Cruz disengaged from Mrs. Silcock, a gray-haired, pinch-faced woman who was punctuating her monologue with lots of finger-shaking. Herded together like this, the group looked very small. They sat stiffly in their chairs as Charlotte Wertz strode to the front of the room. Goldstein stretched, set the reports on the table, then leaned against the wall. The old woman had a firm grip on someone's sleeve and was continuing her *sotto voce* harangue; Cruz escaped to a seat at the far end of the row.

Low murmurs trailed into silence as Charlotte Wertz began to speak. "Thank you for coming out in the rain. Now, if each of you brings in at least two new people tomorrow, we can get the job done. And we really need a file cabinet. But there *is* good news. The Oakley Corporation has given us two weeks rent free in this space, and the office supply company promises to keep us in legal pads and pens." Polite applause acknowledged her achievements. "Oh, and I'd like you to meet Sergeant Carlos Cruz."

Cruz rose, nodded at the crowd, then sat down on the edge of his chair.

"And this is Sergeant Jay Goldstein. If you've got any questions for these gentlemen, now's the time to ask."

Goldstein scanned the group, careful not to avoid their eyes yet wary of seeming to linger too long in challenge.

"We've heard rumors. Is it true that you've identified a suspect but you haven't arrested him yet? We have a right to know." Mrs. Silcock, her cheeks splotched and her back rigid, sputtered and coughed.

Concerned murmurs rose from the other volunteers. *Just choking on her frustration,* Goldstein thought, making his way to the older woman. "She's okay. Move back and give her a little breathing room," he ordered as the other volunteers pressed forward.

"Back off now and let Sergeant Goldstein take care of Mrs. Silcock."

Grateful for the unexpected support, Goldstein glanced at the speaker. It was Toller, with his runner's legs planted firmly in an inverted V and his smart, searching eyes staring down the onlookers from behind his glasses.

"Hey, Toller, who put you in charge?" Dexter Williams muttered.

Someone handed Goldstein a paper cup of water; he passed it to Mrs. Silcock, surprised at the cool and silky feel of her skin. Her color was more even now, the glint in her pale eyes returning with each noisy breath. She sipped the water, dabbed at her mouth.

"Feeling better?" Goldstein asked.

"I'll feel better when they catch the scum and . . ." She nodded. "I'm all right, Charlotte."

Charlotte Wertz patted the woman's hand. "Good, Zena. You had me worried for a minute."

"What about the doll, Goldstein?" Now Dexter Williams took a turn; his voice was strained and his right hand flailed in the air. "The *Tribune* said there was a doll. Doesn't that connect Marianne with that other little girl three years ago, the one in Rockridge? Was there a necklace on that first one?"

"Dexter, these are *policemen,* remember? They know what they're doing," Toller said with quiet insistence. "We want to help, not give them a hard time."

This was going to become baby-sitting duty; Goldstein tried to keep the impatience out of his voice. "We're pursuing the possibility that there is a connection. Right now that's all I'm at liberty to say. As soon as we have any word, you'll know about it."

"You can't tell us anything else?" Williams worked his face into a scowl. "What if two hundred people were here, yelling about their right to know what's happening? Would you tell us then?"

"Police investigations require discretion. You should know that." Toller's tone was indulgent, his head tilted at an odd angle as he directed his steely gaze at Williams.

A smile played at the corners of Charlotte's mouth, but she made no move to mediate between Williams and Toller.

Goldstein matched her silence, compelled by this curious, backlit moment to join her game. He had already given up a

degree of objectivity where Charlotte Wertz was concerned; whether that would eventually be an advantage or a hindrance was unclear right now.

What he did know was that he looked forward to the opportunity to find out.

five

She had to stay calm; blind panic would only lead her into the situation she wanted most to avoid.

She had to figure out, really *understand*, what the police were likely to be thinking. That would help her to prepare.

She trailed her spoon through the fish soup; she'd abandoned the pretense of trying to eat after several attempts to raise her spoon out of the bowl had failed.

Another little girl? Another doll? Linda forced herself to breathe.

Matt dipped a hunk of bread into his bowl. A glistening piece of tomato clung to it; leaning forward, he brought the bread to his mouth. Juices ran down his chin and he wiped them away with his napkin. "This is very good. Fish is real fresh."

Linda's stomach knotted but another deep breath helped the churning settle. "What are we going to do?"

"*Do?*" Matt's eyes registered mild surprise.

"It sounded like they were looking for us. Me. In connection with this new murder." Amazing how easy it had become to say the unthinkable. All sorts of boundaries had been pushed beyond their old limits in the nine months between Amy's death and the end of Linda's trial.

"There's nothing to do," Matt said finally, pouring himself

another glass of cabernet. "The police aren't going to find you here."

The police. A thread had dangled from the sleeve of the police officer's suit jacket; it had mesmerized her—brown, curling at the end. For a while, deprived of her sense of time and place, she hadn't realized that she was at police headquarters. Later, they told her she kept saying the roast would burn, the whole time the matron washed the blood off her hands and arms and all during the fingerprinting process. The flash of the camera and someone moving her head to a different position had broken through her shock, and she had been forced, finally, to admit to herself where she was.

"I feel like jumping up and getting into the car and driving and not stopping until they find whoever did this."

"Are you serious, Linda? It's pouring. You're upset and it's ten o'clock at night. Calm down."

He was right, of course. Still, she longed for the sensation of trees and fences rushing by in a simulation of something changing. Sometimes, when she returned from one of her long drives on unfamiliar roads, an inner shift had occurred and a change really did take hold. More often, the miles accumulated and the hours passed, but everything else remained the same. Reprieve from reality in a rolling box, that's all it was.

"I can't face it again. The whole dehumanizing process. Your body—they want to make sure you don't have drugs, weapons, I don't know what. I could never go through it again, Matt, not—"

He reached out and touched her hand. "Take it easy. Getting worked up won't solve anything."

Solve?

How could she solve the humiliating memories of her arrest and of being cross-examined about her mental health at a time when she was sure she'd lost her sanity to the ravages of grief? Nobody could solve the ugliness of complete strangers spitting at her on the street, the names—

Calm—she would be fine if only she could stay calm.

"Yes, you're right. Even if they did find me, there's nothing, no evidence, nothing at all." After all, *she'd* been the one to find Amy. The bloody knife had *her* fingerprints on it. No, this *was* different.

"If only you had a job or something, some concrete alibi. You were home, right?"

Linda nodded. Probably in the potting shed, mixing bone-meal into the soil and—Oh, no. That's not where she'd been at all.

Yesterday, after she'd wandered back and forth between the house and the potting shed, she'd finally given up trying to focus on anything and had gotten into the Honda and set out on the road that cut east across the coastal hills. Linda had kept driving all the way to Portola Valley before she noticed that twilight was approaching. It had taken sixty-five minutes to find her way home. "Actually, I . . . It was one of the bad ones. The headache didn't start until about one. I remember leaving town but I'm not sure how I got back."

His eyes widened and he sighed.

Was he worried—or was that doubt that flickered across his face?

"Doesn't this convince you just how strange you've let your life become? Most people have things to *do,* Linda. Even a class or something. But that's a different discussion. Look, unless you're not telling me everything, you don't have anything to worry about."

The candlelight made shadows where Matt's eyes should have been. He bent toward her, moving his head so that an oblique gash of light washed over the right side of his face. The illuminated eye stared into space.

"I wish I could stop thinking about it." She twisted the corner of her napkin.

His voice was cold, flat. "I wish you could, too. Look, it'll work out."

Linda jumped up. "Maybe it will," she said more shrilly than she'd meant to, "and maybe it will always be like this." She swept her arm in a gesture that gathered their shared life into a closed circle. As she drew her arm back, her fingers brushed the wineglass. She watched it tip, watched the ruby liquid tilt out of the glass, watched the glass roll as though it were fastened to the table by its base.

"I'll get it." Matt yanked open a drawer, returned to the table, and pushed a white cotton dishtowel onto the puddle, mopping at the droplets near her plate. He dabbed again, picked up the towel by a corner, and deposited it in his empty soup bowl. Matt started to take the bowl away.

Linda screamed.

(It's so late and she's not home and she's not at Jennifer's house. She knows she's not allowed to go to the park without a grown-up. Why is she lying under the bushes? Toss the knife away. Why is it here?)

She looks so cold. The sweater helps. It helps, doesn't it?

(Don't take her. Leave her here so I can fix her. Don't cover her with that. She can't breathe if you put that over her face.)

"Linda, it's just a dishtowel."

Matt's voice broke through to her. "It was her blood, Matt. I covered her with my sweater. Her blood was all over." Rain roared on the roof; wind pattered in nasty puffs against the door.

He sat stiffly in his chair, his fingers rolling the wineglass in a tight arc. "What kind of vine would work on a trellised overhang? Joey wants something colorful." He righted the glass and looked at her.

"It's—" She closed her eyes; he was doing it again, completely ignoring any references to Amy and the day she was killed. No matter how hard she looked into his eyes when he did this, all she ever saw was emptiness. "—the twenty-third. Her birthday's coming. She would be ten. She—"

Matt pressed his back into the chair. "He says he doesn't want wisteria, and Angela doesn't want ivy."

And I don't want to think about another child in Oakland. Matt had never been very good at talking about problems. He'd avoided her every time she brought up how his long hours at work ate into their family time, how Linda had turned to Amy for companionship. He was so good at putting off difficult discussions; she could practically see the tension building. Then he'd toss off a sarcastic remark about providing his girls with the comforts of life or about the secrets his girls kept from him. When pressed, he'd say it had been a joke.

When he was feeling expansive, he boasted that he had it all: a wife and daughter he loved, a job he thrived on, an exciting house in a vibrant and interesting city, friends, his health.

In one cold twilight, it had all changed.

Afterward, he had held her. His arms gave her strength to start building again. The old dream had been shattered, but she wanted to believe that they could construct a new one. She had reserved a small dark corner of suspicion that it might not work. And now, even if he wasn't saying so, he seemed to blame her for the failure.

"You have to understand, Matt. I may always be like this. If you want to leave, find someone else who can smile all the time, who won't be so vulnerable to demons, I won't blame you. You've done your best. You've stuck with me long en—"

His fingers on her mouth cut off the sounds.

"Shsh. I've always known what my options are." He lifted his fingers one by one.

Her lips still felt a phantom pressure, a ghostly warmth where he'd touched her.

"Stop pretending nothing happened," Linda whispered to the flickering candles. "We have to stop telling lies."

PART TWO

Saturday

six

Linda wiped at a misted pane of glass and squinted through the slanting downpour. Matt's van was gone.

She'd sensed his absence in bed; in the dark, she became aware that the weight of the mattress felt different and the temperature of the sheets had changed. She'd driven herself back into the depths of sleep, not yet ready to face the day; now she realized that she had no idea whether or not he'd come back to bed, or when he'd gone off in the van. She'd called his name at the closed door of the back room when she first came downstairs. But, as she knew it would, only silence answered.

She touched her cheek to the glass, hoping to clear the cloud in her brain. As she pulled back, she stared at the window; a graceful arabesque left by an imprint of her hair curled on the steamy glass, like worm tracks in wood.

Matt's sleeplessness and his early morning disappearance were surely connected to the news from Oakland. Maybe he was off somewhere—on the beach or hiking along a trail protected by an umbrella of redwood branches—trying to understand. He was right, of course, when he told her last night that she had nothing to worry about. They'd let their old lives fade to black, like the final scene in a movie.

The only connection they'd maintained to their past was Matt's college roommate. Anton Brodsky opened his veterinary practice in Berkeley the same day that Matt hung his architect's shingle in Oakland. Anton knew all the details of their relocation but he'd never tell anyone, even if, by some unlucky coincidence, the police got in touch with him.

She felt hollow, overcome by an emptiness that could only be filled by contact with Matt. But it would be so embarrassing to call him at the Sharpe house—she hated the idea of becoming one of those women whose husbands couldn't get through a morning at work without the interruption of a phone call. Besides, it was too early. She'd wait until eleven. Four hours.

So much time to fill. She would *not* rush out to the market and buy a newspaper. The longer she could keep Marianne Brandon—and the child's mother—faceless, the easier it would be.

She would have coffee, clean up a little, and then she would call Eugene Sharpe. She set the teakettle on the burner, turned the knob, and jumped back, startled, as the gas erupted with a whoosh. When the water boiled, she poured it into her cup and stirred instant coffee crystals beneath the foam. She drank slowly, and as she finished her lukewarm coffee and stared at the untouched dry toast on her plate, the panic started to rise up into her throat again. *That catchall drawer has been looking like it's caught too much lately,* she thought. *Better tidy it up.*

She sorted nails and screws, rummaged in the cupboard until she found little jars for them, and she didn't think about the mother of the child with the hole in her chest. She secured a coil of picture wire with a twist tie and didn't wonder where Matt had gone so early. The sky lightened, metallic and wetly luminous; in the gloom of the kitchen, her fingers remained cold and clumsy. Her arms began to feel leaden, but Linda continued to move as automatically as she had in the early weeks after Amy's death.

In the beginning, untouched by offerings of comfort from

her friends, she'd devised her own. She had cleaned, sorted, discarded, polished; she kept herself so busy that she'd even missed two appointments with her attorney. Matt started calling from work, to shepherd her through her days. He'd been her tether to reality, and when she drifted too far away, he gently pulled her back. She wanted only to touch his hand now, but he was gone.

She was sitting on the floor surrounded by tablecloths, placemats, paper-plate holders, the two old vases that she and Matt planned to turn into lamps. She'd refold the linen, maybe even iron the whites and the embroidered cloths, wash the dust off the vases, and then . . .

It was no good. She couldn't hide the truth from herself with needless motion. The facts were no less clear for all their strangeness: At a park in Oakland, a child had been stabbed. A doll carved with an *X* was lying beside her body. Just the way Amy had been found. But this time the body had been discovered by two boys playing frisbee instead of by a mother worried about why her child was so late coming home. At least Marianne Brandon's mother wouldn't have those other nightmares— the arrest, the trial—to haunt her. Linda had grown accustomed to the thought that Fate had decided that the fact of her child's death wasn't punishment enough for some unremembered, unnamed deed.

(The shoebox with blunt-nosed scissors and cutout dolls—a mouse ballerina in a pink tutu; a slender mouse nurse in a lab coat with a stethoscope dangling from her neck.)
I can't go in there, Matt.
—I'll take care of it, Lin. You sit here. It's all right.

How foolish to dwell in the past when the present was beset with new danger.

Another little girl? Another doll?

It was only five minutes to ten. The Sharpes were surely up by now; nobody in Pescadero slept in, even on weekends. The number was on the pad beside the phone: Brothers Market, J. Minetta, Wells Fargo Bank, E. Sharpe. After only one ring, a male voice answered with a cheery "Hello."

"We've never met before. I'm Linda Orett and—"

"Matt's wife. I told Jeanie why don't we get together with Matt and his wife sometime. Jeanie makes the best cornbread this side of Santa Barbara. Hey, but that's not why you called. What can I do for you?"

No explanations. Keep it simple. "Is Matt there? I—" Linda stopped; was she really ready? It would all get too hard again and maybe she didn't want to know. *Don't tell me,* she begged silently. *Don't say another word.* She held tight to the receiver to keep from slamming it down.

"Gee, I'm sorry, hon. He hasn't been here since Thursday. Left around ten, I guess. Said he had to buy some materials and do some drawings and I shouldn't expect him again until Monday. Maybe you should—"

"Thanks. Sorry to bother you." She had known he wouldn't be there; she hadn't really expected anything else. She hung up.

It was all slipping away—the careful rebuilding of her strength, the newly established belief in herself. Linda closed her eyes and inhaled, tried to make her heart stop banging in her chest. She needed to know more about what happened in Oakland, and the radio would be a start. She turned it on, then fiddled with the dial until the sound was clear.

A commentator summarized the failures of California elementary schools. The word "schoolgirl" sent a terrible pain raking through her: Amy would never have the chance to sit at a desk and wrinkle her forehead learning fractions.

An oil spill had been averted at a Richmond refinery; San

Francisco was facing a budget deficit; some radical Middle Eastern group was claiming credit for blowing up an American tourist bus in France. It was all so familiar.

The radio was dangerous, though. Even if you avoided the news, a bulletin might interrupt and strike you with a word. *Judge. Arraignment. District Attorney. Jury.* Words of a country enamored of its legal system.

". . . to Oakland where reporter Geoffrey Finn is on the scene."

Linda felt herself trapped; the floor rose and the ceiling descended toward her. *How could a mother allow such a thing to happen how could a mother not protect her after she grew from a tiny seed in your womb and made her way from the wet dark home the liquid safety into the glare of light and the cold separateness and learned to take nourishment from your body dependent on you for all her needs without you she would die and with you she died anyway . . .*

A chill gripped her. She swayed and held onto the counter as she allowed the radio voice to come back into her head. Maybe he would announce that the police had found the person who killed Marianne Brandon.

". . . investigating several possibilities. No arrests have been made. Sergeant Vincent Morella reports that the Homicide Division has canceled all time off. In an interview taped earlier today, Sergeant Morella recapped the situation."

Don't say my name, Linda pleaded as she lowered herself into a chair.

". . . many similar details, like the Smiling Suzy slashed with an *X*. But I mean, not everything's the same. That cameo, the one on a blue velvet ribbon that was hanging around the doll's neck—the doll found near the Crell girl didn't have anything like that."

Linda stared at the radio. *We're sure to come across it when we unpack,* Matt had said as they surveyed the nearly empty living room. All the big pieces of furniture had been loaded onto the U-Haul first; then they'd filled the spaces with cartons. Only the old upright piano was left, staring reproachfully from its position along the wall, as if it knew it was being abandoned.

But the cameo was my grandmother's, Linda had said, knowing that it was irrational to feel such emptiness because she couldn't, right then, before they drove away from Oakland, put the cameo around her neck. She had needed every talisman she could gather that day. Again Matt had assured her that it would turn up when they unpacked. It never had.

Unless she wasn't remembering something, she couldn't think of anyone except Matt who might have had access to the cameo. No one had visited them in Pescadero. No one had come to see them during the last two months they'd spent in Oakland.

Matt had never mentioned it again after moving day. When they finished unpacking and Linda put the jewelry box on the dresser, atop the lace doily her grandmother had given her, she remembered that she had missed the cameo when they left Oakland.

Now, nineteen months after all the cartons had been emptied, their contents distributed in drawers and closets, the cameo still hadn't turned up.

Unless that was it in Oakland, pointing investigators right to her, if they ever figured out its provenance. But *she* hadn't put it there.

In a daze, she pulled on yellow vinyl boots, stuck her arms through the sleeves of the raincoat, and let her legs carry her to the threshold. She stepped into the gusting storm. Rain slashed at her face. Bitter wind followed her to the yard.

Linda entered the shed, flipped the light switch, and began to putter among the fragile young plants that were sending down roots and growing strong. She took a breath and was bathed in the smells of damp earth and rotted hay. She would take each question, like a tiny seedling, and put it in its own growing place and feed it. She would give herself up once again to the small movements of a simple task, to the tiny trowel and the minute particles of loamy soil and the little green shoots.

seven

The blare of the telephone broke through the silence. Linda grabbed the receiver and glanced automatically at the wall clock. Blood pounded in her ears; the face of the clock leered at her as it revealed its obscene secret. More than seven hours had gone by since she first realized Matt was gone.

"Hello?" She stared at her hand, lines embedded with damp dirt from her work in the potting shed.

"Linnie?"

Linda nearly collapsed with relief; her legs buckled and she slid down along the wall, clutching the phone to her chest.

"You there, Linda?" Matt's voice was strained—he was struggling for control, she could tell.

"Matt, I've been so worried. What's going on? Where are you?"

"I'm all right. Sorry—I didn't mean to worry you. I got . . . detained and I couldn't call. I'm in San Jose. Checking out some supply houses. I'll be home late, ten maybe. You okay?"

He never could hide his moods, not from her. Even if his words were calm, his voice gave him away. Now it floated, disembodied and shapeless, across the telephone line. This was Matt's listen-to-how-competent-I-am tone, but she wasn't convinced. Why would he be in San Jose now, anyway?

Was she going mad? Had she imagined the agitation in his voice? "I'm fine. Can't you come home sooner, Matt?"

"Well, maybe, but I've still got a lot to do. Roads are pretty sloppy—fender benders all over the place. Maybe I'll wait till morning. I'll call you if I won't be home."

This was her chance—she had to show him that she would no longer ignore the truth. Her legs quivered and she leaned against the counter for support. "Where are you really? I know you're not in San Jose. Tell me what's going on."

For a moment she thought he'd hung up, but she picked up the faint sound of his breathing keeping time with the tempest of wind in the trees beyond the rain-soaked window. Finally, he answered her.

"Don't interrupt me. Okay?" He sounded like he was struggling to wake up from a fitful sleep.

"Okay," she whispered. Her voice was very small.

"I'm cold and I'm wet and I don't know how this is all going to end, but I have things to do and it may take me a while. I want you to stay inside. Don't go anywhere. Don't talk to anyone. Can you understand?"

Linda let out her breath. "The newspapers—have you seen them? If they're going to arrest me again, I have to know. Do they—" —*say anything about my cameo?*, she thought.

"I haven't seen the papers, but still—you'd better stay put. People might start to . . . If someone recognizes you . . ."

"Come home, Matt. I need to talk to you." *I need to ask you about some jewelry.*

"Now listen, you make sure you've got food and candles and dry wood and stuff. There may be a problem with the storm drain backing up. If you notice the water going down slowly, call John Ostrowski and get him to come out and—"

She wasn't worried about the plumbing. "Tell me what your being away has to do with this . . . this other child." There. She'd said it. *They can't touch me any more,* she thought as she waited for his answer. *There's no more they can take from me.*

"Look, Linda, don't push it. It's only going to upset you."

Make me crazy again, do you think? Linda listened to her own breathing, amazed. No, she wouldn't slip over the edge, she was certain of that. "I want to know."

"Stay right there. I'm worried that someone might connect you to this new . . . thing."

This was a different voice, clearly troubled, obviously tense. All his sounds were sharp, ending with tight little clicks as though his teeth were banging together with every word and his insides were all hard edges and oblique corners.

"I want you to come home, Matt."

"I have things to do. If I decide to stay tonight, I'll call by nine."

"Please come home."

Again, silence followed her words.

"Matt?"

"Stay in the house. Don't go out."

Before she could answer, the line went dead.

She hung up the phone and slumped into a chair. Why was he being so damn secretive? What was he doing? Anton: maybe Matt had been in touch with his old college roommate. She dialed his number in Oakland; the phone rang. *Come on,* she thought anxiously, *pick it up.* Anton didn't believe in answering machines—they made people uncomfortable, he said. How like him to worry about other people's comfort, and how she wished he weren't so thoughtful. After ten rings, she hung up.

Despite Matt's warnings, Linda couldn't bear the thought of being alone now.

The once-red paint was dull and the back bumper creased from an encounter with a fire hydrant, but Linda was sure she had never seen a vehicle as beautiful as Bea's camper, sitting in space 22 of the Sunset Shores Trailer Park.

She parked and ran to the side door, banged hard so that Bea could hear her above the wind and rain. While she waited, she watched rain collect in the cupped surfaces and tiny indentations of the small sea shells perched atop the wooden milk crate beside the camper door.

The door slid open and Linda climbed the single concrete-block step into the camper. No wonder Bea was anxious to get going; it was cold in here. When she got someplace warm, she'd have the whole outdoors for a living room.

Scarf wrapped around her neck, baggy sweatshirt and drawstring pants the same shade of faded gray as her hair, Bea grinned. "Storm blew you all the way out of your lane, did it? Want some tea? Nice rum, a little sugar, a slice of lemon to go in it."

Before Linda could answer, Bea moved to the two-burner stove and turned it to HI; the coil under the kettle began to glow red.

"Feels like it's going to rain forever." When in doubt, talk about the weather. Linda knew that Bea wouldn't let her get away with that for long.

"Probably not forever," Bea said over her shoulder. She dropped tea bags into two mugs. "Only until April."

Don't project the future, Linda reminded herself. Bea is here right now. Don't spoil it by worrying. "Gin rummy? Maybe I can whittle that debt to a more manageable size."

Bea's grin lit her face. "Sure. I was just getting ready to drive into town and have one of those damn gritty things they call muffins at that cafe. But it would have only been an excuse to see another human face. Now that I got one of my favorite ones right here and the extra body heat's warming things up, I'd as soon not have to put on shoes or a bra." As she spoke, she reached around and pulled a deck of blue Bicycle cards from the counter. Her fingers worked expertly, making a bridge, riffling it with the dexterity of a Las Vegas dealer.

Bea had never been in the cottage. She couldn't have taken the cameo, even if it had turned up after the move. No one except the owner had been inside since Matt and Linda moved in, and he wouldn't know a cameo from an abalone.

"You still in this world, child? Can't win if you don't play the game." Bea picked up her hand and fanned it, moving cards until her lips unpursed.

Linda did the same. Damn, this was going to be complicated: three of spades, clubs, and diamonds; four of spades; six of diamonds and spades; seven of diamonds; and three unmatched face cards.

"Alfie used to go out in these storms. Well, not actually *go* out but *be* out when they blew up. If I was with him, it was okay because I knew how we were doing, but if it was one of those trips where I stayed home, then I'd walk around talking to myself until he came through the door." She looked away from Linda, to her own cards. "Your turn."

Linda threw down the king of hearts.

"Forgot to pick one up first." Bea tossed her cards atop the discard pile. "Let's start over."

A flush crept across Linda's face. Can't even follow the rules of a simple card game. What would Bea think? Maybe this was the time to tell her.

She could start with the afternoon in the park. Her arrest and her trial. Or maybe she should go even further back to the months when Matt had been alternately distant or resentful of the time Linda and Amy spent together. Maybe she should just shoot forward to the present: *I'm terrified because another child was murdered and a cameo was found near the body and I think my husband may have put it there.*

"Want a card?" Bea's voice was gentle and her eyes filled with questions.

Linda sorted her cards. The four of hearts and diamonds; seven, eight, nine of clubs; ten of spades; jack of diamonds;

queen and king of spades; and ace of hearts. Of course Matt wasn't responsible for that cameo turning up near Marianne Brandon's body. Linda picked a four of clubs and threw down the ace.

"Aces flying already." Bea cocked an eyebrow, tapped her cards against her chin. "This one's flying right into my hand."

Linda reached for the face card Bea discarded. Fingerprints. The cameo was probably loaded with her fingerprints. The Oakland police had a full set, all ten fingers, rolled one at a time in black ink. She discarded the jack of diamonds.

"You ever been to New Orleans?" Bea took a card. "Nick Talaveros at the market says I should try the coffee and these fried rolls with powdered sugar at some French place near the river."

"Beignets," Linda said absently. She and Matt had spent a couple of hours between planes in New Orleans. It was July, steamy, and the cab driver who directed them to the French Market and to a wonderful, musty used-book shop on a side street had promised to meet them on the corner in two hours, so that they wouldn't be late for their flight. He had been there. Linda reached for a card. Three of diamonds. She lay it down.

"Here's our pick-me-ups." Bea set the mugs on the small table.

It was safe in here; only Bea and the cards and the mugs of tea. The hot tea—sweet, lemony, heavily laced with rum— tasted like heaven. "Am I keeping you from anything?"

Bea shook her head.

"Good," Linda said, leaning back and taking another long slow swallow, "because I want to have a proper farewell party. Let me have a cigarette, Bea. In fact, let me have two or three."

They both laughed. She was feeling better already.

eight

"Don't worry, Cavessena. We won't lose your evidence."

The pretty cop's mouth tightened into a grimace. "Goldstein, it's *my* name on the sign-out sheet. I'm responsible."

"Your choice, Tina. I already told you—our record's impeccable. Not a sliver, not a scintilla of evidence ever lost by Goldstein and Cruz." Hopefully, Cavessena wouldn't have the heart to keep up her end of this struggle for much longer.

Cavessena sighed; her dark brows furrowed above her eyes but her mouth half smiled. Goldstein suppressed his own grin. Department rules, unlike the rules of mathematics or even the highly vaunted and vastly overrated rules of logic, weren't to be applied universally and without prejudice. Some rules—the ones regarding your partner's safety and your own—were inviolate. You didn't mess with rules of evidence. But Goldstein's pulse raced happily at the prospect of finding ways to sidestep the bureaucracy when it threatened to hamper the swift completion of his appointed rounds. It was different for Cruz, Goldstein understood: For even a lapsed Catholic, bending rules was easy to understand in spirit but difficult to put into guiltless practice.

This time, however, moral relativism presented no problem for Cruz. "It's all right, Tina. Honest. Why don't you go home? We've been doing this for a while, you know. You must be real tired." Cruz offered her a winning smile and his most earnest tone.

Cavessena stifled a yawn and muttered something about not sleeping. "Tired, but I'll finish reading these reports at my desk. It's really wild how Linda and Matt Crell totally disappeared. No forwarding address. No IRS filing. His family claims they haven't heard from them. I'm about to check their friends. Been collecting names wherever I go. Weird." She slumped down and rested her head against the back of her chair. "I was sure the cameo would have a clear set of prints, but the kids handled it too much before they found Marianne's body. When you're done, let me know."

If that was the way she wanted it, fine. She had only her own stubbornness to blame for being uncomfortable when she could be home in her bed.

Goldstein held the tagged plastic bag upside down and shook it; eight smaller bags dropped out and rolled onto the pitted wooden surface of the desk. "This was all within ten feet of the body?"

Cruz nodded and poked at the packages with the eraser end of a pencil, prodding matchbooks, buttons, an unopened condom packet, Burger King fries wrappers, a rusty soda can, a nasal spray inhalor, several coins, a BART ticket, an elastic hairband, three unmatched earrings, and the cap from a Bic pen.

"Flowers in the desert," Goldstein mused, sifting the pile. "You don't see what's there until you really start looking. Then, once you start, you're amazed at how much there is."

"How much *shit* there is, you mean." Cruz sighed.

"You're right. It's all too damned ordinary. The BART ticket places it in the Bay Area, but otherwise it's your all-American public park detritus."

Goldstein's frustration had been building all day. At the volunteer center, Toller, Williams, and Mrs. Silcock—who turned out to be a retired immigration lawyer with sixteen grandchildren—had been very excited about a call the older woman took. But they reacted with adolescent resistance—disbelief, mild derision—when Goldstein told them that Donald Von Englehart had been calling OPD headquarters once a day for the past ten months. Frantic reports of crimes-in-progress, culprits-in-flight: Mr. Von E. believed his stories with his whole heart but no one else took a single word seriously. Just another crime slut getting off on his own imagination.

"We might as well give this stuff back and let Cavessena go home," Cruz said, staring at the objects on the table. "She says she's been having nightmares about this case. Kid could use a good night's sleep."

Kid: Even dozing in her chair, it was obvious that Cavessena was no child. Was Cruz slipping into chivalry or merely being parental?

Cruz pushed the plastic bags into a mound. "You done with all this? Too bad there's no—" With his fingers he prodded one of the objects until it slid to the outside of the pile.

"You find something?" Goldstein canted his head; he'd been through the pile twice. Nothing impressive here.

"Take a look. This is no earring. It's one of those lapel pins." Cruz moved a gold hoop out of the way of a green-and-white piece at the bottom of the bag.

Cavessena was out of her chair and standing beside Cruz's desk. "Look at how thick the post is. That wasn't meant to go in a woman's ear. Cloth—it's meant to pierce cloth."

Goldstein shimmied his chair closer as Cruz opened the plastic, carefully pulled the ornament from the bag with the tweezers, and lay it on the desk with the enameled face up. Cruz pointed to the letters below a stylized picture of a balance scale. "CAST. That mean anything to you?"

Goldstein's mind was blank. All right, then; he'd talk it out. "Scales," he said finally. "A judge. Scales of justice, something like that."

"Or maybe it has to do with drugs, a pharmacist or something. They use that kind of equipment, don't they?" Cavessena's big eyes seemed to open wider.

Goldstein rolled the letters around in his brain. "Maybe it's a theater group. You know, the cast of something." He shook his head. If Mr. Yamasake, his meditation teacher, were watching, he would offer that mischievious little smile and push both his raised hands away from his body to indicate that Goldstein should put distance between himself and the problem.

"Okay, Goldstein. It's probably California Attorneys *S* something *T* something. Call Margolin, why doncha, and ask him what this is." Cruz pushed the pin to the edge of the desk.

Goldstein nodded, then sketched a decent representation of the pin into his notebook, labeled the colors, and replaced the pin in the plastic bag. "Why don't you go home now, Cavessena?"

Her long fingers closed around the plastic bag. "I hope it's me that finds this bastard. I just want ten minutes alone with him." Cavessena pivoted and disappeared into the hall.

"I'm going to the head. Be right back." Cruz was gone before Goldstein could say anything. He settled back in his chair, listening to the quiet. The city was holding its collective breath; everyone was taking this case personally. Even Doc Ruiz, the coroner whose thin bloodless lips and cold-eyed appraisal of the most mutilated bodies had earned him the nickname Dracula, had circles under his eyes these days. Everyone offered theories—and they all kept coming back to the Crell case.

He had read the reports a dozen times. Three years ago the mother had been found wandering in a park carrying her daughter's bloody body. Practically incoherent, she had finally been charged by Roberta Herron, then a bright and rising star in the DA's firmament. Herron recorded Linda Crell's wild account of that afternoon; that testimony and the woman's fingerprints on the knife in the bushes constituted the DA's case. Herron sought out experts who labeled Crell's postpartum condition "mental instability." If she'd won, she would have been the reigning *wunderkind*. As it was, she was still trying to work off a reputation for poor judgement. Her career had stalled for the past two years, and she told anyone who would listen that Linda Crell was to blame.

And now, Linda and Matthew Crell were nowhere to be found.

Gone from their Oakland home; gone from their business, Crell Associates Architects. No DMV renewals, no moving violations. No state or federal taxes had been filed in the Crell name, no income reported for their Social Security numbers. How had these people disappeared?

Homicide was convinced: the consensus was that the same person killed Amy Crell and Marianne Brandon. Erikson, the department oddsmaker, was giving three to five that it was Linda Crell.

Jay Goldstein wasn't sure which side he'd come in on. And now the press was setting up a howl, and Morella and Webster were getting crazy about finding the Crells and making the case before any more articles about unsolved murders ran in the *Tribune*.

"Where's Morella?"

The hostile voice startled Goldstein. Had he caused her to appear? There was Roberta Herron standing in the doorway, arms folded across her chest, suit jacket buttoned tight across her small breasts.

Everything's small except her mouth, he thought. She was not quite five feet tall; her waist looked like he could circle it with his outspread fingers. Her nose was tiny. Her ears pressed neatly to her skull and her hair was brushed toward her narrow face in a nondescript short cap.

"Morella's not here."

Roberta Herron glared, then snapped, "What about Webster?"

Such charm. Goldstein shrugged. "He's working on a murder investigation. So's Price, Erikson, Quinn, Smith, Cavessena, Crowley, and McNaughton. They're all out."

"I know McNaughton's out. I already talked to him. He said he couldn't be bothered—what were his words?—to waste his time on a pissant personal vendetta." Her high heels clattered along the floor; she set her fists atop a pile of papers on his desk and leaned toward him. "I have a piece of information that will make the Brandon case, if anyone around here wants to do that."

He was surrounded by women who wanted to engage him in battle. Herron, like Charlotte Wertz, was intent on establishing territorial imperative. When he had time, he'd check out whether he was the one imposing the notion of war on these encounters. Herron's tiny fingers drummed on the desk.

"Do you want to know or what?" Her fury had dissipated into peevishness; she was annoyed that he wasn't slobbering over her offering. Then, as though she suddenly remembered the old flies-and-honey adage, she smiled. "Okay, Goldstein. I know I come on strong sometimes. I'm sorry if I sounded, well, confrontational. This is really important to me. I care about this case."

Touchingly sincere, he thought, *but let's not get maudlin.* "What do you have, Counsellor?"

She yanked a piece of paper from her leather satchel and slapped it on his desk. "Ben Ollinger is a friend of mine. Lost his driver's license when he was twenty—too many speeding tickets or something, I don't remember. One night, at a party, he got loaded and showed me how he beat the system. He applied for a new license with an altered birth certificate; suddenly, he was Ottinger. See?" She pointed to the paper.

This was beginning to interest him. "And?" he asked, knowing what was coming next.

"So I was sitting around yesterday and I started doodling, writing the name Crell. I wrote it ten, twenty times. I thought about my friend Ben and had someone do some checking for me." She paused for a breath and then plunged back in, her face coloring with excitement. "Some guy in Pescadero applied for a Social Security number sixteen months ago. It all fits, Goldstein. Easy for him, trickier for her. Her maiden name was Donner. Maybe the *o* became an *a*. Anyway, I'm waiting for final confirmation from the DMV. I want these people. And don't forget where you got this." She wheeled away from his desk, nearly knocking into Cruz as she barreled out the door.

"What's with Tiny?"

"All right, Cruz. You ready for this? Get a piece of paper and write Crell."

"What the fuck kind of game is this?"

"Humor me. You got it?"

Cruz wrote the letters.

"Okay. Now cross the *l*'s."

"Crett. That's what it says. So what?"

"Good. Now close the *C.*"

"Orett."

"That's it. Matthew and Linda Orett. Pescadero address. Looks like they started their own relocation program: new birth certificates, drivers' licenses, Social Security numbers, the whole package. No wonder we couldn't find them."

"Anybody verify this?" Cruz pulled his jacket from the back of his chair; he tossed a case folder onto the pending pile and flipped a pencil into his desk drawer.

"According to the esteemed Miss Herron, McNaughton dismisses the idea as a product of her fertile and apparently one-track mind. You going somewhere?"

"I think someone ought to talk to Matthew and Linda Orett, don't you?"

Words of warning filled Goldstein's head but he said nothing. Going to look for Linda and Matthew Crell in Pescadero would give Cruz an excuse to visit Elenya and the boys, a little further south, in Santa Cruz.

Cruz could make his own decisions. Goldstein didn't have a brother—and he wasn't about to become his partner's keeper.

nine

"Goldstein, I don't know if there's any connection, but I think it should be followed up." *How do I do this one?* Cruz wondered as he slipped into his jacket. *Do I tell McNaughton I took a little drive on my own time?*

"What will you do if you find the Crells?"

Goldstein's stare was making him uncomfortable. "Man, first I want to see if these are the people Herron thinks they are. I want to take a look at the mother; if it's her, I'll call it in to Cavessena or Quinn. It's not that I'm after the glory or anything, but no one else is around and I don't think this should be dropped." And I ought to be able to at least have dinner with my family, Cruz thought as he buttoned his parka.

"You really think Linda Crell did those children?"

"Looks possible to me. But even if I didn't think so, Morella's hot to find her. And besides, it's only twenty, twenty-five miles from Pescadero to Santa Cruz. You know what I mean?"

"You planning to spend the night?"

"You crazy? I'll try to work it so I can have dinner with Elenya and the boys. I mean, what's McNaughton gonna do— fire me because I followed up a lead on something we've been wanting since this case hit? Nah, he's gonna be glad I took the initiative."

Goldstein shrugged. "At least you're doing something. By

the time you get back, maybe we'll have a whole new assignment."

New assignment? This was the first he could remember Goldstein being more optimistic than the rest of them about a major break in the case.

"The volunteer center," Goldstein said with a half-smile, "isn't worth our time, right? Both of us—for what? Forty calls, then thirty. Tomorrow it'll be maybe twenty, twenty-five. Only nine people signed up for shifts today."

"I forgot about that. Didn't Wertz say she'd close the place after Thanksgiving unless they got more people?"

Goldstein nodded, then squinted up at Cruz. "If anyone asks, do I know where you are?"

"Following a lead, man. I'm following a hot lead."

Carlos Cruz maneuvered the tan Toyota into the middle lane so that two Ninjas could streak past him. Motorcycles like that, on a wet road like this, were definitely trouble. No big loss if the riders spilled all over the road; they were probably drug dealers anyway.

Cruz snapped on the radio, hoping that the music would help take his mind off the anxiety that had nagged at him since Elenya and the boys left this morning. He wanted so badly to be with them, and, for one moment in the volunteer center, he'd realized that he was angry at Marianne Brandon for letting herself get killed and spoiling his vacation.

A spray of water splashed onto the windshield. Instinctively, he took his foot off the gas, waiting for his vision to clear. Maybe he *was* trying to lay it off on Linda Crell. But there was a decent chance she'd been responsible, wasn't there? And if he could wrap this case up, he'd be able to join his family for the rest of the week and for Thanksgiving dinner, wouldn't he?

Nothing else looked good, not the telephone tips, not the

meager physical evidence—dolls, cameos. Talking to Linda Crell might not change anything, but it was the only direction that had a name attached to it.

What would the rain sound like pounding down on the sloped roofs of those huge glass boxes? The neat rows of greenhouses lining the east side of the road must have held miles and miles of flowers—not garlic or even broccoli, but flowers. He'd sent daisies to his mother when she had her hysterectomy; he'd bought Elenya roses maybe three times. Someone else was keeping these people in business, that was for sure.

A big white sign announced *Historic Pescadero*. He took the turn a little wide, corrected the fishtail, and passed a grocery store, a gas station, and a café that looked like it served sprout salad and weedy tea. According to the San Mateo county map, the Oretts lived on a street that ran parallel to the highway, about half a mile east of the main intersection. As he drove on, the houses became smaller, the yards more crowded with rusty swing sets and lopsided picnic tables.

His goal was simply to verify that Linda Orett and Linda Crell were the same person. He'd go to the door, ask directions to Santa Cruz or something; he'd know right away whether or not Linda Orett and the sad, bewildered woman staring out from the picture in the old case file were the same person.

The Orett house at least had a neat and well-tended yard; even the little shack off to the side was tidy, surrounded by plants, like someone spent time taking care of it. That would fit with what he knew about Linda Crell. She used to work as a landscape architect; people didn't just stop being who they were because they were running away from something.

Cruz sat in the car, reluctant to step into the rain. A light burned in the shed, but the house was dark and there were no vehicles in the driveway. It was only six-thirty; maybe someone was napping.

Fuck.

He should have stayed in Oakland.

He pulled the umbrella from the back seat, opened his door, and yelped as a gust blew the door against his ankle. Muttering, he stuck the umbrella into the air and pressed the button to open it. It sprang to attention and then caught on a sudden wind. He stared helplessly as it flew out of his hands and bounced away down the drive toward the road.

He stood up, winced in pain at the sore ankle, and slammed the car door shut. Rain pelted his face and slithered down the back of his neck; he hobbled toward the house and stepped into a puddle so deep it soaked his socks. By the time he reached the porch, only his underwear was dry.

He pounded on the door and waited. No answer. He checked his watch again. Even in a tiny town like Pescadero, people go out to dinner—they were probably out for the evening. That would give him time to drive to Santa Cruz, have a burger or a pizza with Elenya and the boys, and stop here again before he headed back to Oakland.

He limped across the drive to the shed and pushed the door open. Empty.

As he ran for the cover of his car, Cruz cursed the fact that he had no dry clothes with him.

"Papa!"

"Papa!" Carlito and Julio yelled and bounced with excitement at the sight of their father.

"Okay, you two. Now, who's got a pair of dry socks to lend me?"

Carlito's nose wrinkled. "You won't fit into our socks.

Maybe Mama's, if she brought her hiking socks. But what about clothes? Everything's wet, Papa."

Elenya stood back smiling, her face relaxed and even a little playful. She had some kind of surprise for him; he felt some of the tension and the anger of the past few days melt away.

"Go take a hot shower and warm up," she said handing him a towel. The baseboard heater kicked on with a hum. If he had more time, he'd lay a fire. That way, at least he could feel like he'd had a little of the vacation he was missing.

"And put my wet clothes back on? No thank you. I'd rather stay in these things."

"Suit yourself." Elenya opened the closet door and knelt to drag a suitcase onto the rug. "Except I don't know why you'd want to stay in wet clothes when you can be more comfortable." She held up a pair of jeans and a sweatshirt, underwear, white socks, and his Nikes. "I thought maybe you'd wrap things up early so I took your clothes with me. In case."

For just a moment, Cruz forgot that he was looking for Marianne Brandon's murderer. He held Elenya close, smelling the soft spicy fragrance of her, ignoring his sons' giggles as he kissed his wife's warm mouth. Then he remembered Linda Crell and pulled away, mumbling about his wet clothes and a hot shower.

By the time he was dry and dressed, Elenya had produced a minor miracle. A fire blazed in the fireplace; they huddled together on the sofa and Carlito told how they'd put on their raincoats and walked to the tide pool after lunch. He held up an abalone shell and they all marveled at its colors. They laughed and told stories; twenty minutes later, a knock on the door announced pizza.

Cruz ignored the inevitable during dinner but, too soon, it was time to leave. Elenya had understood, Julio had understood, but Carlito, his oldest son, the child who seemed to need him most of all, had been so angry at being tricked that his good-bye hug was stiff and he turned away before Cruz could kiss his cheek.

What if this is the last hug I will ever have from this child? Cruz thought as he closed the cabin door behind him. *Will he know how much I love him?*

Rain still filled the ruts in the parking lot, turning it into a muddy mess. The smell of the ocean and of cut grass, clean and sharp, cleared his head. Cruz skipped around the biggest puddles and hurled his body inside his Toyota just as the wind picked up again. He flicked on the interior light and checked his watch. Ten minutes after ten. If the Crells had gone to dinner they'd be back by now.

As he drove north toward Pescadero, he brooded about Carlito, then shut the thoughts away. He had learned that his feelings were often useful in solving cases. But this time, if he didn't watch himself, he'd identify with that part of Linda Crell, Linda Orett, whatever, who had lost her child—and not with the part that may have murdered her. He'd have to be very careful with this one.

ten

How had the time passed so quickly? What had they done besides play gin and smoke cigarettes? And heat up some chili on the stove. And talk about the French Market, and the storm that broke Bea and Alfie's boat into splinters in 1982, and laugh about how they both tried to read the sandpipers' tracks along the shore. And play more gin rummy and drink tea with rum.

"Bea, did Alfie ever . . ." Linda wasn't sure what she wanted to know when she began the sentence. The camper seemed to sway slightly in the wind, not an unpleasant feeling, but one that reminded her somehow that it was time to go home. Matt was probably worried to death about her right now —wherever he was, whatever he was doing.

Where had the cameo come from?

He might have tried to call to tell her he would be late. Maybe she would just as soon come home to a blessedly empty house.

"What you asking, child? Out with it. I won't even hold it against you that you won back three hundred of those dollars in one sitting." Bea's left eye wandered; the right one looked directly at Linda. Linda had noticed this phenomenon one other time—after she and Bea had drunk several rum-and-cokes.

She couldn't begin to tell Bea. If she started now, she'd be all night. No partway with this one, and she wasn't ready to go the distance. "I better go home. It's late and you must have a lot to do these next few days. I don't want to be responsible for delaying your trip." *Yes, I do. I want you to stay two days, three, a week, forever.*

"Talk about driving—you make it home okay? I got space on the other bed."

A little fresh air was all she needed. "I'm fine. I only had two of your magic concoctions. Or three."

"You want to go, then give us a hug first." Bea stood and held her arms open; a crooked smile lit her face.

Linda stepped closer and Bea's arms wrapped around her; one broad hand spread its fingers on her back. Bea smelled of baby powder and rum and cigarettes, and Linda wanted to sink into the woman's softness.

"I don't know what it is," Bea whispered, "but you're smart enough and strong enough to beat it. If you need anything after I've gone, you leave a message with Martha. The postmistress, you know? Gal with that tight, ringlety perm. She'll get it to me." Bea squeezed harder and then let Linda go.

Linda tossed her raincoat over her head and slid the camper door closed behind her. The rain had stopped and the air was crisp. She hopped off the concrete block and took three steps, pivoted, and hurried back to the doorway. As though it were a separate being, she watched her hand reach out, lift a glistening oyster shell from its milk-crate perch, and stuff it into her raincoat pocket. Then she ran to her Honda.

She pulled out of the trailer park and onto the road, flinching as a passing car's headlights cast shadows around her; eerie shapes loomed in the road and then disappeared.

She had been exaggerating things. The missing cameo, the story Eugene Sharpe told about Matt leaving work early, his irritability and secretiveness lately. It wasn't reasonable to think that she was going to face another chapter as harrowing as the first had been.

No compassionate power would allow that to happen to her.

Surely Matt was waiting for her at the cottage, ready to tell her that he had been upset by the news, had reacted in his own way, that was all. Wasn't it good that something had finally broken through all the barriers he'd so diligently kept in place since Amy's death? Everything was going to work out.

Don't get too optimistic, she warned herself. It isn't safe.

Nevertheless, she was cheered as she turned onto Church Street. A fat, round moon hung in the sky, dangling from a band of clouds. The silvery edges of the clouds closed, then opened as shreds of vapor parted and a slice of the moon peeked through. It was a magnificent show. She'd have to come out and look at the stars, some night soon. She'd had nowhere to go after dark since she'd been living in this town, and she missed the stars.

The house was just ahead. Linda slowed for the approach to the driveway. She peered through the misted windshield. Matt's van wasn't there.

The light inside the potting shed shone bright and yellow as the moon. She must have forgotten to turn it off when she ran back to the cottage for lunch. She parked under the eucalyptus tree and cut the engine and the lights, then dashed to the shed. She pushed the door open, its creak sounding like branches rubbing against each other deep in the forest.

She flipped off the light switch. In the dark, she heard the soft dripping of the leaves in the trees beyond the shed. Maybe Matt had been home when she was at Bea's; maybe he had left a note. Her hand touched the door frame.

Headlights lit up the driveway. Apprehension edged aside her relief as Linda pushed the shed door open.

Her mouth got dry and her throat closed up. That wasn't Matt's van. It was a Toyota. If she waited, the driver would realize that he was in the wrong place; he would turn around and go away. Wouldn't he?

How did the cameo get around the doll's neck?

A man got out of the car. Medium height, a little round-shouldered. Full, dark hair. Casual clothes. He played a flashlight beam along the ground, walked in a zigzag path around the puddles to the front of the house where he banged on the door. He waited, pointed the light, bent to look in the window.

Linda stood inside the potting shed, unable to move.

The man stepped back, then proceeded around the house. The beam from his flashlight moved in jerky arcs until he came full circle.

She was in someone else's dream and the colors became extraordinary, silver and gold rimming each branch of the oak tree, lining the bottoms of the eucalyptus leaves.

He was going now; he was walking back to his car.

No, he was walking to *her* car. He stood behind the Honda, pointed the light at her license plate.

Her hand lifted from the door. Her watch caught the moonlight but she couldn't tell whether it was eleven o'clock or five minutes to midnight.

Did it matter?

The man was walking around her car. Now he stopped, as though he were listening for the footsteps of his prey or sniffing the air for a scent. He began to walk toward the shed.

Linda stepped away from the door. The ten-foot-long makeshift table she'd built for her seedlings was behind her. Beneath it, she had stored twenty-five-pound bags of redwood chips, bonemeal, soil conditioner, vermiculite. She knelt, moved one of the big bags aside, crawled under the table.

A light bobbed nearer the window.

She pulled the bag of bonemeal in front of her and forced herself to breathe slowly. The tightness in her chest relaxed.

The earth floor was damp and cold but not so cold that she couldn't stay here for a very long time if she had to.

Light flashed in the window; the door creaked.

Why hadn't she locked it?

She stared at a pair of blue Nikes as they stepped closer to the planting table. A bug skittered across her leg. The light bounced and swept past the bag of bonemeal, kept going to play against the opposite wall. Then the shoes were gone. The door banged shut, echoing loudly in the quiet of night; footsteps crunched on gravel.

A car door slammed.

An engine started up, the sweetest sound she'd heard in a long time. He was going away. She rubbed her knee, shifted her weight.

What if there were two of them and one stayed behind to wait for her? What if the police accused her of the murder of Marianne Brandon?

—Linda, don't say anything until the lawyer gets here.

Is that you, Matt? What lawyer? We don't know any lawyers. (Those are your arms around me. I know how you hold me. But why are you shaking, Matt? The chair is hard. The lights are bright. I don't like the smells. I want to go home. Where's Amy? I want to take Amy home.)

She still had Mia Honer's number somewhere—the lawyer would advise her. From the beginning, she had known exactly what to say, who to contact, what they should be doing. Mia had found the experts at the Mountainview clinic who explained the temporary physiological nature of Linda's postpartum condition. Mia had kept Linda out of jail. She would tell her what to do now to protect herself.

How would she explain the missing hours when she'd been

driving around trying to shake her headache? Would the cops be inclined to believe her about where she'd been on Thursday?

Not likely. The last time, they had needed a scapegoat and she had been it—but that wouldn't happen again. She couldn't bear the questions, the leering accusations, the demeaning sneers. No, she had to protect herself. Go somewhere safe, far away. Canada. Massachusetts. Anywhere she might be anonymous, just another sad and quiet newcomer who soon became invisible in the stream of everyday life.

It wouldn't be easy—living like a fugitive, always wondering who had noticed you, who had read the newspapers and memorized the pictures. But it was preferable to staying here, so close to Oakland, and feeling all the same terrors. When they found the person who killed Marianne Brandon, then maybe Pescadero would be an option. It wasn't now.

Linda stepped out into the yard. The cool air sent her a surge of strength. As if she were protected, finally, by a great and good power, she walked confidently, avoiding puddles and obstacles, maneuvering by memory past two tree stumps that jutted a foot above the ground.

Clouds streamed past the moon. Exhilarated, moving easily in the shadows of the trees, she went around to the back of the house and unlocked the door. Whatever she had to do, she'd manage in the dark; she knew this house well enough. She pulled the door closed behind her, slipped the bolt into place.

The house had a smell all its own. Wet wood. Furniture polish. Rose petals. Kitchen cleanser.

A break in the clouds admitted a flood of moonlight through the windows. *It is quite beautiful,* Linda thought, as she made her way around the foot of the sofa to the telephone table. The third drawer from the top opened easily. She reached inside. Papers slid around; her fingers closed over the small telephone book. Better to have Mia's and Anton's numbers written down; a trip like this, events like these, she just couldn't trust herself to remember important numbers.

She continued to the bedroom.

She'd need warm clothes. She grabbed three turtlenecks and a thick Aran knit pullover and laid them on the bed beside two pairs of jeans. Wool socks, all the clean underwear, boots, an extra pair of sneakers. Her black wool scarf and her driving gloves. One skirt.

She lay the clothing in a small canvas suitcase, lining the corners and empty spaces along the sides with socks and under-wear. She tucked two cosmetic bags—small one filled with makeup and larger one crammed with shampoo, toothpaste, face cream—into the outside pocket and zipped it shut. She slipped an envelope of snapshots and Amy's school drawings under the clothing.

She closed the suitcase, set it beside the front door, and checked her purse for her keys and wallet. Everything in place. Should she leave Matt a note?

The police might come before Matt did, they might see the note. No, the problem of contacting him was something she'd work out. Later. Now, she had to be sure she had everything she needed to get far away.

Think, she ordered herself. *What can I do to make my chances better?*

She grabbed the road atlas from the bookshelf, pulled a package of flashlight batteries from the freezer.

She was going to make it. Where the hell was Matt? What was he doing now? Well, she couldn't wait around to find out. She was going to save herself, even if he wasn't here for her.

A sleeping bag.

She'd have a lot more flexibility on this trip if she had a sleeping bag with her.

The bags were stored with the other camping equipment in the back room, in the closet. But the back room, where Matt disappeared each evening to work on his sculptures, was secured with a padlock.

Linda hesitated; she'd seen him drop the key into a carved wooden box one day about six months earlier. Going into that room would be like reading someone's diaries, she had decided then, and she had resisted every time she went to the linen closet at the far end of the hall.

Now, that didn't matter. She felt along the row of towels and found the wooden box, then reached inside for the key. She slipped the key into place, turned, pulled down on the padlock, removed it. She pushed the door open.

The smell of wet clay was elemental and unnerving. It got stronger as she approached the plastic-draped forms on the plank beside the shuttered window. Only the light from the window, curtainless and open to the moon, fell into the room, dimming to near darkness by the time it reached the plank.

She'd just grab up the sleeping bag from the closet and then give herself a few minutes to think. In seven steps Linda was at the closet door. There, on the shelf, was the blue sleeping bag. A picture on the wall next to the window caught her attention.

Her eyes were accustomed to the darkness now and she looked around. Buckets of clay beside his kiln. Shelves crowded with bits and pieces of shapes she couldn't make out. And that picture—what was it? When she stepped closer, Amy's face, smudged and satisfied, greeted her. Linda remembered how Amy had pleaded with Matt that day to teach her how to bait her own hook. She'd proudly held up the line with the squirmy, segmented worm body neatly pierced, dangling in the air. Linda turned away.

She couldn't identify the objects on the shelf below the window. Still enchanted by the moonlight, she lifted the plastic sheet and knelt closer to the clay.

Like echoes reverberating at irregular intervals, the same

image was repeated over and over, in different sizes. One piece was at least two feet long, others no bigger than a child's hand. She reached for the smallest one but stood frozen, unable to touch it, unable to catch her breath. Two shelves and the plank —full. There were at least fifty of them. Fifty clay replicas of the doll, slashed with an *X,* that had been found ten feet from Amy's body. On some a white film had formed. Others had dried to a reddish, fragile bisque.

Why was she shaking?

Surely there was a reasonable explanation for these figures.

Linda was stricken by a sudden desire to laugh. She backed out of the room, carefully replaced the lock, and ignored the babble of voices that fought for her attention. Still clutching the sleeping bag, she grabbed her coat and the suitcase and stumbled through a fresh downpour of rain to her car.

PART THREE

Sunday

eleven

The lingering effects of the rum and the repetitive slap of the rolling tires on the wet road were making her sleepy. Struggling to stay alert, she gripped the steering wheel as a truck passed her, creating a gust that buffeted the car. Somehow, she managed to keep the Honda pointing straight ahead. Ahead—onto a succession of strange highways, where she'd always be looking over her shoulder. Into a space where she was free of restraints but also free of connections. Yet, of all her unappealing options, this movement forward was the most comforting.

The mountain road twisted over forested ridges; houses were sparse and the sense of being alone in a spectacular and untamed wilderness overwhelmed her. At one intersection she passed a long row of mailboxes set on a two-by-four on the side of the road and shivered at the thought that she was being watched by an army of invisible houses. She envied the isolation of those people, and their sleep—in their own beds. Delicious warmth, under layers of quilts, listening to the quiet, even breathing of someone beside you. Blessed lack of care.

Her head jerked up; she had almost fallen asleep. Pescadero had been a false haven. If only they'd gone far enough away, she wouldn't be so worried now.

Two hundred feet ahead, a metal fence and an unmistakable POSTED sign marked a fire road. Linda slowed, pulled into the turnout, and looked around. Isolated and quiet, this protected little spot would be a good place to sleep for a while. She turned off the wipers and the lights and let her head rest on the side window.

A mockingbird called out in the darkness, its voice carrying a message of mourning. A branch snapped and the whiffling snort of an unseen creature nearby was answered with another snort. The animals would watch over her. Linda climbed into the back seat, made a pillow of her jacket, crawled into the sleeping bag. On camping trips to the Eel River or along the Sonoma coast, Amy always seemed to absorb the sunlight and cast it back to the world in her smile. *Those clay images. The cameo.* This car would be more comfortable than the rocky ground that had kept her awake all night near Mount Lassen. Linda set her mind to recalling all the details of that campsite: the picnic table with *Thank God I'm an Atheist* carved into it; the mound of pine needles that someone had left beside the fire ring; the half-circle of boulders that formed a natural barrier between their site and the one behind them.

Thought became dream and Linda stirred only when the sun blazed across her eyelids—time to get up. She raised her head and opened one eye. *The sun doesn't move so quickly.* A flashlight beam played along the sleeping bag and then up to her face, the corolla of light obliterating objects behind it.

She tried to get up but her legs tangled in the sleeping bag.

A clenched hand banged on the window. Glad that she hadn't zipped the bag, she freed her legs and pushed up to a seated position.

"This ain't no camping place," a testy voice warned. The flashlight swung to the sign on the tree in front of her car. "You got exactly thirty seconds to get going else I'll have the police here."

The car doors were locked. All she had to do was climb to the front seat, drive away.

He said he'd call the police. He's not a cop.

She moved quickly; the keys were still in the ignition and the engine started right up.

Some fugitive you are, she thought as the flashlight faded to a tiny prick of light and then disappeared. Twenty-five minutes: that was how long she'd been asleep. She'd have to find another place to stop, at least for a few hours.

Maybe she would be less visible if lots of other people were around. Linda headed for a major highway.

Silence seeped around the edges of her consciousness as she became aware of her breath. In, pause, out. And again: in, pause, out. The sky was pale gray and cheerless. Had it been hours or seconds since the steady drumming of the rain on the roof of her car had soothed her to sleep? She couldn't decide. She stretched her legs and reached for her watch from the dashboard as several cars started up, buzzing curiously like a hive after a winter of hibernation.

The space to her left was occupied by a Triumph, its blue paint spotted with rain. On the right, a battered old station wagon rocked as a German shepherd made an ungainly leap from back seat to front, correcting his path in time to avoid the steering wheel. Linda pushed herself up, raked her fingers through her tangled curls, and peered into the station wagon. Three lumpy bundles of sleeping children curled peacefully in the back, their smooth chocolate skin a contrast to the lemon-yellow blanket that covered them. Two women leaned against the front fender; smoke from their cigarettes traced blue tendrils through the air.

Ten minutes to six. She felt as though she had misplaced three hours. Her flight from the Pescadero cottage came back to her, out of sequence, bright and vivid. A careful drive past Langley Hill. The clay images. The gas gauge nearly empty. The irate landowner protecting his territory. Pulling into this rest area on Route 280 to wait until a gas station opened.

Her body telegraphed a message of discomfort. The muscles in her neck felt like they had been shortened, her jaw hurt when she opened her mouth, and her bladder was nearly unbearably full.

She'd feel better if she could just get to the rest room. She opened the car door and straightened by degrees to a standing position. The air was clean and full of promise, and Linda took a huge swallow to sustain her until she could get more substantial nourishment.

All of the stalls in the ladies' room were empty. From habit, she walked to the second door and pushed the bolt-lock into place, grateful that she didn't have to wait on line. The rusty squeal of the front door hinges and the slap of footsteps on the asphalt tiles were followed by the sound of doors on either side of her slamming shut and of unzipping and unbuckling. Linda sighed with relief as a thick voice carried over the top of the stall.

"Yeah, well, none o' mine is blond, that's for sure. Nobody wants a little nappy-headed black thing, thank the Lord."

Linda flushed the toilet and tuned out the voices, hissing with impatience as her shirt caught in the zipper of her jeans. She bent to examine the problem; not too bad. She'd be out of here in a few seconds. She worked the zipper down as far as it would go, pushing back an image of Amy standing in the kitchen, morning after sunny morning when she was three, and practicing the very grown-up art of zipping her own jacket. Linda tugged on the zipper and pulled at the shirt. A piece of it came free.

"Me, I'd keep those kids locked in the house unless it was my eyes that was on them. I mean, every minute."

"Come on, Mabel. That little Brandon child's hair was yellow as a daisy. And the missing one—I forget her name—she's even blonder."

Something was wrong with what they were saying. Something was terribly, dreadfully wrong.

"Cindy. Poor child's Christian name is Cindy. Don't remember the family name. You really think it's the same person did it?"

The woman with the husky voice coughed, spat into the toilet, and cursed softly. "Shit yeah. Killed one kid, then snatched another one yesterday in the same—" The woman's words were drowned out by the flushing of the toilet.

Linda's breath caught in her chest. Another child? A third name to add to Amy's and Marianne Brandon's?

She would have to wait right here in the stall until the women left. If they recognized her . . . Despite the cold, Linda's armpits began to run with sweat.

"You really think that child is alive?"

Water splashed in the sink and the second toilet flushed; the door to Linda's right swung open.

"Maybe the mother of that first little one snapped from sorrow. Been known to happen. She might have been trying to get hold of another child, a replacement."

"I'm in San Jose at a supply house." When Matt called yesterday, he'd told her a lie at first. *". . . haven't seen him since noon Thursday,"* Eugene Sharpe had told her.

How did the cameo get around the doll's neck?

Linda started to choke; an obstruction in her throat kept her from catching her breath.

"Hey, honey, you okay in there?"

Linda coughed again. If she didn't answer, one of them might even slide under the stall door and try to help her. She pressed her lips together and forced herself to swallow. She managed a whispered "Fine," then took a deep breath, concentrated. "Thanks anyway."

"Scared me for a minute." The husky voice just beyond the door was close, too close. Linda struggled with the last remaining bit of her shirt and freed it. With relief, she heard their footsteps recede, then disappear, the soft hiss of the door closing behind them.

She yanked open the stall door and pushed her hair behind her ears. The shorter layers sprang out again; impatiently, she splashed cold water on her face.

They said snatched. They said yesterday.

She looked into the mirror and felt herself being sucked into the cavernous depth of a whirlpool as the door swung open again.

A black woman with short shiny curls and an obviously dentured smile appeared behind her. Linda bent over the sink and splashed more water on her face; the icy shock brought her back to the physical world. She reached for a paper towel and blotted her face.

"Just wanted to make sure you were really okay." The woman wrinkled her forehead in concern.

Linda fought a desire to be sheltered by this maternal, ordinary presence, as she had been by Bea for a while last night. She wanted to tell her how she'd been haunted, how she'd been unable to sleep without medication for eight months, how gradually things had gotten better, and how she was afraid. The burning knot in her chest slackened and cooled but Linda continued to press the paper towel to her face.

Acting-as-if. She'd read in one of the women's magazines that this technique could help you through the worst times. Act as if you really did feel strong. Act as if you really were secure. Then, others would act as if it were true and you'd know how it felt and it would become internal.

Sometimes it worked and sometimes it didn't.

"Thanks for your trouble but I'm fine," Linda said, tossing the wet towel into the trash can and hurrying to the door.

"Hey, hold on, honey. You're forgetting something." Her face scrunched as she pointed to Linda's brown leather purse sitting on the edge of the sink. "You look sick, honey. I don't mean to meddle but you best see a doctor, you know."

Linda reached for her purse, mumbled a hasty "Thank you," and pulled open the rest-room door, half running past a disheveled, sleepy-eyed teenager. From the safety of her car, she watched the station wagon back out of the spot beside her, aware of the woman's scrutiny.

They are all looking at me and I can feel the weight of Amy's legs dangling over the crook of my arm. The button on the top of her blouse is undone but I can't reach down and fix it because my arms are filled with Amy's body and I must keep stumbling forward. I won't ever stop. If I keep going I'll find out that this hasn't really happened.

No, she thought angrily, it *did* happen—and so did a lot of other things she didn't understand. She flicked the radio on to a twenty-four-hour news station. A wave of nausea swept over her as the newscaster spoke. Cindy Forrest, missing from Oakland since late yesterday. Seven years old—the same as Amy, the same as Marianne Brandon. Last seen near the Rockridge BART station wearing a red jacket, black jeans, black Reeboks, her blond hair in braids.

Where was Matt? He was her anchor; he was her protector.

He was the maker of the sculptures.

He was upset and he hadn't been home since yesterday morning, hadn't been at the Sharpe house since early Thursday, was the only person she could think of who had access to the cameo.

As she eased the car onto the freeway, the nausea faded and her brain cleared; she had to get some breakfast, fill the car with gas and oil. East. She'd cross the Sierras, rest until night-fall, and then, after dark, make safe passage through the desert and head southeast to avoid the bad weather of a northern route.

Each raindrop sounded a separate note in counterpoint to the percussion of the windshield wipers. The sky was shaded in a hundred variants of gray, feather-soft or slick and steely or ashen. The smell of bay leaves and eucalyptus filled the car like a green cloud. Each fiber of her sweater drew an intricate pattern on her skin.

Everything was clamoring for her attention, trying to distract her so she couldn't grab hold of her thoughts. Once she had something to eat, she'd be able to think more clearly.

The rain now lashed against the highway in sheets. A wall of water kicked up by a passing truck crashed onto her windshield. She pulled one hand from the steering wheel and shook it to dispel the tension.

Inexplicably, the words of an e. e. cummings poem that Matt used to read to her when they were in college came into her head—his voice floating on the chilly air, the words "rain" and "small hands" echoing long after the rest of the poem faded away. Poetry was no good to her now—why was she thinking about that?

The winding blacktop road twisted, glistening with rain, through unexpected vineyards. Linda passed field after field of bare vines standing in formation like stunted and deformed trees, their limbs jutting out at queer angles. A sprawling white frame house was perched on the hillside above the narrow valley floor. If she could drive around the ruts that pocked the driveway, park the car, hide until the whole situation went away . . .

But first, she had to have something to eat.

There: A towering sign announced TONY'S DINER, just beyond the exit that loomed ahead. Linda spun the wheel and the car followed. The ramp merged with a two-lane highway studded with low boxy buildings; Tony's Diner anchored the far end of the strip mall. She nosed the car into the last parking space; the diner would be crowded with farmers and travelers stoking up for a long day. Waitresses wouldn't have time to stare at her. Linda locked the car and averted her eyes as she ran through the rain past the newspaper racks. *I don't want to see her face,* she thought. *I don't want to see my face.*

twelve

A seat at the far end of the counter was empty. Good—customers would only see her back. She scanned the coffee-stained menu, rubbed the bridge of her nose with two fingers. She'd better make sure this headache didn't get any worse; she needed every bit of clarity she could muster now. She reached into her purse and took out the little pillbox with the glittery elephant glued to the top—one of the thirty gifts Matt had given her for her thirtieth birthday. Four years ago—it seemed like decades. She washed down two aspirins with half a glass of water and put the pillbox back in her purse.

A plump, hennaed waitress pushed a wet cloth around on the counter; with a stub of pencil, she wrote Linda's order of juice, eggs, whole wheat toast, and coffee. Her watery blue eyes never even looked at Linda's face.

Linda stared at the counter streaks, fanned the dampness with a napkin. Behind her, a group of men burst into laughter and a child screeched. When the thick white plate and steaming mug were set down in front of her, she ate quickly, tasting nothing but feeling her strength return with each bite. The waitress moved her lips as she calculated the bill; she slapped it on the counter and trundled away.

Two dollars and sixty-five cents, including tax. Breakfast specials were still a bargain. She should leave fifty cents for the tip. She opened the change compartment of her wallet, pulled out two quarters, set them beside her empty cup.

Revived by the rest and the food, she was ready to plan her route, then stop for gas and be on her way.

She pulled open the billfold section of her wallet.

Three one-dollar bills.

That was what she forgot when she was gathering her things last night: money.

Even if she managed to walk out of here without paying the bill, she still wouldn't get very far with only three dollars.

She handed the check and the singles to the cashier. Sunday—the banks were all closed. Thank goodness for automatic teller machines. She'd stop at a bank and get cash. She flipped through the cards in her wallet.

Library card.

Sears charge card.

Old receipts from Brothers Market.

There it was. Her bank card. She pulled it out and ran her fingers lovingly along the raised letters.

"Thirty-five cents ain't much but I expect you want your change anyway." The cashier peered over his half-glasses and tapped at the money beside the register.

Linda smiled and scooped up the coins. She dumped them into her purse and started to put the bank card away.

This had to be some kind of joke, a punishment for not keeping up with the outside world like Matt said she should, a penance for avoiding the mail.

Beside her account number, clear and bold, the letters sprang up at her: EXP 10/15. The card hadn't been good for a month.

It was a matter of logistics. She needed money. Even if her bank card hadn't expired, the account only had three hundred and seventy dollars, not enough to get her across the country, not enough to keep her safe until she could establish a base. Their savings had been wiped out during her trial—not that they'd ever been serious about putting money away. Rainy days seemed like someone else's bad weather. Now, one income— and a meager one, at that—barely paid the bills. She couldn't use her credit card: that would be like calling the police and telling them where to find her. She shouldn't even try to cash one of her own checks. They would track her, close the net.

Really, it broke down into two problems. The short term question was how to fill her car with gas with only thirty-five cents in her wallet. And she had to get enough money to get far away. Only then would she be able to pay attention to *where* to go to avoid the police.

She turned the key without starting the engine: the gas gauge needle crept up to the E and hung there. One gallon at most. Twenty, twenty-five miles, max.

Where could she get the kind of money she'd need? Anton, maybe, or Bea. Pescadero was more than thirty miles away, Oakland sixty, if she went straight up 280 to San Francisco and across the Bay Bridge. Either way, it was a risk. Bea didn't have a phone; Anton didn't answer his.

It felt somehow comforting to be forced to think in these practical terms, to allow all her half-formed doubts to be pushed into a dark corner. She had an immediate problem and she needed an answer—now. The rest she would think about another time.

Like Scarlett, she would postpone the most troublesome decisions; tomorrow would come soon enough. Maybe she'd get lucky and discover that the tighter the spot, the more resourceful the solution had to be. It was pretty obvious—Bea would be her green velvet curtains.

She'd have to tell Bea everything and give her the choice to say yes or no, but she felt sure that Bea would welcome her as a traveling companion.

It was a sensible plan, even pleasant. Bea was already scheduled to take this trip; nobody would give it a second thought. They'd take turns driving, after they got out of California. And she'd be good company. She'd feel safe someday; maybe then she'd go back.

How could she ever go back to a place where Matt might find her?

That was possible before the cameo.

That was possible before the clay sculptures.

Everything made sense when she fit it into a bizarre pattern that pointed to Matt. If only two and two turned out not to be four this time.

The day that Amy was murdered. Something lurked beyond memory about that afternoon, something to do with the telephone. She couldn't remember. It might be nothing . . .

The cameo and the sculptures and the fact that Matt hadn't been at work when Marianne Brandon was killed and had been God knows where when Cindy Forrest was declared missing—those were all clear enough.

Had Matt been so angry with her because of her growing closeness with Amy that he . . . No, it wasn't possible. He wasn't capable of that.

Had he become so twisted by what had happened to Amy and so eager to blame her that he was now trying to make it look as though she was connected to Marianne Brandon and Cindy Forrest? How could she possibly prove her innocence when she'd been home alone or driving—alone—in her car? He knew very well that she only ventured out on Fridays, to the market. The two recent incidents happened on Thursday and Saturday.

INCIDENTS?

She would tell Bea everything, every last detail. It would take hours but she had to do it. It was only fair. At the least, Bea would lend her money. Their friendship counted for that much. Safety awaited her at space 22, Bea's camper, the concrete block step, the milk crate shelf of sea shells. She reached into her pocket and fingered the rippling roughness of the oyster shell.

Two more children dead.

PAY FIRST-PUMP LATER, the sign said. That was fine. She'd know right away whether or not she would get her gas, whether she would have to think of something else.

The boy behind the counter was olive-skinned, dark-eyed, twenty at most, judging from his unlined face. *Smile at him,* she told herself. *Meet his stare.*

She took out her checkbook. "Fifteen dollars okay?"

His eyes narrowed. "Sure, but a check—I can't take that. A credit card or cash money but no check. Boss gets mad."

"Not even if I wrote it for twenty but only pumped fifteen dollars worth of gas and you kept the rest as a tip for checking the oil?" Sheer inspiration. What could the extra five dollars mean to her? She smiled at him.

Sudden understanding lent a gleam to his feral eyes. "Thirty," the boy said.

He'd risk his job, then, for fifteen dollars, but not for five. All right. It was worth it to her. She'd already been turned down by three other gas station attendants; the gas gauge was now below the *E*.

Two hours; it shouldn't take longer than that to get to Pescadero. As long as she stayed invisible to the police—and to Matt—everything would be okay.

She wrote out the check and passed it across the counter to the attendant. Every line on the skin of his fingers was caked with grease, every ragged fingernail ridged with black. For a minute Linda thought that he might be reaching out to touch her, but he only grunted and grabbed at the check.

"That's a big tip for wiggling your dipstick, lady. Maybe I'm not so sure now that this check is gonna be good." When he grinned, a black hole gaped at the side of his mouth where two teeth were missing.

This mean-spirited boy was *not* going to stop her. "All right. Don't do me any favors. I'll get someone else to—"

His fingers closed around her wrist as she reached to take the check back.

"Hey, lady. I didn't say I wouldn't do it. Go pump your gas." He released her, sucked air between his front teeth, and grinned. "Number three pump."

Her wrist bore the greasy imprint of five separate fingers. Her skin crawled with loathing; she clenched her teeth to keep from screaming. Still, she had done what she set out to do. Short term goal achieved. Almost.

She hurried to the pump, unlocked her gas cap, and grabbed the hose. Easy does it, she told herself as she squeezed the handle and listened to the reassuring gurgle of the gas filling her tank. Eleven gallons. Two hundred plus miles of freedom.

She'd stop somewhere else, wash his marks off her arm. Not here—best to get far away as soon as possible. The numbers chunked steadily until the meter read 11.6 gallons.

She replaced the hose, screwed the gas cap on. *Good riddance, jerkoff,* she thought as she glanced over at the next island of pumps. He leaned against a black trash container, reading a newspaper, holding it up so that she could see the back page.

The pictures were small but unmistakable: Grandma Donner's cameo on a dark velvet ribbon, her own face, staring out in bewilderment.

He dropped the paper to his side. "I'd say you underpaid me." His sharp-toothed grin flashed and then faded; he started toward her.

Linda backed up until she bumped into the Honda. She reached behind her, opened the car door.

"Now, you wouldn't want the cops to know you underpaid me, would you?"

Dear God, he was standing right in front of her, blocking her way. "You're crazy. I paid you for the gas. Now—"

A huge white Mercedes rolled up to the full-service island. "Shit," the attendant muttered.

Linda jumped into her car and sped away.

thirteen

"You think checking the kiddie-porn circuit is gonna do any good?" Cruz broke the silence inside the car in a voice that Goldstein barely recognized.

If Cindy Forrest's abductor turned out to be a pedophile, then the same person probably hadn't murdered Marianne Brandon—it didn't go with the territory. Two perpetrators seemed equally unlikely. The victims were physically so similar, their backgrounds so alike. They didn't know whether Cindy was dead, her body so well hidden that they couldn't find it, or alive. They might never know. Nothing was neat about this case, nothing at all.

One more day until Lois Edelberg returned to her psychiatric practice after her vacation on Maui. She would have something illuminating to say; she read all the journals, attended all the lectures, kept up with all the new psychosocial theories of behavior and therapy. *Tomorrow,* he reminded himself; *I'll see her tomorrow.*

"You still on this planet, Goldstein?" Cruz curled his fingers, talonlike, on the steering wheel and stared out the window.

"Sorry. I've been wondering about the connections between Marianne and Cindy. I think the guy who's got our girl wants us to come looking for her. I don't think he's a sex offender." *Now who's indulging in wishful thinking?* he thought.

Objectivity: it was time to correct the balance a little more in that direction.

"What about the Crells? You know if Quinn or Cavessena got a hit on them yet?"

There it was again, that too-bright sound, as though Cruz couldn't say her name without revealing his interest. That wasn't hard to understand. Even dressed in her rookie's blues, Tina Cavessena had a certain sultry appeal, even when she was trying too hard to be accepted as one of the guys. Goldstein found himself drawn to her, so he could understand that Cruz might feel a strong attraction. Yet he was sure Cruz would give up the job he loved, if that was necessary, rather than risk his marriage. So what was Cruz doing letting himself get confused by Tina Cavessena?

Brakes squealed. Goldstein flew forward, reaching out to keep himself from smashing into the dashboard; his forearm broke his impact. "What happened?"

"I'm fucking tired of trying to talk to you and having you zone out on me, Goldstein. I ask you about how the case is being handled, you take a trip to dreamland. I ask you about the Crells, you're off in outer fucking space, man. You got your investments or something so much on your mind, you're gonna be useless on the case."

"You think you have an exclusive on feelings because you have kids and I don't?" Enough—in fact, it had gone too far. People telling him that he didn't understand this or that because he wasn't married or didn't have children or didn't have to struggle with financial problems. His humanity was being disallowed because he hadn't squeezed himself into the goddamned unrelenting middle class machine. "I wasn't ignoring you. I was thinking about your questions, that's all."

A flush rose up Cruz's neck and spread to his face. The light turned green but Cruz, staring at the sky again, didn't move. "Cruz." Goldstein spoke softly. "Light changed."

Cruz blinked and nodded, and the car rolled out of the intersection, picking up speed gradually. "Hey, man, I didn't mean to blow up that way. Sorry. It's getting to all of us worse than we thought. Shit, I want this one over so bad." Scowling, he turned onto Broadway as a Coors truck cut in front of him.

And when this one is over, Goldstein thought as Cruz eased the car into a parking spot half a block from the volunteer center, *the next one will come along and we'll put ourselves in the middle of the dirty, ugly, stinking cesspool all over again, and never ask what we get out of it.*

They walked in silence to the storefront, Goldstein lost in thought. Maybe it really was different for Cruz. It *had* to be— Goldstein wasn't a parent. Carlos Cruz was, and much as he might pretend that he could imagine, Jay Goldstein knew he could only come close.

Parenthood: he wasn't suited to it. He lived too much in his mind, took too much time mentally playing out scenarios. Police work forced him into a direct relationship with cause and effect: You acted. It worked and it was over or it didn't and you tried again. As a parent, he thought, uncertainty and long-term payoffs seemed more the rule.

Still, he'd begun lately to wonder whether he had it backwards. Maybe he, the adult, needed to learn from a child. He had been protecting the world from his ambiguities for so long he felt married to his own metaphysical dilemmas. Not much to warm your cold feet on, he mused as he pushed open the door to the volunteer center.

There had to be forty, forty-five people in the room. Six phones rang at once; volunteers rushed from table to table waving pieces of paper, cornering each other. The activity quivered with energy and purpose, so different from anything he'd seen here for the past two days. Business certainly has improved, he thought, elbowing his way through the crowd to the rear table. Seated beside each other were Charlotte Wertz, her face drawn and fatigued, and Dexter Williams, tie loosened and sleeves rolled up, looking even more fragile than he had the day before. Albert Toller, his glasses slipping down his nose, hung his plush-collared jacket over the back of a chair and sat down beside Williams.

"What happened here?" Goldstein gestured at the crowd. "Cindy Forrest?"

His pale lashes fluttering with excitement, Dexter Williams bobbed his head. "Suddenly, everyone's concerned. I could have told you what they'd say: If they had paid attention when Marianne was killed, if they'd come down here then, this might not have happened. Now they want to make sure it doesn't happen again."

A frown wrinkled Charlotte Wertz's forehead, casting her deep-set eyes in shadow. "Hell of a way to wake them out of their stupor. But we *do* need all the hands we can get now. A hundred and fifty calls in the past two hours—that's about how many we got in three days, after Marianne."

Goldstein stared at the flyer Cruz handed him. He hadn't made a connection with this child yet, didn't have the sense that he knew her secret self. Cindy Forrest seemed more tentative, more apt to wait for clear cues before acting. He hoped he'd have the chance to match his mental image of her against reality.

"Look at this. I bet it's the same guy someone spotted in the park near Marianne's body on Thursday and then again yesterday at the BART station. Within an hour of each crime." Albert Toller stood with his hips cocked, one long leg bent, looking for all the world like a flamingo decked out in a blue shirt and pants. "Significant, I'd say, Sergeant. I spoke to the second caller so if you have any questions, I'd be happy to answer them."

Dexter Williams peered over Toller's shoulder, then looked

directly at Goldstein. "What about the man in front of the McDonald's on Grand in his car? You follow that up yet?"

"Nothing special about that one," Toller snapped. "They have to pick their priorities, kind of like law enforcement triage." He grinned, apparently pleased with his turn of phrase. "But that guy at BART, what *did* you find out?"

That was the trouble with these volunteers—once they started to believe that *they* were the police, they expected to get the inside dope. "I haven't had time to review all the reports yet, Mr. Toller," Goldstein said evenly.

"They find any fingerprints on the doll, Cruz?" Williams cleared his throat as if to make himself more visible. "Or the cameo?"

Toller chimed in. "You use any of those DNA techniques? Seems as though that ought to—"

"Look, we're not your personal pipeline, Mr. Toller. We're here to gather information, not give it out." Cruz wasn't hiding his frustration any better than Goldstein.

McNaughton had given them this assignment because, together, they were usually so good at community relations. Goldstein wasn't about to apologize now, but he'd better turn the tension down a notch. "We're not authorized to say anything about the investigation. You understand, don't you?"

"One way street, is it, Goldstein?" Red blotches mottled Williams's face. He offered Goldstein a dismissive wave and retreated to the coffee machine with angry, slapping steps.

Albert Toller canted his head. "I guess even detectives aren't perfect," he said with a grin.

Perfect? A discussion of perfection was bound to end in frustration. The only appropriate response was a smile and a nod.

"Don't worry about Dexter. He may have his . . . his flaws, but I never saw him walk away from a commitment. He'll finish his shift. Unless something's really wrong." Toller backed away and nearly collided with a silken-haired young woman.

"The phones covered?" the girl said.

Charlotte Wertz got up and put her arm around the girl's shoulder. "You're scheduled from five to seven tonight, Michelle. You'd better get going. You've already missed part of your gymnastics lesson."

"I hate changing into leotards in the middle of November." The girl's soft features pinched together in distaste.

"Go on. I'll see you later." Charlotte turned Michelle around so that she was facing the door. "Don't forget your raincoat."

The girl looked over her shoulder and flashed a grateful smile. "See you later?"

Charlotte nodded and made shooing motions with her hands until Michelle closed the door behind her. "Sometimes I get the feeling that her mother sells cocaine to the ladies of the PTA." She reached behind her to the papers she'd been reading earlier and handed them in an untidy stack to Goldstein. "This is a sample of what's come in this morning."

Goldstein passed half the papers to Cruz and took the remainder to an empty chair beside the door. Hopeful that the din of voices and the jarring bleat of the phones would fade as he worked, he read through the reports.

A little blond girl in a Cadillac in a shopping center in Moraga, in the back of a Chevy pickup on route 80 near Sacramento, in a small foreign car driven by a woman with dark hair in San Jose.

Forty-three different sightings of a blond little girl riding BART with a man variously described as tall or medium height, with brown or black hair and dark eyes.

Sightings in San Rafael, Petaluma, Emeryville, Concord. These would be passed back to the appropriate local agencies. Several reports mentioned a convertible—white or light blue.

This was coming in often enough so that they should pay attention. The description of the driver was pretty consistent: white male, twenties or thirties, full-faced, wearing a blue knit cap and a ponytail.

"Hey, man, what do you make of this?" Cruz shoved a report at Goldstein and then stuffed his hands into his pockets. Only three blanks filled in on this one. Date: Sun. 11/20. Time: 9:19 A.M. Message: Rabbits on the barrettes.

Goldstein recognized immediately why Cruz had singled this one out. Morella had moaned about how hard it had been to get a detailed description from the girl's distraught mother. The final, official wording included the phrase "red barrettes." Nothing about rabbits, though. If it turned out that Cindy Forrest's barrettes did have bunnies on them, then maybe her abductor was taunting them, thumbing his nose with a bit of information that only he could know. If they were lucky, he'd get bolder, more public, until he made a fatal error.

Goldstein brought himself back to the buzz of voices and the sharp tang of midday sweat and stale coffee. "Let's see if we can find out who took the call."

Cruz slid forward on his chair, leaning toward Goldstein. "While you were reading, I flipped through the rest of these. Handwriting matches Dexter Williams." He pointed to two reports to which Williams had signed his name. "We need to talk to him. First, I'm gonna call Morella and have him check with the parents about the barrettes. When I get confirmation I'll check with Williams."

"These people should know better by now," Goldstein said, trying to balance his frustration with the tiny glimmer of hope that this garbled message might lead to a break in the case. "Williams should have at least filled in his own name. Look." He riffled through the papers; fully one third were unsigned. He glanced over at the motley group of volunteers at the telephone table, wishing they were as competent as they were eager.

Dexter Williams and Albert Toller both lifted their pencils from their reports as Goldstein approached. A frown creased Toller's forehead. Williams resumed writing. "Anything promising?"

His features crumpling, Williams mumbled a hasty, "Same old stuff."

"What do you think?" Toller cocked his head toward Goldstein. "Is Cindy still nearby? Usually, in these cases, the child isn't taken too far, right?"

Goldstein didn't want to say that if a child was found within ten miles of where she disappeared, she was usually dead. "Hard to know, Mr. Toller." He put both hands on the table. Stern and schoolteacherish—that was the tone to take now. Kind but firm. "A lot of these reports are missing the same pieces of information. We talked about why we need names and telephone numbers, but let me remind you. We need them in case we have to contact the caller. And we need the name of the volunteer who took the call. You all can manage that, can't you?"

"Sure. It's just that I . . ." Williams stared at the telephone, as though his glance could make it ring.

Toller appeared to take Goldstein's warning as a personal affront. "It's not so easy. I mean, we've been told to ask, sure, but sometimes people won't answer. What about you guys? You must have learned stuff in the police academy that would work here. You all have guidelines for this kind of situation, right?"

Goldstein sighed and searched his memory for the official language recommended by OPD in one of Phil McArdle's recently revised procedures booklets. "The volunteer should identify himself by name and then ask for the caller's name. This puts things on a personal basis right away."

Toller's stare dissolved to a look of keen interest. "So, the cop becomes real to the caller by having a name, and the caller relaxes and feels like it's a friendly exchange and then he says his name too. This something you thought up personally, Goldstein, or is it police procedure?"

"Procedure, Mr. Toller. Another thing you can do is offer to send the caller a newsletter or a pledge form to contribute money to the volunteer center. That way, they have to tell you their name and address."

"That borders on the unethical, doesn't it, Sergeant Goldstein?" Dexter Williams frowned in self-righteous disapproval.

Goldstein refused his invitation to argue. "Let's just say the method serves a dual purpose, that's all."

"Maybe we *should* consider it. If that's how they do it at OPD." Toller looked for confirmation to Goldstein.

Goldstein used the change of momentum to launch into an elaboration of the recommended telephone protocol, but he was cut short by Charlotte Wertz.

"Dexter, please write up a memo detailing Sergeant Goldstein's suggestions. We can pass it out at the start of the five o'clock shift." She sat down in the chair in front of Goldstein. Her perfume was subtle, eluding him until she leaned closer. She bent her head as she watched Dexter Williams walk away. "Nothing worth pursuing?" she asked, placing a graceful hand atop the stack of reports.

"Everything's worth pursuing. I'll take these with me to the department, summarize them, and have them dispatched to the proper agencies."

She tossed her hair back and looked directly at him, her eyes shimmering. "You don't like me, do you, Sergeant?"

The question startled him, its directness, especially from a woman, unexpected. He reminded himself that this wasn't an ordinary social situation. "Is that important, Miss Wertz? Whether or not I like you?"

"Not at all." She gathered a precarious pile of manila folders and stuffed them into a box. "Not to me," she added, striding to her desk.

He picked up the next report. The words didn't make sense; he rubbed his eyes, then looked up to see Cruz walking toward him.

"Goldstein, Morella called. The parents said yes. The red barrettes that Cindy Forrest was wearing had little rabbits on them. Williams said he almost didn't fill out a report. Said he could hardly understand the guy. It was a man, Goldstein. Williams said the call lasted maybe ten seconds and the guy kept repeating the same fucking thing. 'Rabbits on the barrettes.' That's all he said."

fourteen

If only the Crell couple had stayed put, Carlos Cruz thought, OPD could have written them off. But nobody had been at the cottage. The Honda in the driveway and the fact that the shed light had been turned off between his two visits bothered him—he'd missed something and it sat like yesterday's burritos, just below his breastbone. This business with the barrettes—maybe this would get them somewhere. The barrettes might even lead them away from the Crells, but he doubted that, even though a part of him wished it would happen that way.

The Crells weren't his problem anyway. Quinn and Cavessena had that one to worry about. He was glad not to be in their place. That detail would be harder than putting up with the frustrated eagerness of the volunteers. At least he was staying dry. Teams of patrolmen, wet, cold, and uncomplaining, had spread out in concentric circles conducting neighborhood searches—sifting through vacant lots, poking into junkyards, checking out abandoned buildings. They had come up with nothing more than a score of runny-nosed junkies and a few homeless families taking shelter from the weather in the crumbling shells of old buildings.

"I got it! He's gonna do it!" Morella exploded into the Homicide room, his jowls jiggling with excitement as he waved a paper above his head.

"You got the chief to spring *both* helicopters?" Cruz

grinned, incredulous. Morella was a better pitchman than he'd thought.

"And four teams with dogs. The helicopters have clearance to cover twenty-five miles north, south, east, west. The dog teams, Cruz. That's where I put my money. You ever see those noses twitch? Shepherds they are and so fucking smart, they could go to college." Morella's dance had carried him to his own desk. He slammed the papers onto his blotter; then, as if he'd shorted a circuit, he slumped silent and glazed into his chair.

"Hey, man. You okay? What happened?" Cruz understood the pressures of being in charge of this case. This was one time that Morella's fabled sweet and even disposition didn't stand a chance.

"I keep thinking about the parents, Cruz. The Brandon woman, I swear she aged ten years in four days. I don't know what's worse, the knowing or the waiting. Can you imagine what the waiting's like?"

Sitting in the interview room yesterday, silent and passive, Cindy's parents looked forlorn, dazed, abandoned. Ed Forrest never blinked except to shift his gaze to his wife; Margie Forrest sat beside him, bouncing her fingers against her lips as though she were trying to keep from saying something. As the afternoon dragged on, the couple seemed to get smaller, more drawn into themselves, trembling as though they might shiver into tiny pieces.

The help they'd been given so far simply wasn't enough.

Nothing would be, until they had their daughter back home, going to school, to church, to the park. Thinking about the parents twisted Cruz's gut into a tangle; he had to resist reaching for the phone to call Santa Cruz. Elenya had already hinted that maybe he shouldn't call five or six times a day, as he had since they left. Just hearing the sweet little-boy voices of Carlito and Julio quieted his anxiety, for a while.

McNaughton had tried to convince the Forrests to make a

public plea for their daughter's return, but so far they'd shied away. As long as the papers and the radio and television news were covering the story, they said, they wanted to stay out of the spotlight. The key piece of information that Webster got from Ed and Margie Forrest yesterday was that their daughter was a diabetic. If she didn't get her insulin, she would eventually go into a coma and die.

If she wasn't already dead, Cruz had added silently when he'd heard the report. The papers were running front page stories explaining that Cindy needed her insulin, asking her abductor to bring her to a hospital.

"Ask you something?" The voice was soft; Tina Cavessena's dark eyes flickered with questions.

"Sorry, Tina. I'm a married man." *Smile: let her know you're kidding,* he thought. Maybe he could dissolve this tension that had been building between them, lighten up the general atmosphere a little.

Cavessena made a ticking sound out of the side of her mouth and frowned. "Not funny, joker. We're still trying to get the parents to make a statement on TV, right?"

"Morella is, yeah. He thinks that'll do some good. Why?"

Cavessena's face relaxed and her smile crept up to her eyes. "My friend Andrea knows Margie Forrest. Thinks she can get her to reconsider—if we really want her to."

Cruz was confused. There were too many *hers* in Cavessena's proposal.

"All right, just nod if the answer's yes and shake your head if the answer's no." Cavessena bent a little closer and spoke slowly, as though she were talking to a child.

Cruz felt his cheeks burn. Did he really seem so stupid?

"Should I ask Andrea to talk to Margie Forrest about doing the television thing?" she enunciated.

Cruz nodded.

Cavessena grinned. "And do you want me to . . ." She

laughed and stood back, hands on her tilted hips. "Never mind. Bad timing for that thought. I'll call Andrea. At least it's something to do."

"You and Quinn haven't got a line on the Crells yet?" Maybe he could convince McNaughton that someone should be in Pescadero on an extended stakeout. Sure, the lieutenant would know that his reasons weren't entirely pure, but, shit, he'd still be making a contribution, maybe one that was more valuable than hanging around at the volunteer center.

"We faxed pictures to the San Mateo county sheriff. Local storekeepers made them as Linda and Matthew Orett." Cavessena picked absently at invisible threads on the sleeve of her sweater. "State police and the local cops are sharing shifts with the sheriff's boys to keep the house covered, but I have a feeling that's not gonna get us anywhere. Listen, I'm going to see if I can set something up with the Forrest family." She whirled around and marched to her desk.

Family: Cruz thought again of Elenya and the boys, and of Thanksgiving. Even if they did a turkey dinner, trimmings and all, next week or the week after or whenever the schedules got back to normal, it just wouldn't be the same as doing it on the right day. The *family* day.

Oh, shit, he moaned to himself, *give up the complaining and do something useful.* He could at least make some calls, run down the most promising of the sightings. He started to dial the number of the Fresno police when he became aware of steps behind him. He knew who it was—Webster or Morella or Goldstein in no way sounded like a one-hundred-twenty-pound woman in high heels.

"One camera for each of the networks and one for the wire service. No reporters, no questions, no cops except you and me. Four o'clock this afternoon. At their house."

Cruz sat back and frowned. "What are you—a goddam hostage negotiator? What do you mean 'you and me'?"

"Ed and Margie Forrest saw you on television last month when you were being interviewed about the gang shootings, right? They know you're a soccer coach for your kids' team and that you volunteer in the schools and all that. Me because I'm a woman and I know Andrea. Yes or no?"

Shit, this was complicated, and Tina Cavessena, innocently staring at him with her big brown eyes, was making things worse. Cruz wanted to make this case. But she wasn't even his partner. Had she set this up on purpose?

"What about Goldstein and Quinn? And what about—"

"I cleared it with McNaughton. He said we should go along with whatever the Forrests want. A television spot—it's got to work, Cruz."

How did he get into this, anyway? Nothing made sense these days, nothing was the way it was supposed to be, and he was just barely keeping a lid on his feelings. The thought of being face to face with Ed and Margie Forrest and their pain made Carlos Cruz sweat.

"It's really not that bad." Ed Forrest's potbelly strained against his sweatshirt as he hauled himself out of the captain's chair at the head of the dining room table. His mouth twitched and he jammed his fist against it, gulped down a breath, and went on. "The doc says she'll be all right another twelve to eighteen hours without her insulin. Unless she eats a lot of sugar."

Or unless she doesn't have to worry about her health anymore, Cruz thought again.

"Okay, Mr. Forrest, here's the thing." Cavessena's voice was soothing, soft. "You want to deliver the information as simply as you can. Whoever this person is, it's possible that he's not very bright. He may not know anything about diabetes. So you need to go slow and talk about it in very simple terms."

Margie Forrest grabbed a tissue and blinked her red, swol-

len eyes. "I can't . . . I don't know if I can say anything without crying." Her face sagged and her husband sucked in a
breath and cupped her quivering chin in his hand.

The *Chronicle* articles that McNaughton had passed
around this morning quoted some FBI expert who said that
emotional appeals to kidnappers could backfire if newspaper
and television pleas played to his sense of power, made him
hungry for more attention. Cruz shoved aside his own fear that
Cindy probably wasn't alive as he explained what they should
say. The Forrests nodded at the right times, but he worried that
they might not be able to stick to the script when the cameras
were rolling.

Cavessena put an arm around Margie Forrest. "You only
have to stand here for thirty seconds. Mr. Forrest can do the
talking. You just stand beside him. You can make it. We'll all be
here to help, however we can. Just tell us what you want, Mrs.
Forrest, and we'll do it."

The tissue was beginning to shred in Margie Forrest's rest-
less fingers. Dry-eyed and silent, she pursed her pale lips.

"All right. Let's do it now." Cavessena motioned for Ed
Forrest to take his wife's hand; the Forrests followed her into
the living room.

Technicians adjusted the lights between a faded plaid sofa
and a tan vinyl recliner. The cameraman arranged Ed and
Margie Forrest in front of the fireplace so that a framed photograph of Cindy peeked out over Margie Forrest's right shoulder.
"Don't worry, Mr. Forrest. We can do this as many times as we
need to," he said as he stepped back and reached for the camera.

Her rapid breathing punctuated by occasional muffled
sobs, Margie Forrest didn't look like she would make it past the
first take. Cruz felt his own lungs fill with hot air—the faces of
his sons shimmered in the glare of the standing lights, then
disappeared.

The cameraman shouldered the camera. "Okay, now we're going to roll tape. You can begin whenever you're ready, Mr. Forrest."

Ed Forrest stared straight ahead and gave no sign that he understood. He opened his mouth, then closed it, forcing a sharp breath through his lips. Finally, he began to speak. "This is to the person who has our daughter. Cindy has a health problem that maybe you don't know about. She's a diabetic and she needs her medicine every day. If she doesn't get her insulin soon, she'll get very, very sick. Please, leave her at any hospital with a note saying who she is and that she needs her insulin." He paused to swallow.

Cruz was aware that his own lips were moving as Cindy Forrest's father tried to speak. *Come on,* he urged. *There's not much more to say.*

Ed Forrest seemed to get the message. "If she eats candy or cake or anything sweet, that'll also make her sick. Please bring Cindy to any hospital or police station, wherever you are. Please let her get the help she needs. Let my daughter live."

Before he could stop himself, Cruz groaned. Ed Forrest had been doing so well, until he blew it by referring to the power that Cindy's abductor had over her life and death.

Tugging at the collar of her blouse as though she were trying to keep herself from choking, Margie Forrest reached behind her husband and grabbed the photograph of Cindy, hugging it to her chest. She spoke in a voice that was too loud, too high. "Don't hurt her. She never did anything to you. She's just a little girl and she needs her medicine. Don't you have any feelings? Why would you do this to my little girl? Just let her go."

"Jesus." The whispered hiss from Cavessena startled Cruz.

"Cindy, honey, don't worry. Mommy and Daddy are here and we're going to all be together soon, I know it. And we'll practice your threes table and I'll quiz you on your spelling words and you can tell me about the cotton clouds in a jar and how rain is God's tears and about the tundra and we can bake oatmeal cookies. We love you, Cindy."

The torrent of words was broken by a loud sob and Margie Forrest collapsed against her husband's chest, her body heaving as the sobs became soundless.

Maybe this was right. It was real, anyway. The mother wasn't playing games; she was right out there, telling it straight. It was already on tape and it was so goddam dramatic. It was bound to have an impact.

Cavessena motioned for the video people to speed up their departure. Gently, she led Ed and Margie Forrest out of the room.

Oblivious to the bustle around him, Cruz stared at Cindy's picture. No matter what he did, it probably wouldn't make any difference for her. Maybe for other children, potential future victims . . . he had to keep his mind on that goal.

"Let's go, Cruz. I'll buy you a drink." Cavessena's face looked suddenly old, lined with sadness and anger; her shoulders drooped.

"No." Cruz didn't have the strength to say more or to try to be polite. "I'm going home." *And I wish Elenya was there waiting for me,* he thought as Cavessena shrugged and walked away.

fifteen

She couldn't wear this old baseball cap forever. Still, she was glad she'd found it on the backseat of her car. Matt had a million of them and was forever leaving them everywhere—his calling cards.

The bathroom light was dim; only a fly-specked, naked bulb hung from a ceiling outlet. Instead of a mirror, a streaked and pitted square of stainless steel was screwed into the wall. The whole place stank of urine. But at least she'd washed off the gas station attendant's finger marks. Thank God he hadn't seen her picture before she made her deal with him; if he had, then he'd have been more demanding, crueler. *He* hadn't recognized her in time to cause her trouble, but sooner or later someone would.

She couldn't go anywhere, not yet.

The newspaper picture was two years old, the one that had been splashed across all the front pages after her acquittal—leaving the Alameda county courthouse, her blond curls cascading below her shoulders, a dazed expression on her face. She had gained back twelve of the twenty pounds she had lost during the ordeal, but it was the hair—her beloved hair—that made her instantly recognizable.

She put her hands on the cold enamel of the sink and leaned closer. Frowning, she reached up and yanked the cap from her head. Her hair sprang out, as though celebrating its release.

She could always put it in a ponytail. She gathered the hair and pulled it away from her face. Layered curls tumbled forward; they would never stay back, even with combs or clips. And if they didn't, she would look exactly like the woman in the picture.

She rummaged through her purse, pushing aside coins and lipstick and odd bits of paper. Damn, she always had them with her. Where were those cuticle scissors? A mechanical pencil. An emery board. *There*—her fingers, trembling, touched the cold metal.

You will no longer be even Linda Orett, she thought. You will be nameless, without a home, but you will make it. Bea had said she was smart enough, strong enough to beat it. If this was what it took . . . She gathered her hair into a ponytail, secured it with a rubber band, and started cutting with the tiny scissors.

Snip, clip. A piece of hair fell away onto the floor. There lies the person who knew all the Latin names for ground cover plants that thrive in areas with long, dry summers and interminable, wet winters.

Clip, snip. A chunk fell down her collar; she reached in and pulled it out, tossed it into the wastebasket already overflowing with paper towels. There lies the person who believed she really knew the man she married.

Don't stop—not yet, not until you've banished the childless mother, the husbandless wife, the rootless gardener.

For the first time in years, the back of her neck felt cold. Her head felt lighter. Only a little more now. Now the top— she'd have to do that too. Snick, snick. The scissors took on a life of their own. Her eyes looked huge and questioning, her nose more bony than it had before. Two inches of hair left. She could stop now.

The itching was unbearable. She brushed hair from her

mouth, reached under her sweater and tried to get it off her back and her chest, but it stuck as though glued.

Linda pulled off the sweater and shook it, watched the hair float to the floor like a gentle blond rain. Goose bumps covered her skin; she worked quickly, using the cap to brush as much hair from her back and her breasts as she could. God, what she would do for a shower now. She slapped the cap against her head; more loose hair fell into the sink.

She pulled a paper towel from the holder and hunkered down. *There lies,* she thought as she scooped up fistfuls of hair and shoved the long blond curls under the crumpled paper towels, repeating the process until all but a fine layer of hair was stuffed into the wastebasket. Her reflection startled her—a stark and naked set of features seemed to leap out from the steel square.

A tight little laugh caught in her throat; when she got to the trailer she would have to announce herself. Even Bea wouldn't know, at first, who she was.

She stared at the empty space. Bea would have a million things to do right before a trip, so there was no need to worry. A dark rectangle was outlined on the macadam in the number 22 space, as though the camper had left its shadow behind when it drove away. An oil leak, probably. Bea should have the rings and valves checked.

But she couldn't make that suggestion because Bea wasn't here.

No need to panic. It would take a little more time, a little risk to track her down, that was all. Maybe Linda would just wait here. Park in the visitor's lot and wait. Watch the rain.

And think about Matt and what he might have done.

No, she needed to act; she couldn't sit around and wait for someone to find her. She should go to the beach, drive past the market, past the garage. Find Bea. At least, kill the time until Bea came back. Dusk wasn't that far off.

Linda backed up, cut the wheel, and then put the car into forward gear. A little wooden duck in slicker and rain hat bobbed atop the white picket fence around next trailer, watching her from his perch.

The concrete block was gone. The milk crate and the sea shells weren't in their usual places. That's what was wrong. They were Bea's concessions to permanence; they marked her spot. As long as they were there, she was coming back, even if she had taken off on a three-day jaunt down the coast to San Simeon or north to Mendocino. Now, they were gone.

Linda was almost back in the center of town when it struck her: Bea had started her trip early.

Her windshield wipers pushed sluggishly at the rain, streaking the glass. She drove past Smitty's garage; the light was on. He'd come in today, even though it was Sunday, to fix the carburetor—that's how Bea had managed to leave early. Since he was working, she would pull into the garage and get him to change the wiper blades.

And pay him how?

She rolled past the garage; going inside and talking to Smitty—he would ask about her hair, he would have seen her picture in the paper—wasn't an option. Hunger began to gnaw its way to her consciousness and she looked again through every section of her purse, her wallet, in the glove compartment. That netted her another sixteen cents.

She could go back to the cottage, spend the night, and then go to the bank first thing in the morning as if withdrawing all her money was the most normal thing in the world.

No, she couldn't. What if Matt was at the cottage? What if his advice to stay home yesterday had been a trap?

Besides, she'd need more money than they had in the bank account.

Like a point of light at the far end of a long tunnel, her only real choice became clearer as she drove. She had to go to Anton's; it was the only way. She headed for the highway again. Almost as an afterthought, she cut the wheel hard as she came up on the post office parking area. She scrabbled through her purse until she found the little pad and a pen.

"Leave a note with Martha," Bea had said. It was worth a try. She copied Anton's phone number, wrote the words *Please call,* and then folded the paper several times. On the front, she scribbled another note: *Martha—Please forward to Bea Kelly.* Impossible. Bea would never get it. No stamp. No envelope. Ridiculous. Linda tossed the note into the mail slot and ran to her car.

She pulled onto the coast highway, drove north without thinking. The sky was heavy, all the way out across the gray, crashing sea to the horizon. All the beaches were deserted, no one parked at the cliffs above the surging waves, no one watching the storm strike toward land.

Going to Anton's was really the only viable alternative; he would offer her the balm of his healing powers, the same comfort he gave to the creatures he cared for in his veterinary practice. She'd have to prepare a story, one that accounted for Matt's absence, but if she stuck pretty close to the truth and kept the rest simple, it would work. Of course she would have to drive into Oakland, but it was a risk she'd take, even though that policeman—surely the man in her driveway had been a policeman—had written down her license plate number. They would be looking for her but it was late and the dark would help keep her invisible.

If only she could find a dark corner of some supermarket parking lot and take her own license plate off first and then replace it with one from another car . . .

That was stealing. She couldn't do that. Even driven by her fear of being arrested again and by the confusion that Matt's strange behavior had stirred up, she couldn't let herself break down. She had to hold on to her dignity, even if this crew-cut hair of hers did make her look like a concentration camp victim.

Yellow light gleamed like a welcoming beacon from the swan-shaped fixture beside the heavy oak door. Linda knocked, then leaned toward the curtained window. Nearly giddy now with impatience, she knocked louder and shivered.

The light dimmed as a shadow loomed behind the opaque curtain; the door opened and Anton's round bulk filled the space. Hank, the gray-and-white cat who had been abandoned six years earlier at Anton's office, peeked out from behind Anton's legs.

"Linda—your hair's gone." Anton stepped aside and beckoned her in, then hugged her and pulled back, nearly tripping over the cat as he dabbed at the chest-high wet spot on his burgundy bathrobe. "And you're still as beautiful as ever."

His hugs were one of the forgotten pleasures of her former life. His hair had thinned and his body had thickened, but he still bestowed his calm like a benediction wherever it was needed.

"Give me that," he said, tugging at her raincoat. "You're dripping on my hardwood floor, girl."

He didn't seem at all surprised to see her, but, then, surely he'd been reading the papers and would make a connection between this middle of the night appearance and the headlines.

"You all right?" Anton hung her raincoat on a peg on the hall rack and they both followed Hank past the living room into the kitchen. "Where's Matt?" he asked softly.

This had been a mistake. Anton was Matt's college roommate. Matt's friend first, Matt's friend always, and even though they had all laughed and joked and spent a week together— three of them and Anton's then-current girlfriend, camping in

Yellowstone—Anton's bond with Matt was primary. If it came down to essentials, she was only Matt's wife to Anton.

"He's getting the van fixed." She'd rehearsed the story for the past thirty miles and knew exactly what she wanted to say.

"Linda, I know about these other kids. I tried to call you guys until about ten tonight, but no answer. Listen, you don't have to tell me the whole thing. Just tell me what I can do to help. Come inside. I'll make us some hot milk." He led her by the hand toward the kitchen. "Now, tell me. What's going on?"

She had just enough time, as they walked down the hall, to make certain that all the pieces of her story were in place. Linda stared at her shoes as she spoke, unable to look Anton in the eye. "We decided that the best thing would be to go away for a while until this blows over. Until they find the person who—" She sobbed, then caught her breath and went on. "But the Honda has some kind of carburetor problem and just barely made it here, and the van—Matt's working on the van, changing the points and plugs and getting it ready for a long trip. You know how he is about cars and all, so anyway, that's where he is. We thought it would save time if he kept working and I came here." She stopped for a breath but still didn't look up at Anton. She was rambling, departing from the script; she dug her nails into her palms to remind herself to stick to the story. "You're our only chance. We need to borrow a thousand dollars. For a few weeks. A month or two. Until we find work somewhere. Maybe Maine or Montreal or something. We're better off going really far away this time, he said, and so it will take us a while to get settled and to get jobs and all and he—"

"Linda." Anton's voice was firm, hard. "You can stop now."

Oh, God. Matt had been here after all. The trembling started in her arms and moved to her chest. She must look like some kind of freak, sitting here with no hair, her mouth hanging open. What was she going to do?

"Linda, look at me." Anton knelt at her feet, took both her

hands in his. "Of course I'll lend you the money. Don't worry about when I get it back; I won't miss it. But I can't do it until morning, you understand. My bank card's only good for two hundred dollars a day. Now, you drink this milk, and then you'll sleep upstairs. I'll move your Honda into my garage. And in the morning, I'll go to the bank and get the money."

A sound plan. A good plan. He was a good person and he believed her and everything was going to be all right.

PART FOUR

Monday

sixteen

As soon as Anton touched her hand last night, she understood what a blessing it was to be in a safe place.

Her sleep had been almost peaceful, interrupted once by a dream of a baby crying and voices, whispering. Toward morning she dreamed of Amy, accompanied by two friends who had no faces. All three little girls wore cameos that dripped blood; all clutched clay dolls. Linda awoke in a sweat and tried moving her head to a cool part of the pillow, but she never really went back to sleep.

She uncurled and turned toward the window but could see only the drawn shade; the patter on the roof and the dreary light told her that it was raining.

Voices. Just like in the dream. She stretched her legs, brushed her hand over the stubble of hair on her head, waited for the pounding in her ears to quiet so that she could hear the voices more clearly. They were coming from downstairs. A housekeeper? The police? If she got out of bed, the floorboards would creak. If she stayed where she was, Anton would send them away, whoever they were.

And then she heard the familiar notes of the *Today* show theme music, and she smiled and reminded herself that she was, indeed, in a safe place and could, for a while at least, allow herself to relax. The television . . . Anton must have left it on. She glanced at the clock. Quarter to eight, fifteen minutes after

Anton said he was leaving for his office. He probably just forgot to turn the television off.

No need to get ahead of herself; she had the rest of the day to get in her quota of worrying.

Her bare feet hit the cold floor, sending a shiver through her. She reached for her socks, jeans, a sweatshirt and pulled them on. At the foot of the stairs, Hank greeted her by rubbing his head against her ankles; she knelt and scratched the silken fur at his neck. When she took her hand away, he rolled his head as if to say, "Here, scratch it here," but she ignored him and poured herself coffee from the Chemex on the stove. It was still warm, not yet bitter, and it made her think of the chicory-rich dark brew they'd had in New Orleans. She might find Bea, sitting at a table at the French Market . . .

The coffee cleared the last sleepy cloud from her brain; half-listening to the television story about a Hollywood starlet who was about to enter a Carmelite convent, Linda's gaze drifted around the room and came to rest on the table. Anton, thoughtful, caring, concerned about her peace of mind, had left her a note.

Gone to fix cats and dogs. See you at 11. Help yourself to whatever.—A

She sprawled in the chair, resting the warm cup against her chest. A long soak in the tub would get rid of the grit of travel and wash away the feel of that gas station attendant's fingers. Maybe one of Anton's overnight visitors had left some bath oil upstairs. As she reached to turn off the television, a picture flashed on the screen.

Young girl with blond hair and wide blue eyes. Not smiling, not really frowning, a thoughtful expression on her face.

The missing child. Her parents must be going through torture, imagining the ugliest details of their daughter's unknown hell, knowing they were helpless to do anything about it.

The picture switched to a living room and panned to two

adults; the father was stiff-shouldered, his voice gruff. As he spoke, his mouth quivered.

The camera moved to the mother. Linda couldn't take her eyes from the screen. *You may get her back. Even damaged would be better than never seeing her again.* She couldn't watch this. She reached for the dial but stopped, her hand in midair. The mother was talking *to* her daughter, not *about* her. Good; if the child by some miracle could hear her, it would help keep her hopes alive to know that her parents hadn't given her away.

". . . practice your threes table and I'll quiz you on your spelling words . . ."

No, Amy. You forgot that city *starts with a different letter than* sit. *Remember we talked about it before?*

". . . can tell me about the cotton clouds in a jar and how rain is God's tears . . ."

—*Mommy, the teacher said that the lakes and the rivers and even the oceans went up into the sky and stayed in the clouds and then when God got very sad and cried, that was what the rain was.*

Well, I don't think it has anything to do with sadness, sweetie. It rains when there's too much water in the clouds.

—*You mean, the teacher lied to us?*

No, I think it was just a fairy tale.

That conversation had been so very ordinary, so unremarkable. Amy had chattered on, a milk mustache above her lip and cookie crumbs on the table, about her day in school and what Jennifer brought for a snack and how the teacher made rain jars.

The day before she was murdered.

Blindly, Linda reached for the table, for something solid and substantial to hold on to. Without seeing, she set the mug in front of her and let her hand rest on the cold wood. It was a coincidence, surely. It had nothing to do with Amy. Cindy Forrest was in the second grade in Oakland, that was all. Part of the curriculum, that's right. Learning about rain.

Do they always talk about God's tears? Is that written in the teachers' handbooks?

She was grasping at straws, that was all, desperate for an excuse to think that the facts pointed to someone other than Matt. If she could convince herself that someone else might have done these terrible things, then she wouldn't have to give up the future. After they had been through so much together, that was the hardest part.

Not true, she admitted, shivering. What was most difficult was accepting that, night after night, she had slept beside a man who might have done unspeakable things. And she had never known, hadn't even guessed, what he was. Shared her bed, her body, her most intimate thoughts with him. She had believed, until yesterday, that despite the difficulties of the past few years, they could learn to talk to each other again, to remember all the things that brought them together.

Then why did a cold fist twist her insides when she considered the things he might have done?

Name them. Go ahead. That's the only way to banish them.

No, not yet. There was still a chance that it wasn't Matt, despite his disappearance, despite the cameo and the clay statues and that odd, dissatisfied note in his voice when he talked about the boredom of his work and living in Pescadero. If only she could make sense of what she'd just heard on the news. It was a straw, but she'd cling to the chance it offered.

Surely the police had checked whether the girls had the same teacher. They'd be looking for patterns, connections. Linda pressed her icy fingers against the still-warm mug.

She glanced at the wall clock. She had to fill two hours somehow, had to quiet the whispering voices that kept Matt's name in the front of her thoughts. She couldn't go out for a walk or a ride. Even if she put the cap back on, wore dark glasses—in the rain?—she wouldn't take the risk of being seen.

She took a bath, washed the tub, threw the towels in the dryer. She scrubbed the kitchen sink with Ajax, cleaned the grout between the tiles with a Q-tip, tried to make the face and voice of Cindy Forrest's mother stop haunting her. Now, Hank in her lap, she sat watching the clock. The sound of Anton's key in the door roused her from a reverie; she had been driving somewhere in the Louisiana bayou. Spanish moss. Thick swamp. Looking for Bea, trying to find New Orleans.

"Sorry I'm late. You talk to Matt?"

"No, I—" *That was dumb, not to think that he would expect you to talk to Matt. Think of an excuse.* "I didn't want to slow him down. You know how he gets when he starts working on something. He wouldn't hear me anyway, working out in the yard. Probably right under this big eucalyptus tree we have. Keeping dry." She was rambling again; maybe he would chalk it up to nervousness.

His back to her, Anton scooped cottage cheese into Hank's dish. "Have you thought about going to the cops and explaining where you were? What you're planning . . . it means having to run all the time. I guess you know what you're doing but I have to say it, as a friend."

If only it was that easy. She couldn't go to the police, especially with that cameo sitting on some shelf in their evidence room. "I was alone both days, all day. I saw no one. That's not going to impress anyone."

He nodded. "That's what I figured. Okay, one more question. Maybe you should wait until dark before you try going back there. What with the Oakland police looking for you and—"

"No, Matt's waiting for me. I better go right now, in fact."

"Let me pack you some sandwiches."

A genuine laugh welled up in Linda. "For a two-hour trip? I can make it all the way to Pescadero without starving to death. But thanks for everything. You're a lifesaver." She hugged him and pulled away quickly, before she let herself say the rest: *Thanks for helping me save myself from your friend, my husband. Thanks for not asking about the cameo.*

She'd head for the Interstate, drive south for four hours, and then cut east at Bakersfield. All the northern roads, the ones through the Sierras, would be closed for the winter; she should have realized that yesterday. It was a good sign that she had the presence of mind to think of it now. She would do this. Each mile she drove would put distance between herself and Pescadero, herself and Oakland, herself and Matt.

His brows knitting together in a frown, Anton followed her to the hall. "You sure you're going to be okay to drive? If you want, I can take the afternoon off and run you back home."

I'm going farther than you imagine, she thought, but before she could say anything, the doorbell rang.

She stepped back, as though whoever stood on the other side of the door couldn't see her if she was a little farther away. Anton's frown deepened; then, he seemed to realize that she was afraid of being discovered by the police and his frown faded.

Thank God she hadn't moved her Honda out of the garage yet. It would be all right, had to be all right. She couldn't bear to be taken to Seventh Street, to sit in one of those interrogation rooms with men leering at her and questions hurtling across the room, piling up one after another and burying her.

She put a finger to her lips, then pointed down the hall in the direction of the small bathroom. Anton nodded.

She stepped backward down the dark corridor and into the half-bath, pulling the door shut behind her.

Get hold of yourself, she warned. Most likely it wasn't the police at all but a Jehovah's witness or a salesman, making the rounds of the neighborhood. She examined the chips in the tile, counted the number of black squares, tried to hear what the voices at the other end of the hall were saying.

A low hum of conversation—male voices—then footsteps.

She held her breath and hugged her knees to her chest from her perch atop the toilet lid.

The footsteps stopped in front of the bathroom door.

There were one hundred twenty-eight black tiles. She started counting the white ones.

"Linda?" Anton knocked once, softly; the doorknob handle turned.

Thirty-seven, thirty-eight white squares. Thirty-nine.

The door opened and Anton smiled down at her. Thank God. She had certainly overreacted that time.

"Linda," he said quietly, "come on out. Matt's here."

seventeen

"I've been so worried. Why didn't you call me?" Matt's face contorted. "What is . . . your hair . . . what did you do to yourself?"

It's only my stigmata, she thought. A better actor than he used to be, Matt was the picture of solicitude. He was putting on a good show, one that she couldn't bring herself to believe. If only she had told Anton everything last night; maybe then he would have come up with a way to help her get far away. Instead, Anton had betrayed her. She'd heard a telephone ring in her sleep and had dreamed it was the sound of a baby crying. The voices: Anton, talking to Matt. Telling him where she was. Well, she needn't waste any more time on "should haves" or "could haves"; they made no difference now.

"Linda." Matt's voice was almost stern; now he was beside her, touching her arm, bending to kiss her cheek, trying to gentle her out of her position on the toilet seat lid. "Anton said you were upset but I didn't expect this. I'm so glad I called him. It's going to be all right, Linnie. I'll make it all right." The pulse at his temples beat visibly under his skin.

If she didn't do something besides sit folded up into herself, Matt and Anton would both become more watchful, more wary of her. She had had enough of their scrutiny already. If she looked too distressed, Matt would try to comfort her, touch her. She needed to think but she also had to avoid arousing his suspicion or even his curiosity. She had to at least *seem* in control. "When I didn't hear from you," she said, "I got worried and I came here. I was afraid the police would find me and you were gone."

"Well, I'm here now. And there's a lot we have to talk about." Matt's voice was soothing, his eyes crinkled with concern.

Talk—maybe she could handle *that*. It was the rest of it— touching his hand accidentally, feeling his breath on her neck . . .

"Why don't we find more comfortable quarters for your conference?" A smile lifted Anton's apple cheeks. "I'm used to meetings in small spaces, but this is a little too, well, intimate."

Had he used that same genial tone when Matt called last night? How stupid she had been to feel safe here. *Had been*— that was the key phrase. If she didn't start learning from her own mistakes, she might as well walk into police headquarters right now and save Matt the trouble of leading them to her.

Matt held out his hand. Pretending she didn't see it, Linda uncurled herself and stood beside him. He reached for her; in the tiny room, it was impossible to avoid contact.

"I'll make some fresh coffee. You two come join me when you're ready." Anton backed out of the bathroom with Hank's steady purr coaxing him down the hall.

"Where have you been, Matt? I was worried about you."

"*You* were worried about *me*? You should have left me a note or called me. I thought I was going to go out of my mind."

Sure. Because you thought your precious setup wasn't going to work. "You haven't answered me."

"I was in Oakland—what's today? Monday?—I was in Oakland when I called you on Saturday. I got back to Pescadero in the middle of the night. That was Sunday morning. You were gone, and when I saw that some of your clothes were missing, I didn't know what to think. I went to Santa Rosa, to your cousin's, but nobody had seen you. I didn't think you'd come here."

He had lied about being in San Jose; she knew that when he called. But Oakland—Cindy Forrest had disappeared from Oakland. On Saturday.

"Why did you disappear without leaving me a note or calling me?" When he ran his hand over her hair, she gritted her teeth to keep from pulling away. "Why did you do that, Lin? I waited at the cottage until I couldn't stand it anymore, and then I drove around looking for you. I didn't sleep more than ten minutes both nights, thinking: Something terrible has happened to her. Then I called Anton, all upset that you were gone."

His eyes flickered, and she wondered what part of what he'd said had been the lie. He wasn't telling the truth, at least not about all of it. Well, let him think she believed him. If she could just get away, she'd go straight to the bank. Three hundred dollars would get her to Nevada; the resorts always needed waitresses. She'd dye her hair, what was left of it.

"Linda, did you hear me?"

"My head is—let's go see if the coffee's ready. Maybe it will help my headache."

"Headache bothering you again?"

She nodded and followed him into the kitchen. He'd forgive her apparent inattention if he thought she had a headache; that would buy her a little more thinking time.

Anton was pouring the last of the water through the Chemex. "Be ready in a minute. Have you two decided what you're going to do?"

"Maybe I should forget talking to those people and take Linda home," Matt said quietly. "She needs rest. And she's getting one of her monster headaches."

Anton looked at her quizzically. "Headaches?"

Matt nodded. "She's been getting these attacks for a while

now. Past week or so, they've been more frequent. Sometimes it gets so bad she can't remember hours at a time."

Don't speak for me, she wanted to shout. I'm not a specimen. "It's not that bad. What Matt means is that sometimes I get these headaches. But it's no big deal. Lots of times, I feel better just driving around. I don't know why but it's soothing, and then I go home." *Same difference, jerk. Matt was pointing out that you can't account for where you were on Thursday and on Saturday.*

"Coffee should help. Dilates the vaso-whatevers, that's why they put caffeine in aspirin." Anton pulled three mugs from the cabinet and set them on the table.

"I'll get the milk." She filled the small, flowered pitcher and inhaled the rich coffee aroma—so civilized, redolent of all those after-dinner conversations they'd had around this table. It wasn't like that now.

"Did I hear you say you were in Oakland Saturday?" Anton stirred sugar into his coffee and looked at Matt. "And you didn't call me?"

"They should have started looking for her earlier." Matt's voice was tight with sudden anger. "The police knew she was missing at, what, four o'clock. But they waited until nine to do something."

Linda's hands trembled.

Anton looked merely puzzled. "How did you know that the little girl was . . ."

Matt stared at the table. "Her mother was running around the streets. It was pouring and this woman stopped everyone she saw on College Avenue, describing the little girl, asking if anyone had seen her."

How could Anton sit and listen without suspicion or surprise to Matt talk about those events? But his round, calm face was only intent on the story, not its meaning. "I saw the mother on television last night. Hard to watch her without feeling her pain. I mean, especially after you and Linda . . . I . . ." Anton shook his head. "Seeing her on television brought it all back."

The television interview. The mother's anguish and her sweet words as she talked to her daughter. *Rain jars.* Maybe there *was* another explanation; maybe she had been trying to force the facts into a shape that would accommodate her worst fears about Matt.

"Linda, what is it?" Matt stared at her now, his eyes dark and small. "What did he say?"

She had no right to keep it from him, no right to play God in a universe whose rules changed often and unpredictably. She doubted that she understood how the past became the present, and in any case, she no longer knew which future she would choose.

"The teacher," she said flatly.

Matt's face twisted into a perplexed frown. "What are you talking about?"

"Amy told me about the rain jars, too," she replied.

"Linda." Matt's fingers dug into her arm.

"Maybe you'd better lighten up a little," Anton said. "Maybe you should let go of her."

Matt turned to him. "Jesus, what am I doing? I'm so worried about her. I keep thinking I'm going to lose her too and—"

With a shrug, she disengaged from his grasp. "You don't have to hurt me anymore. I just have a headache. A lot has happened. We're all upset."

The veins on Matt's forehead stood out, blue and thick. He rubbed his hand over the stubble on his chin. "I'm so exhausted I can't think straight. Maybe I should go upstairs and lie down, try to rest a little."

"Good idea," Linda said, knowing that *she* wouldn't rest until she was far away. The biggest problem would be getting the Honda out of the garage. If Anton went back to work, if

Matt did fall asleep, she would do it. He would sleep deeply, if he was telling the truth about not having slept for two nights. But why should she assume that he was telling the truth about anything?

Anton lay his hand on the table. "I'm still confused. All that talk about a trip last night—that was just Linda being upset?"

"Trip?" Matt echoed. "We're not going anywhere, not even back to Pescadero. I need to sleep and Linda needs to get rid of her headache. These headaches—whether they're caused by stress or what, we don't know, but she can't go anywhere now. The blackouts and all."

She'd never had blackouts. Maybe she'd lost pieces of the hours immediately surrounding Amy's death . . . was he calling her inability to remember how she'd gotten home after one of her drives a *blackout?* That wasn't fair. "Matt, I—"

"Linda, you should see your face. You look all panicky, like you're being held against your will in the enemy camp or something. We'll talk later."

Anton lowered his eyes. "Then you won't be needing the money," he said softly.

Now it was Matt's turn to look bewildered. "Money?"

Don't blow it, she thought. You still have options. "I was scared. I thought that when you got back, going away would be the best thing for us. We don't have much cash so I asked if we could borrow some from Anton."

The silence felt interminable.

"We aren't going anywhere." Matt sounded like he was being as patient as he could with an especially stubborn child. "I'm here now and everything is going to be all right."

Light from the colored crystals in the brass chandelier glinted on the wall like stained glass in a church.

"I'm going upstairs." Matt rose from his chair.

Don't touch me, she wanted to scream. He bent to her but she didn't flinch when his dry, warm lips brushed her cheek.

Maybe she was making this all up.

Making up the cameo?

Inventing the sculptures?

Making up the fact that Matt was unaccounted for when Marianne Brandon was murdered, when Cindy Forrest disappeared?

She had to find Bea. Three hundred dollars, if she was careful, would get her to New Orleans. If she had to use credit cards, maybe that risk was worth it, better than staying here with Matt. He might be spinning a tale, concocting a web to catch her in. As soon as she got a chance, she would fly away.

eighteen

Jay Goldstein rolled up to a white zone on Franklin Avenue and flipped the visor so that his Police Association card was visible. He dashed between fat, lazy raindrops to the canopied entrance of the building where Lois Edelberg had her office.

The lobby smelled like wet shoes and cigar smoke. Goldstein wiped his feet on the runner that bisected the corridor and headed for the bank of elevators. He first met Lois twelve years ago when his father, Aaron, found out that Jay was joining the Oakland Police Department. Certain that his son would never choose to be a policeman except in response to severe emotional trauma, Aaron had insisted that Jay see a psychiatrist. Jay had struck a bargain with Aaron: After four visits, if the doctor found that there was no need for Jay to continue seeing her, Aaron was never again to mention his displeasure at Jay's choice. For his part, Jay would continue treatment if that was the doctor's recommendation.

Toward the end of that first hour, Goldstein discovered that despite the considerable difference in their ages he and Lois shared a common fascination with Kierkegaard. They spent the remaining time discussing the aesthetic/ethical polarity in *Either-Or*. By the end of the second visit, Lois admitted to Goldstein that she felt guilty about taking Aaron's money, but she agreed that two more visits would keep the bargain honest and wouldn't violate *either* her ethical *or* her aesthetic sensibilities. Three years ago she'd shifted her focus to teaching, which still left her time to meet Goldstein several times a year for dinner or to take long walks on the beach, to talk philosophy and to catch up on their very different lives.

And sometimes, he even consulted her, as he would today.

The elevator deposited him on the third floor; the lighting was dismal, which was just as well, he thought, since it made the peeling ochre paint less noticeable. He made his way to the pebbled-glass door with her name neatly lettered in the lower right corner. He knocked, then entered her office.

It was as though the room were part of a different, more careful and elegant world. The walls were covered in pale blue paper with delicate, irregularly spaced white stripes. An oak paddle fan with a globe light in the center hung over a rolltop desk. A woman wearing earphones, her eyes closed and a dreamy smile spread across her face, lolled in a leather chair.

She had to be seventy-five, her hair thinning and white. The flesh around her mouth was pouched and wrinkled, but her eyes, as they flew open and looked directly at him, were still the same intense violet that had captivated him twelve years earlier.

"Jay." She removed the earphones and straightened herself in one easy motion, standing to receive his hug. Lois Edelberg was one of the few people not related to him by blood whom Jay Goldstein embraced without restraint.

"Thanks for seeing me on such short notice, Lois. I know you've changed your schedule and I—"

Her pale eyebrows rose with each word. "If you keep prattling, Jay, you're going to get yourself in trouble. Now, I have fifteen minutes only, so let's talk killers." Once, she had admitted that she envied policemen their macabre humor. If you had to deal with death everyday, she said, the least you could do for yourself was to make jokes about it. "I know you've asked the obvious questions already, right? What do the children's parents have in common? Do they all work at the same place? Did the children all go to the same school? Did they all use the same day-care center? The same baby-sitter? The same grocery store?"

Goldstein nodded. "You're right. We're checking those things. The department shrink presented a profile, standard stuff that you could have come up with in the middle of the night when you had a hangover on top of the flu."

Her smile always made him feel as though it was something she saved for him and no one else.

"But I'm still not convinced," he continued, "that the same person would have committed both these crimes. The Brandon murder and the Crell case three years ago have an obvious link, like the killer was leaving his calling card, symbolically—the dolls. Both children were stabbed only once, in the chest. The bodies weren't concealed very well, as though he was flaunting what he'd done. Or wanted to be caught."

"Or both." Lois's voice was quiet, her face an immobile fixture in which her extraordinary eyes darted from thought to thought as he spoke.

"But with the Forrest child, there's been no sign of a body. I want to believe it's the same person because one arrest would wrap up everything neatly, but it doesn't fit."

Lois tilted her chair. "It *is* highly unusual that someone who would murder in this way would also kidnap a child and not make his actions public. You're right. But maybe there's a scenario where all the elements fit."

"Maybe he's feeling remorse about Marianne, and he wants to make it up by taking care of Cindy Forrest. In a warped way, that seems possible." Although he'd never been particularly adept at the method-acting school of detection, Goldstein now and again found that he had made an unexpected leap into the heart of the person it was his job to apprehend. More often, random stabs at plausibility turned up at least one interesting theory.

Lois shook her head. "Don't try so hard to make it complicated, Jay. He wants attention—a major factor. Part of the attention is that he knows a crime against a child—any crime, any child—is fodder for the media."

"And it's also the most intense motivation, except for the murder of a fellow officer, for all policemen." Goldstein was constantly reminding himself that he was doing all he could in this case. "Did you know that this particular child is a diabetic? If she's not dead already, she will be soon."

As though she were trying to keep everything else out so she could concentrate on getting closer to the killer, Lois hunched her shoulders together. "The person who commits crimes against children . . . often there have been frequent episodes of childhood abuse directed against him. Classically, the only way such a person can feel powerful even as an adult is to act out against other children. It's so transparent that it blinks like a neon sign." She sat back, her shoulders relaxing momentarily. "Does that qualify as a mixed metaphor? Anyway, I'm sure this is nothing new to you."

"That's where the department psychologist stopped. It took him twenty minutes to cover the same ground you just did in twenty seconds."

Now it was Lois's turn to beam with the pleasure of being in the company of someone whose intelligence was a match for her own. "You, of course, have already expanded on the theory and refined it, yes?"

"Of course," Goldstein acknowledged. "Not only is our killer likely to have been a victim in one way or another himself as a child, he probably has wildly distorted thought patterns: black-and-white perceptions, magical mind-reading, labeling, generalizations."

"Good, good. Don't stop, Jay. Keep going."

Despite her bright encouragement, Goldstein hit the same wall that he'd run into whenever he thought about this in the past few days. "Could be an indication of *my* pathology, but that's as far as I can go."

That Lois didn't stop to chide him or examine the underpinnings of his inability to press on was one of the things he most valued in her.

"If it is the same person," she said, "it's likely that he grew up in an alcoholic or otherwise dysfunctional family. He may have assumed what the current jargon calls a co-dependent role. Because the family history has created a world in which the only acceptable roles are either to be in need or to provide for the needs of others, he may have taken the second choice.

"As long as someone else is in trouble, he can fit himself into the role of rescuer. It gives him validity. Now here's where it really gets twisted. If people close to him aren't in trouble, this co-dependent may encourage or even manufacture trouble."

"So that they can get their rocks off by being saviors?"

"Rocks off? This means what, Jay?"

Her worldliness was so uneven; Goldstein unfolded his legs and grinned. "Figuratively, it means they have a peak pleasure experience."

"I have made a nimble mental leap to the literal meaning," she said, eyes sparkling. "What about the dolls? Have you any thoughts on the subject?"

"The ritualism—that indicates to me a desire to establish an identity and a need to be caught and punished. I think he'll do something to give himself away. That's not a guarantee, mind you, but we're all watching for the next sign. I figure it's coming soon. He's going to tip his hand."

"We keep saying 'he,' don't we?"

As her hand moved toward her mouth in a gesture he had seen countless times when she was engaged in sorting and ordering her thoughts, Goldstein had a momentary vision of Lois as a young woman, an electric presence who lit rooms. *She can still do that,* he thought.

"That's a major assumption, Jay, but it's based on the statistics and the literature. It could be a woman, but I bet it isn't. I haven't been much help, have I? It's not an area I know a lot about. I called several colleagues, but they weren't much help either, I'm afraid. I'm sorry that I couldn't—"

"Now who's going on and on? If you keep talking like this, I'm going to feel compelled to act out as the rescuer, and then I'll have you suspecting me." He took her almost weightless hand in his. "You're the only woman I know who doesn't want to prove something at my expense or get me to make a commitment of some kind."

"Don't be so sure, darling. Don't be so sure." She was readjusting the headphones as he pulled the door shut.

Cruz stepped around a cardboard carton of papers and draped his raincoat over a wooden folding chair. "Quinn and Cavessena asked us to show these around. They're making a big deal again about trying to locate the Crells."

Cruz handed him a blow-up of a grainy photograph; Goldstein recognized it as a two-year old newspaper photo from the final phase of Linda Crell's trial. "Your shrink friend have anything to say?"

Goldstein summarized his interview with Lois Edelberg. "It's complicated," he concluded. "Why don't we talk about it on the way to the four o'clock briefing, okay?"

Cruz nodded and went off to a table set up along the rear wall, where eight volunteers, each with a phone clutched between shoulder and ear, all wrote busily on their yellow pads. In the far corner, her champagne-colored sweater and skirt casting a golden glow around her, Charlotte Wertz sat opposite the girl he'd met yesterday morning. Did her mother really sell cocaine? to the ladies of the PTA? He nodded a greeting as he approached, but the girl looked away. Did all adolescents think that adults of the opposite sex wielded some mysterious power? Shy—but she'd outgrow it.

"I'll be right back," Michelle said. She jumped out of her chair as though she were a startled doe and he a clumsy hunter; Goldstein watched her make a production of taking a soda from the small refrigerator beside the door. He handed Charlotte a photo of Matthew and Linda Crell and studied her face as she squinted at the page, tracing the movement of her green eyes from the mouth to the hair to the eyes, always returning to the eyes. "Have you seen either of these people recently?"

Finally she looked at Goldstein. "Yes. I'm sure I've seen *him*. I can't remember where, though. Maybe it will come to me later. Now about that report yesterday. Is—"

"Here? Somewhere in the neighborhood? like at the supermarket or in a restaurant?" This was one conversation he didn't want her to control. "If you could narrow down where you saw him, come a little closer . . ."

"That would be remembering, Sergeant. I'll think about it, and if I come up with anything, I'll let you know." She sighed and leaned back in her chair, her gaze calculating and direct. "This isn't easy for any of us. Now it's my turn to apologize for being snappish."

"Accepted. How's your little friend doing?" he said, nodding toward Michelle. "Good kid," he said, suddenly uncomfortable with the silence that sprang up between them.

Charlotte lay both hands flat on the table. Goldstein noticed for the first time that she wore no rings.

"Too good, I sometimes think," she said.

Goldstein's skin prickled. "Too good?"

"She cares too much and she'll get hurt over and over

again. It will keep confusing her because her only mistake will have been to care too much."

Lois's words came back to him; hadn't Charlotte Wertz, on a grand scale, taken on the role of rescuer? "And she'll try to protect others from getting too badly hurt by being there to break their fall, as you're doing for her—and for the Forrests and Irene Brandon. Is that it?"

Charlotte Wertz turned crimson.

He'd better back off. He'd need more than a fit between Lois's theory and the very common and easily understood desire to help before he'd allow himself to consider Charlotte a potential suspect. He handed her five copies of the Crell photos. "Show these around, would you? And let me know if anyone's seen either of these people. Sergeant Cruz and I have a meeting in twenty minutes. We'll check back with you later this evening."

Charlotte snatched the papers from his hand and whirled away as Cruz, tapping the face of his watch, maneuvered toward the coatrack near the door. Goldstein nodded, grabbed his raincoat, and made his way around a carton—the volunteer center was sprouting cartons filled with reports much more quickly than he and Cruz could do anything about it. As he reached for the door, it flew open and Dexter Williams hustled inside, shaking rain from his shoulders. Albert Toller followed a few steps behind. Despite his paleness, Williams graced Goldstein and Cruz with a brilliant smile.

"Never fails to amaze me." He wiped his face with a handkerchief and shook his head.

"What's that, Mr. Williams?" Cursing himself for getting started on a tiresome conversation, Goldstein backed toward the door.

"Beginner's mind. Every winter, I'm surprised all over again by the rain and how long it lasts and how dark it gets and how cold it feels. Same with summer. Like I've never been here before." The man's pale, drawn face became more animated as he spoke.

"People who don't learn from their experiences—that's who has beginner's mind," Toller snapped. "You didn't sign four reports yesterday, Dexter."

Williams looked away. "If you can tell that it was *me* that didn't sign them, then there's no problem, right? Why don't you stop minding my business, Al?"

"Finding the killer, finding Cindy—isn't that your business here? We have to do it right, don't we, Sergeant Goldstein?"

If they paid half as much attention to the task as they did to the petty rules, they'd all be better off. "I have to go now, gentlemen," Goldstein said, his hand again on the doorknob.

Williams screwed up his already tight mouth. "And we'd better start answering the phones."

Glad for a statement he could heartily endorse, Goldstein nodded and stepped into the rain.

"Sergeant Goldstein, wait. Michelle has something to tell you." Charlotte gave the girl an encouraging nod.

Goldstein followed Cruz back inside.

"The man in this picture," the girl said, flush-cheeked and whispering, "was in my father's hardware store the other day. He was asking about Mrs. Brandon."

Somehow the news didn't surprise him. "What day was that, Michelle?" Goldstein asked.

"Saturday." Her voice was barely audible. "The day Cindy Forrest disappeared. Around three, maybe a little after. I know because that's the time I get to the store every Friday and Saturday. I work there."

"Thanks, Michelle. You've been a big help." He patted her shoulder and followed Cruz out the door. Now he *was* surprised: The fact that Matthew Crell, a man he'd never met, had moved onto the short list of suspects, filled Jay Goldstein with a deep and heavy sadness.

nineteen

"See Cavessena."

"Where is she?" Cruz jogged after Webster, who was flying by with a phone book in his hands.

"Fuck do I know," Webster muttered as he disappeared around the corner.

"Quinn." Cruz straight-armed a tall, red-haired man as he sprinted toward the Homicide-room door. "Where's Cavessena?"

"Dunno, but she wants to talk to you. I don't have time to explain; she'll tell you. Gotta run, *amigo.* Some poor jerk in the lockup at Kaiser Hospital is talking that he doesn't want to hurt any more kids, so I get to go check him out. See you later."

Quinn ducked out the door. So much for trying to avoid Cavessena. Cruz pulled two messages from his in box and read them without interest. The Fresno police had checked out the sighting and were sorry to tell him that it wasn't Cindy Forrest who had been seen in a pickup truck. And the Kansas City liaison officer was sorry, but they didn't have the personnel to do more than include the request for information in morning summaries. He reached for his case folder; at this rate, he'd need a whole file drawer just for the volunteer center dead ends.

Despite the bustle in the hall, the Homicide room was

eerily quiet. "Got a chocolate bar in your pocket?" Morella called as Cruz sat down.

"Have a cup of coffee. Don't blow it, man. McNaughton'll be after your fat ass if you gain back that fifty pounds. Think of it, Morella—that's five bags of potatoes."

"You know, when you put it that way, it's like not carrying a six-year-old kid around all the time." Morella swigged from a Pepsi and grimaced. "I want to get this fucker so bad. I'm afraid of what I'll do if—" The phone rang on Morella's desk. He dabbed at the sweat on his forehead and picked up the receiver. "Morella. Homicide." He frowned, then nodded and put his hand over the mouthpiece. "For you." Grumbling, Morella handed Cruz the phone and then began pecking away at the typewriter.

Cruz leaned against Morella's desk. "Cruz. Homicide."

"Listen, Cruz. Could you call Ed Forrest and tell them that they did fine? Andrea says they're worried they blew it. I already called, but they still sounded shaky."

Cavessena, going a hundred miles an hour. If there was one thing Cruz didn't want to do, it was talk to Margie Forrest without bringing her news of her daughter, but if he could help her feel better, then he'd do it. "Okay, sure, Tina. I have to—"

"Did you get to any of those names on the list of the Crells' friends? Any new leads?"

"Cavessena?" Cruz wished she'd hit him with one thing at a time. Better yet, he wished she'd remember that he had his own work to do. "I did two names. Noreen Kimball and Margaret Masters. Neither of them know where Matthew and Linda Crell are, haven't seen them since before the trial, they said. They each gave me two names already on the list and that's that. Okay?"

"Good, because when you have a chance, there are three new—"

He could almost see Cavessena running her pink fingernail

down a list. "Look, Tina, I've got plenty of my own work to take care of already. I've got maybe fifteen new sightings I should follow up on. The best I can say is I don't know."

"I already said when you have a chance. I know what the load is. Everyone else said they'd try. One more name."

Would he be sitting here grinding his teeth if it was Quinn asking him to do this? But it wasn't. It was Tina. "I'll try. One name. That's it. That's all. *Finito.*"

"Anton Brodsky. He's in the book, out on Ocean View. Thanks a lot, sport." As soon as Cavessena's words were out, the line went dead.

First Cavessena's anger and now he had Margie Forrest's pain to look forward to. Ignoring the activity around him, Cruz dialed the number. Get it over with, he told himself. Don't think. Just do it.

The phone was answered on the first ring.

"Hello?"

It was Ed Forrest and not his wife who answered; relief flooded Cruz. "Mr. Forrest, this is Carlos Cruz. I wanted you to know how effective everyone thought the interview was. It went great. In fact, since it's been shown, we got probably three hundred calls. We're going through them as fast as we can."

"But no news, right?" Ed Forrest didn't want to hear about police procedure; he wanted to know about his daughter.

"As soon as we hear anything, Mr. Forrest, we'll—"

An angry, unexpected dial tone buzzed in Cruz's ear. *Thanks a lot, Cavessena,* Cruz thought. *I really needed that.*

He rubbed his fingers in tiny circles to erase the jolt of pain in his head, then looked up. The briefing was scheduled to begin in five minutes, and, one by one, the members of the homicide squad were sliding into their chairs. Morella was starting in on a sugar doughnut.

"What about that nurse report?" he asked between bites.

"You know, the one from the male nurse on Pill Hill. Something about a pediatric surgeon?"

Erikson sneered and shook his head. "Fuckin' crazy, man. You go to a hospital to be taken care of and they got fuckin' crazy people working on you."

"Shut up, Erikson." Webster's tie dangled loosely from his neck; his cocoa skin glistened with perspiration. "The guy was an army medic who worked on a bunch of kids in Saigon who were burned in an explosion of a munitions warehouse. He's no suspect. First of all, he was in the O.R. all day Thursday and all day Saturday."

"They call back from Seattle yet?" Goldstein asked.

"No." Morella looked up at the clock on the wall. "Cop who called said that if he didn't get back to me by six, either they ran into a problem or they didn't have a chance to follow up on it yet."

"What's the latest from McNaughton?" Cruz asked.

"Lieutenant said the high mucky-mucks finally agree that it's the same person." Webster rocked a little in his chair. "I'm still not so sure, myself. I don't see why he'd do in one kid and not the other. If he's a killer, he's a killer. If he's a nut case who kidnaps little girls, then that's what he is. But I don't think he'd just wait and wait. I think the kid is dead, only no one's found her body."

For Webster, this was a major speech. *Funny,* Cruz thought, *in this kind of case, feelings run so high that some people do a total about-face.* Morella, who was the one he usually counted on for stories and chatter, had been very quiet, almost subdued since this whole thing started, while Webster continued to run off at the mouth with nervous energy.

"Looks like we unofficially started this briefing." Webster pushed himself off his perch and paced to the wire-covered window at the back of the room. "So let's sum up the news. We're nowhere, folks. The helicopters can't go out as long as the weather is so bad. The dogs got confused with all the wet weather, too, ended up going in about twelve different directions. We got a couple guys from Vice in deep with the kiddie-porn trip, but they got nothing so far." His pacing brought him around to the front of the room; he planted his feet wide apart, clasped his hands behind his back, and leaned forward from the waist. "The only thing that's looking real is this Crell business. Goldstein says a kid saw the husband the day Cindy disappeared. It was the wife's prints on the knife and the wife who had the kid in her arms—their kid, I mean. It gets weird to think that . . ." He frowned. "So if everyone would cooperate with Quinn and Cavessena and take one more name, that would help. I want Matthew Crell. He's the *man* of the hour, folks, because that kid saw him here in town. But I want the *wife,* too. I'll personally do the paperwork for an entire week for whoever pops them."

"A week's too cheap. Make it a month, Web, and I'll bring them in." Smith's joke seemed to signal an end to the briefing. The Homicide room buzzed with conversation but it was nothing more than meaningless talk; Cruz felt jumpy, irritated at the noise, annoyed by Erikson's braying laughter.

"I gotta get some air. Anyone want anything from the store?" If he didn't get outside and move around, he'd drown in all the chitchat. No one answered. Possibly no one heard him. Exasperated, Cruz left his raincoat and umbrella in the room and trotted to the hall. He jabbed at the elevator Down button, and tried to shift his thoughts away from Ed Forrest and Webster, away from Goldstein and Morella, to Elenya and the boys, but the elevator arrived before he could get into a fantasy of joining them at the beach cottage. The doors slid open; Cruz nodded to the two uniforms who leaned against the rear rail.

"That's the third ambulance since September," the tall one said. He didn't look more than seventeen.

"Junkies. Whole fucking lot of 'em oughta be electrocuted.

Take 'em out and zap 'em all. Stealing. Going nuts. That ambulance coulda been needed somewheres else and they make this fucking false call, just so they can get spikes. What a fucking sorry world."

Cruz remembered what it had been like early on, the need to come up with sweeping solutions to wipe out all the junkies or whoever happened to be in your face on that particular day. He tried to form a picture of Julio in his mind; when the chin was round enough, he started working on Carlito.

"Funny thing, though. They're going to be in for some surprise. They got their needles, all right. But whatever they thought was in those vials, they couldn't read or what, I don't know, but they're going to be fucking disappointed. Insulin. That's all." He snorted derisively.

With a hammering that resounded in his ears, Cruz felt his heart thud. *Insulin.* Someone had stolen insulin from a paramedic vehicle. He whirled around. "You guys checked out another ambulance job?"

The short cop nodded. "Coupla hours ago. Call came in direct to Providence Hospital. Some guy shrieking about he can't move, he's got pains in his chest and he's seeing black spots, and they talk him down till he's calm enough to give them directions. Cottage in front of the house on Opal near Thirty-eighth, he says. Ambulance gets there, both paramedics rush out with their bags, get chased by a dog, and find fucking nothing. It finally dawns on the assholes that they been had and they rush back to their vehicle and sure as fucking shooting, the back doors are busted open and a stash of hypodermics are missing. They call it in and when we get there, they do an inventory. At first they think it's weird because the usual stuff the cocksuckers go for is all there. I mean, nothing else looks like it's been touched. So Lynch tells them, go over your list, like you were stocking up. Maybe fifteen seconds later they discover that their stash of insulin is missing."

The chubby cop broke into peals of merry laughter. "Stupid asshole fucking junkies. Serves them right."

Cruz would have bet a month's pay that it wasn't someone looking for a high who had taken the insulin.

twenty

The streetlights had come on twenty minutes ago, seconds before the Seth Thomas clock above the mantel chimed five. Until Amy's death, Linda had loved the quiet comfort of the early dark of winter. Now she settled into the bentwood rocker in Anton's shadow-filled living room and tried to recapture that feeling, but an image of Matt and the echo of Margaret Forrest's voice intruded on the silence.

Her legs tucked under her, a cup of tea cooling on the table, she let her hand drift down to stroke the cat's head. He ducked away, leaped under the gauzy curtain, and settled on the sill of the window, where he proceeded to lick a paw and then rub his ear, over and over again. Beyond the window curtain, everything was soft-edged, blurred by the filmy fabric. The lights of passing cars threw figures and objects into sharp relief.

Now, the rhythmic, even sound of Matt chopping vegetables in the kitchen punctuated the quiet. Unable to sleep, he had paced the living-room floor, listened to the four-o'clock news, and then disappeared into the kitchen muttering something about stew. The Honda was still in the garage, and she still didn't know what she thought, really, about the cameo and the statues and the stories Matt offered to explain where he had been.

A car passed on the street, headlights cutting through the rain. She rocked and watched, thinking about Matt. She had never seen him mistreat an animal, a child, an old person, couldn't imagine him pulling wings off flies or tying tin cans to puppies' tails. His most effective weapon was his ability to retreat beyond reach, beyond truth. Confusion settled in with her for the evening. She rocked, watching, thinking.

The rocking chair tilted forward as she strained to see past the curtains. A car pulled up to the curb across the street. It was a Toyota, like the one that stopped in their driveway in Pescadero the other night. Her mouth became cottony, her palms damp. The man who got out and locked the car door— yes, he could be the same one, the man with the flashlight who had walked around her car to check her license plate.

He dashed from the Toyota across the street to Anton's walk, his shoulders hunched together as he loped easily to the door. He wouldn't be able to see her through the curtains as long as the lights in the front of the house were dark, but if the cat decided to jump down from the window and if he pushed the curtains aside, someone standing at the door would have a fleeting but unobstructed glimpse into the living room. She could barely swallow, her breathing sounded like a bellows to her but she sat, unmoving, in the rocker.

The bell rang.

Had Matt sent them after her?

The cat stood and arched its back, then settled onto the sill again as the man pounded on the door; maybe he would go around the house to the garage and find the Honda or see the lights burning in the kitchen. Maybe Matt would come in to investigate the noise.

Nobody's home. Go away.

As if responding to her command, the dark-haired man turned and ran with that same easy stride back across the street to his car. The Toyota sputtered once, then started up, and he drove away.

"What was that?" Scowling, Matt stood in the doorway.

"Salesman or something, I guess. It seemed better not to answer it."

Matt nodded and looked as though he was going to say something but a frown wrinkled his forehead. A sweetish smell —of onions about to burn, of seared meat—had followed him into the living room. "Oh, shit, I better turn down the flame under the stew." He whirled around and was gone, Hank trailing after him down the hall.

Linda sprang from the rocker; as its blades slapped back and forth on the parquet floor, she knew, at last, what she had been hiding from herself since the day of Amy's death. She paced the length of the room in long, hard strides. The memory had been pried loose when she'd heard about the cameo, was shoved closer to the light by the sight of Matt's workroom filled with replicas of the dolls. She had tried to push it away but here at Anton's, it had surfaced anyway, and now she recognized the wrong note, the disharmony in the memory that she had pieced together about that evening three years earlier.

I don't understand, Anton. They said he was at your office.
—I expect him any minute, Linda. Calm down. Is there anything I can do for you?
No, nothing. Ask him to give me a call, would you?
—Sure. Kiss Amy for me, okay?

She no longer knew whether it was memory or fantasy. So much of that day remained buried, stored in inaccessible niches in her mind.

She remembered making several phone calls that evening. The first was to Amy's friend Jennifer; there had been no answer. Then, Matt's secretary said that Matt left over an hour ago and Linda should call him at Anton's Berkeley office.

Yet, when she did call, Anton told her that Matt wasn't there. He promised to have Matt call as soon as he arrived.

Matt's office was only ten minutes from Anton's. Where had Matt been?

The picture, sharper now and brighter, made her sick with fear and anger.

Matt lied to her about where he was the afternoon that Amy was killed.

Matt wasn't at work when Marianne Brandon was murdered, was somewhere in Oakland when Cindy Forrest was abducted.

Her cameo was found around the neck of the doll beside Marianne Brandon's body.

Matt's studio was filled with replicas of the doll.

Could you live with someone for years and know so little about him? Surely she would have seen signs. Coming up with *reasons*—that was harder. Perhaps he had been jealous of the closeness that she and Amy had developed in reaction to his devotion to his work. Maybe he was so angry at being excluded by his wife and daughter that he'd extracted a twisted retribution. Since she had been acquitted by a jury, maybe he needed to find other ways to make sure she'd be punished.

In fact if she had answered the door a couple of minutes ago and invited the man in—to talk to Matt about what he was doing in Oakland on Saturday, and about where he'd been when he was supposed to be finishing the work at the Sharpe house on Thursday—she might have saved the police a lot of trouble. *And what about the missing child?*

A warning broke through the barrier she was working so hard to erect. The little girl might be alive. She should tell the police about Matt. It might save the child's life.

Her hands were steady as she reached for the telephone book. She flipped past the first-aid and earthquake emergency sections until she found the city government listings.

There it was. Oakland Police Department. The long column of numbers swam before her, and she jumped as a current of hot air blew out from the floor vent when the furnace went on. Pots and cabinet doors slammed in the kitchen; Matt was busy, at least for a while.

She clutched the receiver and dialed the Homicide number. The sound of each ring pierced her.

Finally, a businesslike voice answered. "Oakland Police Department. Hold, please."

More waiting. Linda held the phone tight and was reminded of her mother, hair rolled away from her face in an old-fashioned style that made her round cheeks shine and her eyes stand out. It was odd, that way she had of hopping from one foot to the other when she talked on the phone. Her mother was usually tranquil, but even the simplest telephone transaction so stimulated her that she couldn't stand still.

"Smith. Homicide."

The brusque tone startled her, and she almost dropped the phone. So much like the cops who had questioned her. So much like the guards at the city jail.

"Somebody there?" The voice was annoyed. If she waited another second, he'd hang up.

"My husband . . ."

The words that might stop Matt wouldn't come. She could put herself physically in his way, but she couldn't tell this faceless voice that she was troubled about what Matt *might* have done.

"Lady, look, you don't have to give me your name if it makes you feel better. Just tell me whatever you want to, okay?"

"I . . . I have information about someone. You've been looking for him but he's changed his name and—"

"Ma'am. What is this in reference to?"

"It's about the Brandon case," she said softly.

"Ma'am, I didn't hear what you said. Please repeat that."

Linda lay the receiver back in the cradle, her fingers curled around the hard plastic. Tiny bubbles of panic burst along the length of her arms and inside her head.

She couldn't betray Matt, not until she was certain.

She huddled in the chair, as though she could make herself invisible while she was figuring out what to do. Doing nothing seemed by far the worst alternative.

The phone rang. Without thinking, Linda reached for the receiver and said hello.

"Can I talk to Linda?"

Bea. Everything was going to work out—unless Matt picked up the kitchen extension. This was the sign she'd been waiting for, the answer offered by a provident power; all she had to do was seize the opportunity and keep things simple. She listened for a click, a change in the sound.

"It's me. Oh, Bea, I'm so glad you called."

"Well, Martha gave me your note. Twenty minutes ago. Said she was gonna charge me for personal delivery service."

"I came by to see you but you'd already left for New Orleans and then I had to—never mind. Where are you now?"

"I'm at Smitty's. Might have looked like I left, but I went and gave the concrete block to Mrs. Chow next door and then took off for Santa Cruz to visit with a friend. I swear, it takes Smitty a week to think about something and then another week to do it." She laughed. "We're into the second week now."

Bea was still in Pescadero. Now, despite the rain, despite the racket of confusion in her brain, the world looked infinitely brighter. But she'd better make arrangements quickly.

"I've been thinking, Bea. You want some company on your trip?"

Bea chortled. "Didn't know Joanne Woodward was giving Paul so much freedom these days."

"My eyes aren't as blue but—"

"But you need to get away for a while, right?" This was a

different voice. No jokes; all business. Bea knew more than she was saying.

"Yes, I do need to get away. I'll be at the trailer park by, say, seven tomorrow evening."

"You be careful, honey. You take care not to call attention to yourself, hear? Now, do you think it would better for me to come get you?"

"No, I'll be there by seven. If I'm not, you go ahead without me." She hung up and stood at the window, unseeing. She couldn't leave now, unless it was without the car, and then she'd have to hitchhike in the rain. Hardly a solution. She'd wait until morning. In the morning, she'd think of something. And she'd meet Bea in Pescadero. Long before seven o'clock.

"Who was on the phone?" A wooden spoon dangled from Matt's hand; his face was in shadow.

"Someone selling light bulbs," she said. "I told him we didn't need any."

PART FIVE

Tuesday

twenty-one

Linda pulled her legs tighter toward her body. If she made herself small enough, Matt might continue to sleep soundly without touching her. In the dark, holding herself away from him, she had hit upon a plan; its simplicity was beautiful. She'd say she needed tampons; Matt hated buying them for her. It was pouring, and Anton's house was several blocks from the nearest store, so it would make sense for her to drive. She had nearly a full tank of gas, enough to get her to Pescadero to meet Bea. Missing cameos and clay statues and all the other signs of her apparently endless capacity for self-deception would be left behind.

She was going to save herself with a little help from *her* friend, not Matt's.

He mumbled something and reached for her, his hand brushing her shoulder before she rolled away. She'd have to leave without extra clothing. Maybe when Matt was in the shower she could take the snapshots of Amy, but probably that was all. She'd stuff some clean underwear into her purse, too. Dress in layers—T-shirt, turtleneck, cardigan, jacket—that would help.

Once past the obstacle of Matt and Anton, the next problem would be the Oakland cops. The rain was in her favor; minor accidents would keep them busy, if she was lucky. She'd get out of the city if she could only get out of the house. As she lifted her clothes from the back of the chair, Matt stretched and opened one eye.

"Headache better?"

Linda nodded and struggled into her jeans.

"You going to start the coffee?"

She nodded again, pulled on a clean sweater, and went down to the cold kitchen, where she attended to the coffee preparation, her movements deliberate and sparing. The quiet soothed her.

"Want some O.J.?" His hair flattened on one side and his cheek wrinkled from sleep, Matt stood in the doorway. Stubble darkened his chin and his jaw. He opened the refrigerator, poured juice into two glasses and handed her one.

All so normal. Linda sipped at the tart juice, busying herself at the stove so that she wouldn't have to turn around and face him.

"After I shower," Matt said in his velvety morning voice, "I have to go out and talk to a couple of people. I'll be back later, about noon, maybe a little after. We'll see then about going back to Pescadero."

What people? And are you really going to just talk? Last week that statement would have sounded perfectly innocent. But now she was listening differently to everything he said. Perhaps she wasn't being fair; maybe she should back off a little. This was Matt, after all, not some monster.

Why did you make those clay images? Where were you when Amy was murdered? How did my cameo get around the doll's neck?

If she kept him talking, maybe he would convince her that she was mistaken about the signs and portents she thought she saw. And if she was *asking* questions, she wouldn't have to answer any. "Where are you going?" she asked, turning to face him.

His face closed up as though he'd drawn a shade over it. "Just to talk to some people." He drained the last of the juice from his glass, rinsed it, and stared at the coffee carafe before he filled two cups and handed her one. "Anton said we could stay as long as we needed to. You be okay for the morning?"

Linda nodded and accepted the coffee. Signs and portents: Better to face facts and keep her own good counsel. If everything went as she planned, she'd be okay for longer than this morning. "Fine. I'll be fine."

"I have to get moving." He brushed her cheek with his lips and then was gone up the stairs; shower water pounded above her head.

By small degrees, the tension seeped from the muscles along her shoulders, her jaw unlocked, and Linda allowed herself a full, clean breath. She wouldn't have to tell Matt any lies, not anything at all because he was going out. Anton would leave for work. And she would go meet Bea.

Hank's toenails clicked on the hardwood floor as he padded to the hall, purring noisily to encourage Anton to come downstairs. Round, bright-eyed, they both pattered into the kitchen.

"Wonderful morning," Anton said cheerily. "Nobody's talking drought for the first time in years. Going to be a great year for lawns and fruit trees."

He had always been one of those people whose energy level hardly changed, whether it was seven in the morning or seven at night. No precipitous ups and downs, no slogging through the haze of morning until that caffeine jolt shook him awake. Marvelous—and a little annoying, especially in someone who was so facile a betrayer. He carried his cup to the table and sat down beside her. "You sleep okay?"

She shrugged. "Not bad, considering." *Considering that you set me up so handily. Considering that I spent the night sleeping next to someone I hardly know anymore.*

Matt, dressed in a blue shirt she hadn't seen before and his dark slacks, stuck his still-wet head into the kitchen. "I'll be back in a couple of hours at the most. Need anything?"

Linda shook her head; no need to mention tampons or anything else now that both men were being so cooperative.

"How about a brunette, about five five, with brown eyes and—" Anton waved away his own attempt at a joke. "Nothing. Thanks. And you be careful out there."

Matt didn't react to the change in Anton's tone. "I'm off. See you in a few hours." He pivoted and was gone as quickly as he had appeared.

When the front door banged shut, Linda could barely suppress her smile. She lowered her gaze, stared at the swirls of wood grain on the tabletop.

"He'll be all right. He's worried, that's all."

Anton's voice startled her and she looked into his clouded eyes. Perhaps she had been too eager to censure him for telling Matt she was in Oakland. She hadn't asked him not to. When a friend—and she *was* Anton's friend—appears on your doorstep in the middle of the night, upset and anxious, *of course* you'd tell her husband—to reassure him, to invoke his help.

"Anton, I know you can hear in his voice that something's bothering Matt. Where did he go? What's he doing?" Hank, who had been staring at her with his yellow eyes, made a dainty leap onto her lap, then curled himself against her stomach.

The refrigerator motor hummed; the gas jet under the Chemex hissed and sputtered. Anton turned it off. "I don't know. That's the truth." He fussed over the Chemex, peering into it as though the answer would come bubbling up from the coffee. "He's been clucking around all morning like a brood hen too stubborn to get up from a cracked egg."

Stroking the cat, Linda looked at the closed cabinet doors, searching the kitchen for memories of the days when she and Matt and Anton and assorted friends had served up imaginative meals and clever conversation. But it was no use. It was today, the day after she heard Margaret Forrest talk about God's tears, two days after she saw her own picture in the paper, and too many things didn't make sense.

Anton's voice pulled her back. "He said he had to even the score." Like a puppet being jerked to life, he twitched and bumped his knee on the open bread drawer.

"What is it, Anton?"

Mutely, his eyes still fixed on the stove, he shook his head.

The cat's ears perked up; Hank hopped down from her lap and meandered out of the kitchen. "Tell me," Linda whispered.

"Matt said that he was going to kill two birds with a single stone. I'm not sure what he meant."

Dreamily, Linda tilted her head and met Anton's gaze. "He once told me that he felt that Amy's murderer also took the person he'd married away from him. I suppose," she said, her voice sounding to her as though it belonged to someone else, "that's what he meant by the 'two birds' part. But do you think he really meant 'kill'?" she asked before her words drifted off.

They sat together in the silence of the kitchen, each holding onto their mugs.

Anton had given her an opening; maybe she *could* trust him. She felt stranded, afraid to move for fear of falling through the ice. She'd take another step and see if Anton's support was real. "He's been so far away, it hardly seems to matter whether I'm sitting right next to him or in another room. And it's gotten worse lately. Every night after dinner, he goes—" Her hand went to her mouth to stop the words.

A quizzical expression on his face, Anton moved the salt shaker, rearranged the pepper mill, folded his napkin in half. "We've both seen him upset. Some of the things that have happened, anyone would be."

"Don't you think this is different than it was before? That was his own . . . Did you mean even before Amy—" Linda was becoming even more confused.

"Before Amy? I thought he handled that remarkably well, all of it."

All of it? All of *what?* She clutched her coffee cup as if it were a talisman. She would confront it now, while her courage was strong, or never. "Handled what?"

"He told you, right?" Anton's eyes avoided hers; something was putting him off-balance, making him uncomfortable with her questions.

The tempo had changed; it was her turn to lead. "You've gone too far already not to tell me."

Hands on top of the table, he pulled himself forward and tilted his head as though he didn't understand the language she was speaking.

She pressed on. "Anton, I know you've been Matt's friend for twenty years, longer than I've known him. And I appreciate that you care about him and that you're loyal. But even though it may seem like *I'm* the one who's losing it, I think it's Matt who's close to some dangerous edge. And I think it's all connected to Amy.

"The day that Amy was murdered, I called Matt's office. His secretary said he was with you. That was a little before six. She said he'd been gone for about an hour, but when I called and asked you if I could speak to Matt, do you remember what you said?"

All the color drained from Anton's face and his eyes burned into hers as if to say "Don't do this to me." He sighed and stared at the table, bobbing his head, opening and closing the fingers of his left hand.

Linda had time; she would get what she needed, now or later. "Anton?" she prodded gently.

"I thought he told you. No one ever mentioned it, after that night."

"I know," she said softly. "You told the police that Matt was with you, though. Didn't you?"

Anton didn't move, didn't make a sound.

"Matt may be in trouble, and covering for him is no help. You're no friend if you think you're protecting him by lying."

"Linda, you're remembering wrong. I didn't tell you that he wasn't there. I said he stepped out for a moment." When Anton turned to face her, his eyes gleamed with a cold and penetrating light, as though his sternness would convince her to accept his version of the truth.

Linda faltered; perhaps she had reinterpreted Anton's words in the light of her own growing fears. Maybe the ugly replicas of the doll had colored her memory, forcing her to seek the ineluctable comfort of an answer, even a wrong one, instead of the void of not knowing.

"I don't believe that's what you did say." She waited, suspended, hardly breathing, gathering certainty.

"Well, I did and—" Now it was Anton's turn to waver.

Let him see for himself that she recognized lies. "No, you didn't. You said he wasn't there yet. Where was he? What was he doing?"

The shrill cry of a siren rattled the air somewhere to the east. Linda's hands remained steady, her eyes watchful for a change in Anton's expression. Time stretched; finally the set of his mouth softened.

"What I'm about to say . . . I'm telling you this so you can stop thinking whatever it is that's making you suspicious. Done is done and there's no need for you to turn an old mistake into a case against him.

"Matt wasn't with me at all that afternoon. We'd worked out this signal. He would call and tell me when he needed my help. That was the first time. He . . ."

She could guess what was coming next; it was so predictable that she almost laughed. She gestured for Anton to go on.

"She was a student of his from Cal. It had never happened

before, as far as I know. That's the truth. He asked me to cover for him between five and seven. And that's all. When the cops questioned me, I hated doing it but I stuck to the story."

How ironic that the news that Matt had been having an affair was one of the best things she'd heard in a long time. Maybe she could let go of her suspicions now, forget about Matt's sculptures and his strange behavior, look at the same facts in this new, harsh light.

"What was her name?" Funny, how important that scrap of information seemed.

Anton shook his head. "I don't remember. He'd been feeling terrible for weeks, maybe even months. It really upset him to lose the commission on the maritime offices; he was so afraid that you would worry about money, about his future."

All this goddam protection; she'd never asked for it. Or had she? Perhaps she had encouraged Matt to feel that he should shield her from difficult truths.

"We used to have lunch every Wednesday. For months, I could *see* the changes. He'd always been so flooded with work that he had to turn things away, and then bam, wham, slam, three in a row that he lost to other firms. He felt terrible about losing his touch and he was worried about money."

"And that's why he had an affair?"

The corners of his mouth turned down; Anton's features seemed to spread toward the edges of his face. "Men can be pretty touchy where their egos are concerned."

Linda didn't want platitudes and banalities. She wished she could scream, and almost resented that she had reached a place of quiet sadness. "I'm not interested in excuses; I just want to know what happened. Matt became involved with someone two weeks before Amy was murdered and he asked you to provide him with an alibi"—she shuddered at the word—"if he needed one, right?"

Anton's head fell forward. Linda took the gesture as a nod of assent.

"And he called to ask you to cover him from five to seven that evening."

"That's right." A plea to let him off the hook filled Anton's eyes.

"And you don't know the name of the woman—girl, really —he was with or where they were or any other details. So, as far as you know, Matt might have been anywhere at the time you provided him with the alibi."

His eyes grew so wide that the almost-black pupils were completely encircled by white. "Are you suggesting that maybe Matt killed Amy? Because if you are, Linda, you'd better think again. I'll go to my grave denying that I ever told you any of this. Matt couldn't do a thing like that. And I won't let you turn it away from yourself onto him."

Away from yourself. Linda reeled with the meaning of Anton's words but she forced herself to go on.

"Matt never mentioned her name?" Her voice was cold; she was pleased that she was able to say anything at all.

Her husband's friend shook his head, then sighed. "Lisa? Laura? I don't remember. Something like that. It was almost three years ago."

Three years ago—a lifetime. Amy energetic and blossoming; Matt building his reputation as an architect; Linda dividing her time between home and an occasional landscape design job. But that was the year it had changed. They no longer spent weekends wandering through museums, watching the sea otters at Point Lobos, learning to ski at Northstar, all three of them, all together.

The signals were subtle. Matt, the amateur actor, was good at hiding things for a while, but when had she noticed that he'd become just a little irritable? He spent more and more time away—networking with his buddies to stimulate new business, he said. He was tired, a little anxious, hardly worth remarking on then. They made love less often, but they'd been through such cycles before.

Why hadn't he come to *her?*

twenty-two

She accepted Anton's apologies with relief. He had to hurry, he'd said, or he'd be late for his ten-o'clock: a German shepherd with an arthritic hip. Grateful for the time alone, Linda watched Anton's Thunderbird drive off and wished away the headache that started to beat behind her eyes. Until now, the fear of the Oakland police and of her own husband had made her choices seem limited. Protect herself. Meet Bea. Run away. Easy . . . until Anton offered her a plausible but distressing explanation for where Matt had been when Amy was killed. Taken together with the odd business of the teacher's words, maybe she could construct a picture of what happened to the children that didn't include Matt. What if Marianne Brandon, too, had learned about the rain being God's tears?

If additional facts came to light, leaving to meet Bea might be cowardly rather than brave, a desertion of Matt rather than a means of protecting herself from him.

Suddenly she was spinning her wheels, and perhaps digging a rut that would eventually swallow her up.

Goddam him, anyway—a college girl. If only he had said that he was upset, that business was off, that he was feeling shaky.

If only she had recognized what was happening to him. The clues were surely there in ordinary gestures, the day he forgot to ask Amy about her first ballet lesson, the weekends when he got up later and later as if he wanted to sleep time away, the way he rolled away from her after sex, without touching her or talking.

If she took Anton's word for where Matt had been on the day of Amy's murder, then maybe there was a reasonable explanation for all the other things that seemed to make such a damning case against him.

Lord, how she wanted that to be so. How she wanted not to have to throw away their marriage in order to save herself. The pleasure of living with someone who illuminated unknown corners of the world, the compromises they'd worked out, the years of struggle—she didn't want to discard these. But she couldn't let nostalgia seduce her into jeopardizing her own sanity and, ultimately, her safety.

The past is behind me, she reminded herself. *I can move forward.*

The throbbing in back of her eyes grew sharper, but this didn't feel like one of the bad ones, not yet. She should do what she could to keep the headache manageable.

Rummaging through her purse for the pillbox, she reached an interim decision. She would take a walk, clear her head, and by the time she returned to Anton's, she would have figured out whether or not to meet Bea and drive with her to New Orleans.

She dumped the contents of her purse onto the bed. The pillbox wasn't there. Maybe she'd unpacked it when she arrived, but she had no memory of doing that.

She looked in the upstairs bathroom, checked under the bed. This was ridiculous; it was no big deal that she couldn't find the pillbox. She'd just take two aspirins from Anton's medicine cabinet.

Another of her things, missing.

How had her cameo gotten around the doll's neck? Would her pillbox turn up beside another child's body?

A wedge of fear pounded against her chest; her stomach

twisted again into a painful knot. The note of accusation in Anton's voice echoed in her head, filled it until she clapped her hands over her ears as though that would stop the words.

Away from yourself. She had already resolved her own questions and put them to rest. She'd read those stories about people with multiple personalities; during her trial, she had looked inside herself again and again and asked whether she might have murdered Amy. The hours before and after finding Amy in the park that day were a shadowy blur, yet she had somehow convinced herself that she couldn't have done such a thing without it leaving a permanent mark on her. Still, she had avoided the park and the streets around it, fearing the power of unremembered incidents.

Was *anything* really possible?

She had to do *something.* She swallowed three aspirin from Anton's medicine chest and ran down the stairs to the entry-way. *Move.* She had to work off some of the tension that was building in her arms and legs, deep inside her belly and her scrambled brain. If she left now, she could meet Bea in less than two hours. But answers to her questions about Matt and the secrets that were locked in the missing pieces of her memory wouldn't be found in Pescadero.

She jammed the baseball cap onto her head and pulled her raincoat on. Walking would help her think, and she needed to think: about Matt's affair, about being truthful with herself, about what she was going to do next.

Surely the pillbox would turn up later.

It was hard to remember that, beyond the heavy gray clouds, a sun shone; intermittent rain appeared to be a perpet-ual condition. Come on, she thought, it's just plain corny to think that the sky is weeping too.

She headed for College Avenue; when she reached the wide street, she turned south. New restaurants and stores had sprung up, but the area was still friendly, down-home, qualities that had attracted her to Rockridge in the first place, even though, like so many other neighborhoods, this one had moved toward gentrification since she and Matt had lived here.

And Amy, don't forget. Amy had lived here too.

She and Amy had walked down this street every day, several times a day sometimes. Time to catch up with *House and Garden*? Out onto College, to the newsstand on the corner of Shafter. Did Amy want to visit Jennifer? Out onto College before turning down Lawton. This street had been the major thoroughfare of their days and nights and she was walking it now for the first time in years and she was numb from trying to keep that other life away.

She paused at the steamy windows of the Rockridge Cafe. A man in a trenchcoat and a black beret pulled the door open and she was assaulted by noise: clanking plates and silverware, the buzz of conversation, the jangle of the cash register. When the door closed again, she moved on, heading north now toward Pendragon.

She'd spent so much time in the bookstore that the owner once jokingly threatened to charge her rent. She pressed close to the window and looked inside. A woman sat cross-legged on the floor, backpack beside her, a book on her lap and her green hooded rain jacket unzipped. At the far end of the aisle, another woman reached for a book as she pushed a toddler in a stroller.

Chilled, frustrated, weary from the effort not to bolt and hide, Linda trudged to the corner.

She made herself go forward along the glistening sidewalk, oblivious to the rain and the traffic, unheeding of the cold and the clamor of warning voices in her head that urged her to go back. The park, half a block away now, was deserted.

. . . As it had been that evening in the lowering dusk when she found Amy . . . As it had been when she was found by the old man walking his dog along the path as she staggered toward what she thought was home with her child in her arms, her eyes vacant and unable to recognize that she was walking away from her destination. Later she had understood that she was prolonging her acceptance of the truth by moving in the opposite direction.

Her steps slowed and rain fell onto her upturned face; the wind sang to her but she ignored it. She was entranced with her past, bewitched by her pain. She was returning to the place where everything had changed.

She stopped at the intersection of two paths, captured by a landscape she didn't recognize.

The trees, whose multitude of branches hung over the walkways, were different; the contours of the land rose and fell with an unfamiliar rhythm, and the benches weren't placed in an arrangement that matched her memory.

Frightened, she started toward the street and then stopped, looking back over her shoulder through sheets of rain, and turned around.

One step and then another. She forced herself to go forward into the park again.

They were the same trees, the same benches that she saw in that terrible twilight almost three years ago. She walked down the path again, toward the flowering quince. It had grown taller and it needed pruning, but she recognized it now.

There, to the left of the path, where the edge of the cement was broken off, was where she'd found the doll. And under the quince tree, the knife. Beside Amy's body.

That was the way it had happened. That was how it had been when she walked this path three years earlier.

She had forced herself to come back to this place—and the memories were unspeakably painful—but she knew now that she didn't harbor any secrets. She wished she could say the same for Matt.

twenty-three

"I hear they got that Crell guy down the hall." Erikson sneered and curled his lip. "Roberta Herron says the asshole barged in on Cindy Forrest's parents. Scum. Checking to see if they were hurting bad enough."

Morella scowled. "Back off, Erikson. Herron's just foaming at the mouth. The guy was popped before he ever got to the house. Picked up half a block away."

"So he's made, right?"

"Not yet. It's still just talk at this point. Look, we got some real work to do, but first I want to acknowledge our man here." Morella's flat voice suddenly rang with pride. "Pretty sharp, Cruz, picking up on that ambulance case. We checked that empty cottage and talked to the guy who rents the house at the back of the property. He was at work. The perp must've called from some local pay phone. Paramedics swear the ambulance response time was under five minutes. We can't be sure, but I got to think that Cindy Forrest is somewhere in the neighborhood, and whoever boosted the needles and the insulin is the person who's responsible for our crimes here."

Cruz listened to the progress summaries and tried to look like he was paying attention. Cavessena's eyes followed the lazy arc of his foot swinging back and forth; she turned away when he met her gaze.

Morella rambled on, referring lovingly to "the multiprong

team approach." Even half-listening, Cruz knew that Morella's news was no news. Except for Crell. Maybe he'd have Thanksgiving, after all. Crell was the only hope. None of the search teams had turned up anything. None of the calls claiming to have seen Cindy Forrest had panned out. Rumors of child pornographers working out of a motel in Daly City had netted three middle-aged hookers and a small-time crack dealer but no Cindy and no leads on Marianne Brandon's killer. The stack of unconfirmed sightings and pending material was growing quicker than the mold on the ceiling of the apartment he and Elenya rented when they were first married.

If Crell wasn't charged or if some other break didn't open up, then Elenya and the boys would drive up on Thursday, just for turkey dinner, and then go back to Santa Cruz for the remainder of the vacation and that would be that.

"The rest of you, I know you're waiting to hear about Thursday. I got nothing new to say. You know as well as I do that this kind of thing is real hard on families. It's tough on all of us to have to work through the holiday, but if you can live with the idea of Cindy Forrest being out there somewhere while you eat your turkey, then you're a better man than me." Morella shook his head. "Sorry, Cavessena. You know what I mean."

Tina Cavessena didn't smile this time. "It's okay, Morella. Forget it." She ran her hand along the back of her neck, pulling out the hair that had slipped inside her collar; when she tossed her head, Cruz thought he caught her looking at him again.

Morella shuffled to his desk, his back bent and his face sagging. "Oh, and McNaughton told me to tell you to keep away from the goddam reporters, understand? You all been doing pretty good about that so far, and McNaughton figures he can feed them stuff for another day. So just plain duck out if anyone wants to talk to you."

An unaccustomed silence followed everyone back to their desks. Cruz filled up a page with doodles of daisies and crosses, trying to get back into a working frame of mind before he and Goldstein left for their afternoon stop at the volunteer center.

"Got a second, Cruz?" The sleeve of Cavessena's white blouse was the first thing he saw when he looked up.

"Yeah, sort of. Just a second." When Elenya came back, it would be easier to keep his distance from Cavessena; he would feel less vulnerable. Maybe, he thought, it was really the other way around. With Elenya away it was easier to resist Tina Cavessena because the situation was such a cliché, one in which a lot of guys would have stopped trying to do the right thing a long time ago.

"Can we go somewhere?" Her eyes were wide and trusting.

Maybe that was part of her plan. It made him uneasy, not knowing what the woman wanted; something about her had bothered him ever since she started in Homicide. Why had she singled him out?

Maybe he should force her to play her hand. Better sooner than later, when she might let her thoughts run away with her even more than they were now. By then, it might even be harder for him to say no. She was, after all, an attractive woman . . . no, a *beautiful* woman.

"I'm waiting for a call, Cavessena. How about if we go out in the hall? Best I can do for a couple of hours."

Tina Cavessena fidgeted with her gold hoop earring. "It's not exactly your private conference room, but if that's what you want, okay."

Certain that everyone was staring at them, Cruz led the way out of the Homicide room into the poorly lit hall. He stopped midway to the elevators. "What's up, Tina?"

She folded her hands in front of her, slid one foot out of her shoe and rubbed her stockinged toe along the other foot. "I guess I knew that one of the dangers of being the only woman in a division with nine men is that some of the guys are gonna see me as a kind of sex object." She blushed and shook her head. "Damn, that sounds so egotistical, but it's one of the realities, right, Cruz?"

Carlos Cruz nodded. Where was she going with this?

"In a way, you can probably understand how it might be the same for me, working with all you guys. I don't know if this is bad timing or good timing or what but it's *my* timing and I don't want this to go on forever without doing anything about it."

"Tina, I—" He stopped, not so much out of concern for what he was going to say as from a paralysis that constricted his throat and made his collar feel too tight.

"Wait, Cruz. Let me finish. So here's what I want to know. I mean, I've been feeling this attraction since I first walked in to the division. But I was waiting to see if I liked the *person* as well as I liked the *package,* if you know what I mean."

Cruz started to sweat.

"I held back until now. Maybe it's the pressure of the case that's making me feel like I have to do something about this or I'm going to explode, so I wanted to ask you first."

"Tina, I—" Cruz wished that Morella, Goldstein, somebody would walk by now and give him the chance to divert this conversation for just a minute. He swallowed hard. If he didn't say something soon, she might think he was encouraging her.

"Listen, Cruz," she said, lowering her voice, "do you think there's even a chance for me with Goldstein?"

"Look, Tina, I—" Cruz backpedaled furiously as he sought time to let Tina Cavessena's words register. The first feeling he recognized was overwhelming relief.

The second was a small but distinct pang of disappointment.

"I can't speak for Goldstein. Honest. I mean, you can probably tell that we're not the kind of partners who share all the gory details of our private lives."

Cavessena nodded. "Sure, but maybe he's said something

about me to you . . . or about a girlfriend. I hate like hell to get turned down, Cruz, so I play the percentages whenever I can."

"Tina, anyone who'd turn you down would have to be crazy." He blushed. "Or married. I don't know anything about Goldstein's current love life. Honest. But good luck."

Tina Cavessena saluted and strutted away toward the elevators, her back tall and straight, her hips swinging.

With a twinge of regret, Cruz went back to the Homicide room. *Better get to work before I start feeling really dumb,* he thought.

"Cruz, didn't you hear me? I said pick up the phone. Some guy, says he's from the volunteer center? He's breathing so hard he can barely talk. Says he's gotta talk to you or the Professor." Erikson scratched his chin and went back to his paperwork.

With a sigh that was louder than he meant it to be, Cruz grabbed the receiver.

"Listen, it was only a little while ago so maybe you can still find him, but I doubt it because he took off in a hurry. This guy in a convertible. Well, I saw him, Sergeant Cruz. Near College and Broadway. Thirty minutes ago."

Toller. Erikson was right; he sounded like a heavy breather about to explode.

"Mr. Toller, slow down. Details—try to give me *details.* That's the only way we can follow up. Think you can do that?"

"This guy's face—I'll see it in my sleep, the way his eyes narrowed, the forehead. He wasn't wearing his cap and he must've cut the ponytail. I mean his hairline alone, it stands out in my brain right now. Widow's peak, receding over these blue veins where his hair is thinner. I'll see that face in my sleep. Don't you think you'd better get someone on it right away?"

No cap? No ponytail? *What makes you think this sighting is any different than the others?* Cruz thought. *Just because it happened to you, do you think it's got any more value than all the*

others? "I appreciate that it's important, Mr. Toller, but I can't move on this until I've got *details.* Why don't you start by giving me the information. Like you were filling out one of the center forms."

"Sure, fine, but I think we'd better move fast."

How can I move anywhere, Cruz thought angrily, if you're not going to give me the damn data?

"The convertible was blue. It was just sitting there, on the corner of Broadway, like I said. I was coming up College approaching Broadway on my way to Safeway, not really thinking about anything. Anyway, I'm stopped for the light and I see a guy maybe five ten, five eleven, medium build, brown hair, big hands. It's raining so I figure the guy's in a hurry to get someplace dry. He's sort of running down College. Then he turns the corner and jumps into this convertible. Just before the light changes, he pulls out quick. I'm two cars behind the corner so I can't do anything. When the light changes I try to follow him, but there's three cars between us and even though I try to keep up with him for a while, he just disappears into traffic. I lost him."

Of course you lost him, Cruz thought, angry that Toller had played at being the cop. Still, Toller did a pretty good job of filling in the details when it was his own sighting he was reporting. "What time was this, Mr. Toller?"

"Three o'clock. Like I said, not more than twenty minutes ago. I drove down here as soon as I realized I wasn't going to catch him."

"Down where?"

"Oh, I'm in the lobby. Didn't the fellow on the phone tell you?"

Cruz was annoyed; he didn't have the patience to baby-sit all the do-gooders who thought they'd earned special treatment by answering a few goddam phones. "I'll get the information out to the dispatcher, and we'll see if we can find this blue convertible. But without a license plate number, it's going to be a little tricky. You understand, I know you do."

There was a moment of silence. "This is different." Toller's voice was teasing, as though he was sharing a naughty secret. "The car, when it was idling at the curb. The reason it attracted my attention when the guy got in. There was a blond kid sitting in the back. I'm sure of it."

Didn't this guy read the reports? Three quarters of them involved little blond girls. Cruz would humor Toller a bit longer, but he wasn't going to enjoy it. "I see," he said.

"And she was holding a piece of paper up to the side window. Big green crayon letters. It said HELP. "

Cruz's heart banged in his chest—this *was* different.

"Wait there, Toller. I'm coming down to get you."

"Sure. I'm right by the—"

Cruz broke the connection and rattled off the bare-bones facts of Toller's sighting to Morella. Then he ran down the stairs, his mind speeding. What a break this would be! A witness who had taken scores of calls and knew what kind of information they were looking for—Toller could be the key to making this case. Cruz offered a hasty prayer that Shirley Johnson, the Department artist, was in the building. The fresher Toller's memory, the closer the picture would come to capturing the quirky details that would set this suspect apart from hundreds of other men.

Please, he prayed silently as he leaped down the last three stairs, *please let Johnson be here. Please let her be sitting on her tall stool, bored and eager to work. Together, we can make a beauty of a sketch, a work of art.*

Toller's eyes lit up when Cruz burst through the door.

"That was fast. You fly or something?" Toller smiled and stuck his hands in the pockets of his Bay Security jacket.

It was a good thing the case didn't depend on Toller's sense of humor.

"Mr. Toller, can you come upstairs with me? I've got to check first, see if our sketch artist is available. If we can put together a decent likeness of this man you saw, then we'll be in great shape."

Toller bobbed his head, his chin brushing against the blue plush of his collar. "You sure that's all right? For me to come upstairs, I mean."

"Of course it's all right. It'll help get things rolling. You ready? Is there something wrong, Mr. Toller?"

The frown on Toller's face had twisted his features out of shape. "No, nothing's wrong. I better call the center first, though. It's just I'm supposed to be there for the four o'clock shift. I ought to let them know I'm not coming in for a while."

"We can do that from upstairs. You ready?"

Toller nodded, then frowned. "Is it always so . . . I don't know, so low-key around here? It's quieter. That's it, it's quieter than I thought it would be. Even with my hearing aid turned all the way up, it's much quieter. You know, if not for my hearing problem . . ." His voice trailed off.

"Wait till you get upstairs." Cruz tried to cover his surprise at Toller's mention of a hearing aid with a smile as he stole a look at the earpiece of the man's glasses. Goddam—there it was. "I bet you won't think it's low-key when you get up there."

twenty-four

"The nose is a little too long." Toller tugged at his ear and then reached for the Styrofoam cup and took a long swallow of coffee. He slumped in the chair, his long legs splayed out. A thin film of mud caked the rim of his shoes; brown flecks dotted the cuffs of his blue trousers.

With maddeningly deliberate strokes of her pencil, Shirley Johnson worked on the nose. She was a large woman; Goldstein cast her as the benevolent Tante whenever he saw her. She had once described herself as "God's pencil," an instrument in making these drawings. Trouble was, she'd said, the trance state lasted for hours after she finished working. In July, after spending half a day with the latest victim of a rapist, she'd almost run her car off the freeway. Goldstein would make sure she didn't have to drive this afternoon. Erikson lived out in Walnut Creek; he could take her home.

The sketch that was emerging was finally starting to look like a real person instead of an odd collection of mismatched parts. He had seen this process eight, nine times before. The elements that made up a human face—shape, contour and spacing of features, texture of skin, hair—were, by themselves, only physical details. You could put any combination together and somehow know that you didn't have it because the pieces weren't working together. A drawing was only marks on paper until the last detail—a slight downward twist to the corners of the mouth or the lowering of the tip of the nose to create a shadow—was added, and in a single moment the whole picture suddenly took on new life.

"Okay, now the mole is in the right place, but the eyes are off. I think they're a little too close together." Toller sounded tired but determined to get it right.

Squinting tightly as she erased the inner corners of both eyes, Johnson leaned toward the drawing table, the tip of her tongue edging out from between her teeth. With a few deft strokes, she drew in the new eyes and then sat upright.

"That's it! That's him—the guy I saw. This is amazing!" Toller jiggled with excitement, looking from Goldstein to Cruz to Johnson.

But Goldstein wasn't at all amazed. In a fragment of time before Toller said anything, Goldstein had recognized the face in the drawing. Perhaps it was that intangible burst of anticipation, but even before the eyes were moved farther apart, he realized that he was looking at a pretty decent likeness of Matthew Crell.

The only problem was that when Albert Toller claimed to have seen this man in the blue convertible with the little blond girl, Matthew Crell was in the interrogation room on the second floor, with Webster and Quinn. In his zeal, Toller must have dredged up Matthew Crell's face from newspaper photos. Goldstein didn't remember a mole; he'd have to check.

"Have you ever seen this man before?" Arms folded across his chest, Cruz leaned against a desk.

So Cruz saw the resemblance too.

Toller's frown deepened the cleft between his eyes. Then his features relaxed and he smiled. "I know. He looks a little like that fellow in the picture you guys brought around the other day." He shook his head. "This guy's got a mole. The other one —I don't think he did."

"Well, you did great, Mr. Toller." Johnson packed away the

pencils and erasers; she sprayed fixative on the drawing and held it up, never taking her eyes off her work. "Very observant."

"It's my job to notice things." Toller cocked his head as though trying to make out a half-heard conversation. "I'd better get over to the center now. They were short-handed and I want to fill out the shift."

"If you still have enough energy left to put in a shift. That was pretty intense." The man looked wilted, crumpled. Goldstein had heard from other witnesses who had worked with Johnson just how draining a task it was.

"Energy?" Indignation stiffened Toller's shoulders. "Of course I still have plenty of energy. Don't you need me to sign a statement or something? Take a deposition? I don't know, whatever you people do about these things, I still have plenty of energy left to do it."

Goldstein reminded himself to be grateful for Toller's information and his perseverance. He didn't have to like him, too. "Nothing else for you to do here, Mr. Toller. We'll get the sketch printed up. You can go to the center whenever you like."

Toller yanked his jacket from the chair and brushed invisible lint from the shoulder patch. "Okay. You'll bring copies of the drawing down later?"

"As soon as they're ready," Goldstein said curtly.

"Guy could be halfway to Nevada by then," Toller muttered as he stepped into the hall behind Cruz.

"What do you think?" Goldstein stared at Johnson's picture, held it up beside the photograph of Matthew Crell.

No doubt about it; Toller had let his mind play tricks on him. Eyewitness reports carried heavy emotional weight with a jury but they were the least reliable indicator of the facts. Certainly, the human mind was a miraculous machine, able to make leaps so that the symbol became inextricably entangled with the object itself, and the whole thing lost reliability. Fun, but he hated to count on a witness, even one who sincerely believed in the validity of his own experience, to make a case.

"Why don't we go see if the person matches the picture?"

Cruz laughed and his face reddened. "Tina said something almost exactly like that a few minutes ago."

Cruz, embarrassed? Something about Tina Cavessena had made him blush.

"This could get very weird," Cruz said. "Maybe Toller was wrong about the time. Maybe Crell has a twin brother. Maybe, maybe, maybe."

"Maybe we better hold off until we see him, hear him, all right?" Goldstein put the drawing on the top of his desk and walked to the hall. "Coming?"

"On my way." Cruz pushed his chair back and stood up. "God, I hate this."

"I told you. I was just walking. Thinking. You can understand— things have come up for me in the past week that open up a lot of painful memories."

The man in the chair was alert, controlled. He was good-looking, in a dark, dissipated way and he did have that damned widow's peak and the veins on his forehead beneath his taut and shiny skin were blue and prominent. He looked like he had lived too hard and life had taken its toll. Or maybe, Goldstein thought, it was only lately that things had gotten out of hand. His posture was erect, his gaze directed at Webster's face. He was clean-shaven, neatly dressed in dark pants, a blue shirt, cordovan loafers and belt. A loden green raincoat tossed on the back of his chair finished the picture. A child-killer? Anything was possible.

Goldstein hated these one-way mirrors; for one thing, you missed details, smells, seeing the sweat on someone's palms. But they couldn't barge in on Webster and Quinn, not in the middle of an interrogation.

Webster narrowed his eyes. "Why *that* street, Crell? Why come back to Oakland after all these years, after all those painful, as you call them, memories?"

The muscle below Matthew Crell's left eye twitched and his fingers gripped the arm of the chair. Finally, he opened his mouth. "My lawyer has advised me not to say anything until she arrives. I already told you that."

Now it would be Quinn's turn. It would be interesting to watch a soft-spoken fellow with freckles and red hair play the Bad Cop role.

"If you have nothing to hide, like you say, then why don't you answer that one question, Crell? I mean, were you going shopping, going to the doctor's, coming to pick up your wife, what?"

This time, the only movement was a clenching of his fists. Matthew Crell's body was a pretty good polygraph. It appeared that the mention of his wife's name made him tense.

"When my lawyer arrives—"

"—she'll make the cops stop harrassing you." A striking, dark-haired woman, dimples flashing, stood in the open doorway, hands on hips, smiling down at Webster. "You aren't giving my client a hard time, are you, Sergeant?"

"You sure got here fast," Quinn said.

When she nodded, Mia Honer's silky hair brushed her face. "There are only two things I do slowly and one of them is shaving my legs."

Webster scowled. "Honer, you know we've been looking for Crell and his wife for six days now. To talk. You advising your client not to answer our questions? I wonder why. You already know where we picked him up, right?"

"I get five minutes with my client, don't I?"

She was too pretty, that was the problem. Goldstein remembered running into her on cases before; each time, he had to learn all over again that she was prickly, sharp. Maybe he was a sucker, but he didn't much like to be in an adversarial relationship with a pretty woman. He was a throwback; his father wouldn't hesitate to try to mop up the floor with Mia Honer. That's why Aaron Goldstein was a good lawyer and his son had chosen not to mind the family store.

Webster signaled to Quinn; as they reached the door, Mia called Webster's name.

"A *private* interview with my client, Webster." She jerked her head in the direction of the mirror. Goldstein flinched and then smiled at Cruz.

"Sure, sure." Trying to hide his grin, Webster stepped into the hall.

Goldstein took a last look at Mia—no dimple flashing now. She was beautiful anyway.

"What's this? Why you got a drawing of my guy?" Webster's face was puzzled. He held the picture at arm's length and squinted. "Left my damn glasses upstairs."

"Witness said this man was in a convertible with a blond girl."

Webster's brows shot up and he grinned. "And we got him sitting right here. Shit, yeah! What took you so long telling me?"

Goldstein's smile was sardonic. "Witness swears the sighting happened at three o'clock."

The hall was silent. Outside, a siren screamed and then died. Goldstein could almost hear his watch ticking the seconds away.

"Brought him in at 2:28. Sheet says he was picked up at 2:11. Fuck, piss, shit," Webster muttered.

"You get a feel for him before this, Web?" Goldstein watched as the man's dark face put itself back together. "Talking to him, what did your gut tell you?"

"Bupkus." Webster leaned against the wall. "He's not

showing much of anything. But there's a light, a gleam, I don't know what to call it. It's there in his eye and it makes me feel he ain't no ordinary carpenter up from a small town for a visit to the city. But kill children? I don't know."

"What you mean—a crazy gleam?" Cruz leaned against the wall and folded his arms across his chest.

Webster shook his head. "Can't say. Let's get back to it. They've had enough time alone. What you think, Professor?"

He had seen it too, the light in Crell's eye. It could have been pain or vengefulness as well as anything else. "Too soon to tell. But I think you'd better keep an eye on him, Web. Find out where he was, what his wife was doing, and then put a tail on him. Something doesn't feel right about this guy."

Webster's jaws tightened. "You think I need instruction on how to do my job, Goldstein?"

Goldstein sighed. "I didn't mean that. You asked and I was thinking out loud, that's all."

Webster grunted and pushed open the door. "Well, Miz Honer, we have your permission to talk to your client now?"

Mia Honer nodded. "Sure. But first let me ask you a question. Do you have any reason to think this man knows anything about the murder of Marianne Brandon or the disappearance of Cindy Forrest? Any evidence? Witnesses? Confessions? Hair or fingerprints? Anything at all, Webster, because if you don't, maybe you have better things to do with your time than harrass a citizen who happened to be walking on the wrong street. He'll answer your questions. I'd feel comfortable giving you, say fifteen more minutes. After that, well, it's gone beyond the friendly discussion stage."

It was a good thing that Webster closed the door just then; it wouldn't do for Mia Honer to see the expression on Jay Goldstein's face as he headed for the elevator.

twenty-five

She tried to make tea, to warm her and to help break the logjam of her thoughts. The long walk had accomplished one thing: She was certain now that she didn't have anything to do with Amy's death. But she was no closer to deciding on a plan. Only three hours remained until the seven-o'clock deadline, but in her heart she knew that Bea wouldn't leave after dark. She had time, and it looked like she would need it.

Steam rolled out of the kettle spout and she reached for a cup. It clattered on the counter as she set it down. Even if the cameo and the sculptures and her missing pillbox didn't tip the decision in favor of leaving, then why should she stay with a liar and a cheat? What else did you call someone who slept around and then came home and pretended that nothing had happened?

She spilled tiny, fragrant strands of loose tea all over the stove when she tried to fill the infuser. She brushed the mess into her hand, dumped it into the garbage, and was about to try again when the phone rang.

She looked at the door, at the stairway, at any means of escape. She didn't want to talk to anyone, didn't want to hear anything that would require another adjustment. The phone rang again. She reached for the receiver and her elbow bumped the open tea container; it teetered and then crashed to the floor, scattering tea all over.

Tears streaming down her face, she picked up the phone. "Hello?"

The voice on the other end was strained, but she recognized it at once. "Linda, this is Mia Honer. Everything's all right now but we have to talk. Problem is I've got a list of things to do longer than Princess Di's wedding dress. You planning to be there for a while?"

"What's going on, Mia? How did you—"

"We'll talk when I get there. Make me some coffee, would you? I'm running out of juice. Gotta fly. See you in twelve minutes." A click and then a dial tone buzzed in her ear.

First Anton's story and now Mia, about to bring another piece of unwelcome news, no doubt. How did Mia know where she was? Matt must have gotten in touch with her, feigning concern—unless he'd had to call her in her professional capacity.

—*Yes, even your underwear. Look, lady, I don't have all day.*
(I can't believe they're going to do this to me first they violate my mind my heart my soul and then they violate my body and poke me and prod me to check for things I can hurt myself with I can't hurt myself there's nothing left to hurt and if I just think about something else maybe I won't feel this but what is there to think about that could make it better when everything is so—OH!)
—*Don't move. I'm almost done.*

Linda squeezed her eyes shut. That was where her memories of that evening started again. When it was all over, Mia had patiently explained that full-body searches and in fact all the intake procedures were designed to make detainees feel powerless. They certainly had succeeded with her. After weeks of hot showers and nightmare dreams, the trembling persisted when anyone touched her. The memory of those hands still made her jaws clench and her throat close up. Even now a great, wordless shame swept over her when she thought about the details.

She cleaned up the spilled tea and then made coffee, her mind ricocheting between questions about Mia's mission and pictures of Matt and his coed cutie. Every few seconds she rushed to the front of the house and peered out the living-room window to the wet, deserted street. Finally, she saw the lawyer, tall and slender, striding briskly up the walk, her long black raincoat flapping behind her.

Mia Honer's huge eyes brimmed over as her arms folded around Linda. Dry-eyed, her own tears all cried for now, Linda pulled back from the taller woman's embrace and almost caught the cat's tail in the door as she snapped the lock into place.

"Lord, I could use that coffee. Hey, I like your hair but, you know, you should accent your eyes more. Try a pencil liner underneath." Mia flung her coat onto the stair rail, then pulled a tortoise-shell comb out of her hair, fixed it in place again, and followed Linda to the kitchen, talking as they walked.

"They picked Matt up for questioning. He demanded to call me and after ninety minutes, it was clear they were fishing. They had nothing and I told them so. They wanted to drag you in, too, but I snarled so loud, they gave up. Matt left with his friend Anton about when I did. Right before I called you."

Linda poured coffee; only a few drops spilled onto the saucers. Had they badgered him and prodded him, assaulted him with so many questions that he said things he didn't mean to get them to stop? What would he say to keep them from those clay monsters in his studio? She would find out soon enough whether Matt had mentioned anything about her or about the cameo.

Mia poured milk into her coffee, then added two spoons of sugar and stirred as if she were scrambling eggs. She took a long sip and leaned back in her chair. "You holding up okay?"

"I'm fine. Tell me what happened." Linda warmed her hands on her cup as she watched the lawyer's eyes.

"That minibitch Herron was skulking around hoping to sink her pointy little teeth into Matt's ankles if she couldn't have yours. She's a goddam embarrassment—nothing prudent about her juris. It warmed my nasty heart to have a bird's-eye view of her face when her boss refused to charge Matt." Mia's eyes sparkled and a broad smile deepened the dimples where the corners of her mouth met her cheeks. "I really shouldn't be so happy to see another human being lose. But she's not—oh well, I never could deny myself any sort of pleasure."

Roberta Herron, chagrined. That was a thought to savor . . . later. Other, more pressing matters needed her attention now. "Why did they pick Matt up?"

"They'd been lying in wait for him. They've been looking out for both of you all week, circulating your pictures. The surveillance team almost didn't identify Matt until he was half a block away from the Forrests' house." Mia smiled and tossed her hair. "He's a little more muscular than he was when their pictures were taken. All that fresh air and physical labor, right?"

Was Matt on his way to see Cindy Forrest's parents? Why would he do that? Linda could barely follow the lawyer's words without crashing into her own speculations.

"Did you hear me, Linda?" Mia sounded annoyed.

"Sorry," Linda said, "try again."

"I said I think it's wise for you not to call attention to yourself now. Don't confuse them. I made the point that we'd sue their asses from here to Kathmandu and back by way of Podunk if they harrassed you or Matt. And they made the point that if they turned up a single shred of physical evidence linking you or Matt to either of these children, they were prepared to climb Everest barefoot if necessary to bring you in.

"We may get some advance warning. I have a contact who can probably tell me what they've got up their sleeves. Now, don't look at me like that. It may not be in the rule books, but that's the way things are done."

The world was so much more complicated than she'd ever imagined; her own naïveté seemed boundless. Mia Honer, with spies in the DA's office? No wonder she was feared and respected. "I'm really glad it was you Matt called."

Mia shrugged and nodded. "I'd been thinking about you two all week, ever since the news broke about Marianne Brandon. I didn't have a number for you or I'd have called."

Linda pushed her coffee cup away, then ran her finger along its edge, embarrassed again at her own innocence. As quickly as she made an adjustment in her perception, something else required fitting in to the picture; she hadn't recognized, until just a moment before, that Mia hadn't come here to tell her that Matt had been picked up and then released. Matt himself could have told her that. Or Mia could have delivered the news over the phone.

"Mia, you came to see me for a reason, right?"

The lawyer sat back in her chair and sighed noisily; her red lipstick was wearing off where she'd been biting her lip. "You remember talking about my tricks, the ones I learned to protect myself?"

Linda nodded. In conference rooms, in the courtroom, in hallways and in elevators, she and Mia had survived the endless waiting by talking about the weather, books, shoes, the school board scandal. When they ran out of small talk, they talked about more intimate things. Linda rambled on about Amy, and Mia discussed why the practice of criminal law turned her on.

"You remember that sometimes I have to detach, so I can listen for what my clients forgot to tell me. So I can pick up on the clues, on the cues, right?"

"Like my postpartum depression. You knew Herron was going to use that." It felt good to be with someone who had been through so much with her. Bea was wonderful—funny, kind, undemanding—but since they'd moved to Pescadero, Linda had missed talking to a woman with whom she had a shared history, even a disturbing one.

Mia's smile crinkled her eyes. "You were an easy one, Linda. Everything you were thinking and feeling, maybe even everything you had ever thought or felt, was hanging right out there, written all over your face and your body." She pushed the coffee cup toward the center of the table. "And I got to know Matt a little then, too. So when I saw him today, I guess you'll understand my shock."

"What do you mean?" *Shock:* that was a pretty strong word. Linda suddenly felt lightheaded; Mia, too, was aware of something troubling in Matt. In an odd way, she took some comfort from the thought that at least she wasn't imagining strangeness where there was none.

"He's different. Through all the months of your ordeal, the man I saw was staunch, strong, with only one purpose—to see you through unscathed. Well," she said, staring into her cup, "the Matt I saw today has the same kind of tunnel vision, only this time, I don't know what's driving him. Something is blinding him, skewing his judgment."

"What do you mean?" Linda barely got the words past her dry lips.

"I don't know if it's an act or what, but he seems to have this idea that he's got to be policeman and prosecutor because no one else can or will get to the truth. I have to confess I was tempted for a minute to let them arrest him for his own protection. Only because your friend Anton pretty well convinced me that Matt was just reacting to the terrible stress did I go all the way for him."

Mia saw it, too. Didn't know what to make of it, either. It was a relief . . . and Linda's decision became clear. She couldn't run away now, not when things were so unsettled. Matt needed her. After all these years, after he'd helped her through the most difficult time of her life, she *shouldn't* desert him. That didn't mean that all her questions had evaporated; she had a sense that they were about to multiply. "This may sound crazy," Linda said, "but I need you to tell me something. Please don't laugh. And please be straight with me, okay?"

"Sure." Instead of making a joke as Linda expected, the lawyer was quiet, her eyes expectant.

"Do you think I had anything to do with Amy's death?"

"Lord, no." There wasn't a moment of hesitation before Mia answered. "Never crossed my mind and I can always tell when a client is shucking me."

Gently, Linda took Mia's hand and placed it above her heart. It pounded wildly; Linda watched the surprise that gathered in the lawyer's eyes. "Good. And do you think that Matt had anything to do with Amy's death? Or with Marianne Brandon's? Or with the disappearance of Cindy Forrest?" She let go of the lawyer's hand.

"Two years ago, I would have scoffed at the thought. After seeing him today—his intensity, his . . . I guess it's an emotional veneer—I'm not sure how to answer you." Still touching Linda's chest, Mia lifted her other hand to her own heart, closing the circuit between them. "I can't say for sure, Linda," she said softly. "I really don't know."

"Pass me that plate, would you, Linnie?" Matt pointed with his chin to her nearly untouched dinner. He and Anton, working with the same frenetic energy with which they'd produced the meal, cleaned up under Hank's watchful eye. "It wasn't as bad as you think. They sat me in a small room, two cops, and asked me the questions you'd figure they'd ask."

Matt calmly recited the tale of his afternoon adventure as he loaded the dishwasher. Yes, the police had asked him about where he was the day Marianne Brandon was murdered. He'd been at the Sharpe house, finishing the interior work, then working on new elevation drawings for Joey Minetta. No, no one could verify seeing him there, except the work got done, didn't it? And, yes, they'd asked about where he was the afternoon that Cindy Forrest disappeared. He'd been walking around Rockridge. No, again, no one could say for certain that he'd been in a specific place at a specific time, but they should try the hardware store or the real estate office because he'd stopped to ask questions in those places.

"They don't have a clue," he concluded. "Amazing—exactly like last time."

What conclusion would they reach this time if it turned out that certain "facts"—about the cameo and Linda's headaches, for example—were dropped during the interview? And would the police simply ignore the information that a teacher told Cindy Forrest and Amy the same strange story? Without a link to Marianne Brandon, it didn't make a very strong case.

Anton sprayed window cleaner onto a paper towel and ran it over the chrome toaster. "This time, they don't have a scapegoat, no one convenient to blame, so we're going to have to find the convergence in the lives of the children. That's why Matt was going to see Edward Forrest. It's out there waiting to be discovered and we're going to find it."

As if things weren't already difficult enough, now it sounded like Anton shared Matt's version of reality, with this talk of finding convergence.

Maybe they weren't so mad—did the fact that Cindy Forrest was taught that rain was God's tears qualify as convergence? *What if someone told Marianne Brandon the same story?*

Matt squeezed water from a sponge and swiped at the counters; it was all so . . . casual. Linda couldn't stand the cozy domesticity a second longer.

"I'll be upstairs," she called over her shoulder as she ran up the stairs and into the bedroom.

The chintz curtains, drawn open earlier in the day, framed the scene below. A single street lamp partway down the block cast a pool of light on the deserted sidewalk; soft rain pocked the surface of a large puddle. The door of the black car across the street slammed and a figure emerged from the shadows and moved toward the light. He glanced up at her window, paused, and then ambled away.

If she had gone to meet Bea, all of this still would be happening but she wouldn't be here to be upset by it.

The figure disappeared down the street.

She tensed at the sound of footsteps on the stairs. What had Matt told the police about her? Asking him would be an exercise in frustration; he would answer but she wouldn't believe anything he said.

"Hey honey, let's shed some light on the situation." Matt flipped the wall switch and Linda blinked at the flood of light that filled the room. "What's up, Linda?"

She could play casual too. "I was just about to look for my pillbox. You see it?"

Hands outstretched, Matt shrugged. "Not since I got here. You sure you took it with you?"

Linda nodded. "Maybe it fell out of my purse. I'm sure I had it when I stopped for breakfast the other day."

He stood beside her, put his arm around her shoulder, pulled her into the circle of his warmth. "Something else is bothering you. I can tell."

If you really want to know . . . "I was wondering whether they asked you about the cameo."

"The cameo? What do you mean?" His arm dropped from her shoulder and fell to his side. "The cameo. I never connected them—Grandma Donner's missing cameo. No, nobody said anything about it. They never asked."

So, now she had asked him. And she had gotten an answer, of sorts.

"Stop worrying," he said as he reached for her hand. "It was no big deal, I told you. They'd been looking for us. They found *me* and they let me go. I didn't do anything so they couldn't hold me. And when they asked about you, all I told them was that you were home last Thursday and on Saturday. I didn't mention your headaches or the long drives. There's nothing for you to worry about."

PART SIX

Wednesday

twenty-six

The rain this morning was steady, dreary, numbing.

"Linda." Matt turned her gently by her shoulders and took her in his arms, his cheek resting on the top of her head and his legs planted far apart, giving both of them balance. She lingered in his warmth and breathed his sweet, faint scent before she stiffened and pulled away.

"I've been up since five o'clock," he said, "trying to figure out what Amy would want me to do. She'd be ten years old now —well, next week."

So he *did* think about her. And for the first time since her death, he'd said her name aloud.

His breath caught but he went on. "And I realize I don't know what she would want. Isn't that amazing?"

"You do, though. She was always saying that if you did something you knew was wrong even if nobody else saw you do it, you'd feel bad later."

"Right. Guilt. We did a good job of giving her plenty of that, didn't we?"

Where had this come from? Matt had never said anything like that, not while Amy was alive and not after she died.

"We weren't such perfect parents. I've been hiding a lot of things from myself all these years." He pulled out a kitchen chair and sat, his hands between his knees and his head bent.

Somehow, she hadn't recognized the sorrow in his eyes

and the dispirited cast of his mouth, until now. Had they been there all along?

"Anyway, we're coming close to something interesting." Matt raised his head; a surge of energy seemed to pass through him. "The beauty of what's happening is that the information is going to come to us; we don't even have to go out to get it."

"What do you mean? What information? And how is it going to come to you?" She had to make him understand; she didn't consider herself part of this "us" he was talking about.

He jumped up and did an intricate quick-step that ended with him facing her, hands on his knees and dark eyes glittering. "The telephone. It's all going to happen over the phone. Anton and I are going to set an investigation in motion this morning."

She held her body very still. "Who are you going to call, Matt? What will you know?"

"When you mentioned something about the teachers and the rain jars the other day, it got me thinking. I saw that interview with Mrs. Forrest on the news. It was too weird to be a coincidence. So I'm going to call the schools and introduce myself as Andrew McCafferty, head of the state Education Department survey team studying the teacher shortage. I'll even toss in some statistics for good measure. The information is going to come to me. And then I'm going to go out and make things right again."

"This isn't a game." Finding out the truth was one thing; setting out to restore order was something else again. Aside from all the moral questions, he'd be endangering himself and the Forrest child, unless he was assuming that she was dead. Linda took aim with the one piece of ammunition she hoped would stop him. "A little girl's life may be at stake."

"That's exactly why I can't give this up." He smiled and spoke slowly, clearly, as if he were trying to soothe an agitated child. "Pretty soon we'll have something concrete to work with, I can feel it."

"I know how much you want to find an answer, Matt, but you can't manufacture one. Please stop this whole damn investigation and let the professionals take care of it."

Instead of nodding in agreement, Matt bent to stroke the cat, who prowled uneasily between his feet. As it always did when he was trying to postpone giving her an answer, his gaze flitted from her to the floor and then back again. "I don't know, Linda. I don't know what to do."

She rose to stand beside him; gently, she touched his arm. "*I* know this time. I *know,* Matt. What you're doing is dangerous to you and to the girl."

Matt pulled away, his shoulders rigid; darts of steely light glinted from his eyes. "I said I don't know!"

Reeling under the assault of his shout, she put up her hands to protect herself. Matt's face twisted with rage and his cheeks burned red. Gradually his breathing slowed; the sudden intoxication of his fury seemed to pass, leaving him vague and disoriented.

When he reached up and touched her face, a burst of unexpected anger filled her. "Were you fucking some college girl the afternoon that Amy was killed?"

His hand fell away from her cheek and all the color drained from his face. His mouth opened but no sound came out.

Linda was nearly as shocked as he was. She hadn't planned this, but the words had spilled from her mouth and there was no retreat now. "Answer me."

"It was—" He seemed unable to catch his breath. Through pale lips, he whispered, "I never intended to hurt you."

"I don't want to hear it! It's too damn convenient to keep me propped up with lies that are really excuses for your own weakness! You either tell me the damn truth now or it's all over." A ragged pulse pounded in her head, then slowed. "We have a chance to make things clean again. Please, just tell me."

He raised his arm, smashed his fist down on the table, uttered a cry of pain. When he finally spoke, his words bumped against each other in his rush to be rid of them. "It was all so weak, so shameful. I used her to make myself feel successful. It was like I was in a competition with you and you were winning because you were so happy whatever you were doing—working on a landscaping project, walking along the waterfront with Amy, or cooking dinner with her. I can't believe I was so childish. I had to do something that would get the better of you."

All right, now they were making progress. No more denying the past. Things hadn't been perfect—that was a first step. "Why didn't you tell me before it got to that point?" Linda shook her head. "That doesn't matter now, does it?"

"Every day there's a moment—I never know when it's going to come—when everything goes black. It's frightening. But it's always connected to this dirty, terrible shame that while my child was being murdered, I was—" He choked and sobbed, his hands opening and closing against the air as though he wanted to grasp something that eluded him.

Torn between his anguish and her own rage, Linda waited for Matt to regain control. "She was in one of your classes?" she asked.

"Linda, I can't. Why do you want to go through all the minute details *now?*"

He reached for her hand but Linda pushed him away; she wasn't ready for his touch. Not yet. "I need to know the truth, Matt, and this is a good place to start."

Some color crept back into his face but his eyes still avoided hers. "The truth—I *told* you the truth. The details aren't going to make it easier to understand. I was weak; I couldn't bear to tell you about it. It seemed so insignificant."

Now his dark eyes met hers; she didn't know if she could stand firm against the urgency in his face.

"It was the only time—never before and certainly not after,

I swear. It's your choice, Linda. I hope you can forgive me. I hope you don't feel like you have to keep dragging me over the coals to make me pay for something I've paid for a million ways, a million times."

Hot, unfamiliar rage swept through her again. Surely he couldn't think that forgiveness would be such a simple matter. He had years to think about it; she'd had barely a day. "You'll have to give me a little time, Matt," she said stiffly.

His uncomprehending eyes met hers.

She *did* love him. Lord, how she wished things were different; they needed each other now, in this terrible time. If only she could toss away the last vestiges of suspicion and offer him her trust . . . but she wasn't quite ready to do that yet.

The sculptures—she still hadn't asked him about them.

Did she really want to know?

Yes. She was tired of the pretenses that rose up in dark moments to throw impediments in her path.

"Matt." Her throat felt as if it might close up, and she swallowed to help ease the words out. "I never told you about the night, last Friday, when you were away."

His face contorted with the effort to speak. "We don't have to do this now, do we? I want to hear what you have to say, but I have to get back to business. You said you needed time to think. Well, I'm willing to give it to you—if you're ready to take it."

"Don't!" Linda shouted, her anger and her fear colliding to create a powerful new explosion. "You're doing it again. Can't you simply say you want to get out of here without twisting it around to be *my* doing?"

Pale and slack, Matt seemed to be trying to blink away her words. Was this for real or was it his best performance ever?

Linda fought the exhaustion that was making her eyes heavy. "Friday night, I wanted to get the sleeping bag. That's the short version. You remember where we put it? In the closet in the back bedroom. Before we turned it into your studio." She watched his face for a sign that he was furious or relieved or anything but she saw no change.

"My studio? The sleeping bags were in there? I thought we—"

She could almost see his mind racing to fill in the blanks of her unfinished story. It was like watching a silent movie. First his mouth closed, then his eyes narrowed and his chest deflated as if someone had stuck him with a pin.

"You saw them?" His voice was hardly more than a whisper.

"Yes. I saw all those figures, Matt. They frightened me." A sense of small triumph filled her; at least she'd gotten that much out.

"Linnie, I—" Matt's eyes flew open and he reached for her.

Linda let him take her hand in his, let herself take the full measure of his pain as he stared into her eyes.

"It's been hell," he whispered, but his voice barely drifted in through her fog. He squeezed her hand so hard she winced. "They were only a way to express feelings that I couldn't allow you or anyone else to see." He let go and buried his face in his hands.

Linda felt flung back into the cold kitchen. She had to make an effort. For his sake. For her own. She gripped his shoulders and felt his tears on her neck. Then, his body stiffened and he pulled away, took a deep breath, stood back. She groped in her pocket and handed him a tissue; he blew his nose.

"Those figures—they were some kind of exorcism. It wasn't anything that made sense. It just happened one day and it scared me. I destroyed the first three or four, but then I started feeling like some of my anger and a little bit of my pain was dissolving as I worked on them. It was so hard to keep a lid on my own feelings, but I had to, in order to help you."

Linda wanted to cry out that she was sorry. She knew,

dimly, that the fault wasn't entirely hers; Matt had chosen to play the strong and silent role, and she had encouraged him to sustain it. Their tacit agreement had kept them both locked in a strange dance all these years.

"I'm so sorry, Matt. You should have cried then. You should have been allowed to feel your own pain, your anger."

"And my fear," he added as he stroked her arm. "The fear that something would happen to us, when we needed each other so badly. I was afraid you wouldn't think I was strong; I was terrified that you might look somewhere else for comfort."

His comfort; her comfort: they'd both been so bad at guessing what the other needed. A warning light blinked on; maybe the very notion that they should be able to guess was the real problem.

"I'm going to find him. I don't care what it takes. I'm going to find the link between these girls. I don't know what it is yet. A bus driver. A teacher. A delivery boy. Something. There has to be. And I'm going to find it, I swear."

Linda listened, waiting for the throbbing pain behind her eyes to subside.

"I'm carrying a banner for all of us. I'm finally going to feel some—" he searched for the word "—some closure."

"You won't do anything, will you, if you think you've discovered who did all these things? Appearances aren't proof, you know. Circumstances aren't evidence. What if you're wrong?"

Matt shook his head. "I'm just gathering information. You can either accept that and trust me or not. But I'm going to do what I set out to do."

And who is going to bring me the news when you've done it? Linda wondered.

"He's right, Linda." Anton appeared from nowhere, his moonlike face lit by the overhead fixture. "It's waiting out there. And we're going to find it, aren't we? You find out anything yet?"

"Nothing useful." Matt's voice was flat, resigned.

"Useful?" Linda didn't like the sound of that.

Anton's bushy eyebrows shot up and he leaned against the door frame, arms folded across the expanse of his belly. "Useful. As in nothing we can use to get closer to the killer. As in nothing of use in seeing that this never happens again."

So Matt had a fellow warrior, a boon companion to accompany him on his quest. A lot had changed in the past few days, but Linda Crell knew one thing for sure; she would not turn this *folie à deux* into a *folie à trois*.

Amy would have giggled at the sight of Linda's fuzz of hair.

Sitting on the closed lid of the toilet, peering intently as Linda drew a mascara brush across her lashes, Amy had watched her mother's morning transformations with alarm until the overwhelming evidence had proven that Linda would come back from work every afternoon.

What will Irene Brandon think when she sees a grown woman with practically no hair standing at her door?

Linda pulled her sweater over her head and clutched it closer to her chest, as if to fill in the empty space where her daughter should be. At least her hair didn't need recombing after she got dressed.

Shoes in one hand and purse in the other, Linda padded down the stairs, glancing out the window at the rain bouncing off the lids of the garbage cans in the alley. It had been easier to talk to Irene Brandon than she expected; she had managed to keep the woman on the phone long enough to explain who she was and what she wanted. At first Irene Brandon sounded wary, suspicious, but finally she agreed in a quiet monotone to a brief visit. Maybe it was stubborn and cruel to subject Marianne Brandon's mother to questions, but beyond feeling compelled to find out whether the apparent convergence *did* exist, Linda felt drawn to the woman.

Facing Irene Brandon's fresh grief would be the price she'd pay. If only she could demonstrate a link between all three girls —the rain jars, the teachers who talked about God's tears. She'd get the information to the police so that they could stop this monster and make sure this didn't happen again. When long shots were all you had, you played them.

What was she going to say to Irene Brandon?

More important, what was Irene Brandon going to say to her?

twenty-seven

The square little bungalow could have been transplanted from the working-class neighborhood of any town. Attention to aesthetics was minimal; the paint was tan, the trim dark brown, and a few rhododendron bushes along a cement path were someone's concession to landscaping.

She knocked twice and stood back from the door, ready to turn and retreat down the street, if necessary.

"Yes?" The voice behind the door quavered.

"Mrs. Brandon? It's Linda Crell." Her own voice rang too bright, too sharp.

The door finally opened. Old orange peels and coffee grounds—that's what she smelled. Irene Brandon probably hadn't taken the garbage out all week. She was shorter than Linda, her brown hair pulled into a lumpy ponytail at the nape of her neck. Her cheeks and her nose were round, as though her features hadn't yet developed their adult sharpness, except for her thin, pale slash of a mouth. She tugged at the waist of a stained green cardigan and said, "We can sit in the living room."

Linda followed Irene Brandon's shapeless form down a dark hallway. The shades in the living room were pulled to just above the windowsills; slats of light fell onto the carpet at odd angles. All the lamps were unlit. Shapes soon became sofa, wall unit, chairs, a narrow bench, then a coffee table in front of the sofa, a large framed print on the wall between the chairs, a ceramic ginger jar lamp. She couldn't distinguish color, texture, anything but the gross bulk of the objects.

Linda set her wet raincoat atop the wooden bench before she sat down in the chair across from the one Irene Brandon had chosen. She could barely make out the woman's face; neither of them spoke for what felt like a very long time.

"I'm so sorry about Marianne," Linda finally said. "It's harder than anyone can imagine. You have no time to prepare; it's . . . I saw her picture in the paper. She was a beautiful child."

Irene Brandon's breath ratcheted across the room. "Everyone pretends she never even existed. You go along and you think you have it all together and it's just the two of you. You think how hard it is, taking care of everything. When she's sick. Summer vacations when you still have to work. Hard."

And then you learn that so many things you used to complain about are meaningless. Your values shift completely. "I know. You figure if only you can work harder, stop time, be a better person, maybe you can bring her back. That's what I thought in the beginning."

Irene Brandon's limp hands rested in her lap. She stared at them, then sighed. "I can't believe I'll never see her again."

Never. That was the part that Linda still couldn't understand. "I used to walk into rooms and expect her to be there." *When had it stopped?*

"It's a pretty exclusive club we're part of, isn't it?" Irene Brandon's chin dropped toward her chest and she began to cry. She accepted the tissue Linda offered and withdrew her hand quickly.

Linda felt the first tingle of anticipation as she waited for the sniffling to stop. Maybe together, in an alliance forged from their shared pain, she and Irene Brandon could help see to it that another parent wouldn't have to go through this. "My questions may not make sense to you but please understand—I'm not being frivolous. After you answer me, I'll tell you why I'm asking. If I say too much now, I may influence you."

A flash of white teeth—Irene Brandon was smiling. "I don't know how much help I'll be. My memory doesn't work too well anymore. I can't remember where I put the mail or if I turned off the stove or the tap on the bathtub. Yesterday it overflowed."

What a terrifying time it had been—Linda was certain then that it would last forever. "That part gets better after a while. Took me two months to feel safe near the stove and another six before I didn't have to wonder where my car keys were. After a year and a half, it got *much* better."

"I feel like I'm going crazy."

That was part of it, too. "You're not the only one. Sometimes craziness seemed like the only escape I had. I went away, into a dark place"—*like this living room*—"and it took months for that to change." Lost in the shapeless memories, Linda was startled by Irene Brandon's voice.

"What do you want to ask me?"

Finally. "Did Marianne talk to you about school, about what happened in class, things like that?"

"Every night at dinner. One day, when she was five, we made a rule. We had to tell each other one funny thing and one serious thing while we were having dinner. We took turns." A sob washed over her, building until Linda bent beside Irene Brandon's chair to put her arm around the shivering woman and stroked her hair. When the wave ebbed, she moved back to her own chair.

"Just a few more questions. Did she ever tell you about learning about the weather? About the sun and clouds and rain?"

Thick silence dimmed the already-faint light and hung in the air, dense and suffocating.

"What a joke," Irene Brandon said bitterly. "God. Her

teacher told her that the rain was God's tears. What God? God wouldn't have taken my baby from me."

It was true, then. This same bizarre story, told to each of the girls. But they went to different schools, had different teachers. What would Matt have to say about this information? *How did the cameo get around the doll's neck?*

Irene Brandon hugged her ribs, rocked back and forth, then sat up straight and still. "I'd spit on God, but I don't want to mess up my carpet."

"A person—it was a person who did this." Linda understood the anger, the sense of betrayal. God and Irene Brandon would work out their relationship later; right now Linda Crell needed more facts. "What about the teacher—what was her name?"

"Her teacher's name was Miss Anderson. But I already know that it's not the same person as . . . Martha Anderson came to Oakland this year from Martinez. She never taught in this city before."

Linda nodded. Amy had adored Keith Genetti; he was twenty-four, eager, fun, and fair. This was too confusing. Still, all the children—Amy, Marianne, and Cindy—had been told exactly the same strange thing.

Irene Brandon resumed her rocking, eyes closed and fingers gripping the fabric of the slipcover that bunched on the arm of the chair.

"Tell me about Marianne," Linda said softly. "Did she like animals? Amy loved animals, especially whales."

A corner of her mouth turned up and Irene Brandon stopped rocking. "Puppies. Spotted puppies. I don't know how it started. Maybe in one of those Golden Books, I'm not sure, but she had a collection. She kept the pictures in a scrapbook. Brown and white, black and white—all puppies. That's how she learned to use scissors. I'll never forget . . ."

Talk about it, Linda thought, settling back in the chair.

*Keep her with you in those memories. It helps, it really does, to
remember the good things.*

"One whole hour—it doesn't seem possible. I got carried away,
didn't I? I'm sorry. It's just that—Are you going to be in Oakland much longer?"

"I'm not sure about my plans, but if it's all right with you,
I'll keep in touch." Linda scribbled Anton's telephone number
on a scrap of paper. "Call me if you want to. Anytime." She
stepped forward and hugged Irene Brandon. Take some of my
strength, Linda thought, and keep it for a while, to use when
you need it.

Irene Brandon pressed her cheek against Linda's. "Thank
you," she whispered, before she slumped back into her chair.

Linda let herself out and closed the door gently, wondering
what to do with the news. Mia Honer seemed the most sensible
place to start. Linda would explain everything she had been
reluctant to say yesterday, everything she had discovered today,
and Mia would help figure out what it meant.

Rain pounded the pavement; a strong wind tossed a sheet
of newspaper into the air, pinning it to the side of a car, but the
cold air was welcome after the intensity of the morning. Drops
of water clung to her lashes as she looked at the sky—pearly,
swirling with colors, alive—and offered her face to the rain. Her
arms swung freely as she approached her car.

"Mrs. Crell?"

Linda turned; a uniformed police officer stood beside her, a
fresh-faced young woman with blond curly hair, like the hair
she had left in that gas station trash can in what seemed like a
long-ago dream. Linda fought the impulse to cover her head
with her hands.

"Mrs. Crell, please come with me. We have some questions. In connection with several incidents."

"My car is—"

"Someone will bring you back to your car. Please come with me."

She wouldn't just roll over because this woman was wearing a uniform and had a gun on her hip. Mia had warned them yesterday about harrassment.

"Am I under arrest?" She ignored the rain that ran down her face and looked the officer in the eye.

"No, ma'am. But there are some questions that—"

"I'll answer your questions, but I'm going to drive down to Seventh Street myself. In my own car. Voluntarily. If you're going to arrest me, that's different. Are you?"

A smile—of approval?—crept into the woman's eyes. "Okay, that's all right. I'll follow you."

"I know the way," Linda said softly. "I've been there before."

Good, that was very good. Better than she'd done three years ago, certainly.

The drive to Seventh Street was easy, the streets deserted in the downpour of rain. They entered the building together, the blond cop fluffing her hair with her fingers as they approached the elevator. Another interview, only this time Linda wouldn't be the one asking the questions. A trio of garishly dressed women, hooting and screeching, wobbled out of the elevator; Linda followed the officer and they rode to the second floor in silence.

Sweat coated her palms; she rubbed her hands against her thighs. It was cold in here, goddam freezing, and she was shivering in this thin raincoat and she couldn't possibly make it on such uncertain legs all the way down the hall where they would—

No, she wouldn't let that happen this time.

Her breathing was labored, quick, like Bea's when they'd climbed the sand path back to the parking lot. Just a few days ago . . . she should have gone away with Bea when she had the chance. Now they were going to ask her about where she had been when Marianne and Cindy—

She wouldn't shatter. This time, in fact, she had something to say that might actually make all the difference in these cases.

The door marked Homicide loomed ahead. No searches, no fingerprinting, no sitting in the room on the chair, alone, with strangers in her face for hours, with blood on her blouse, on her hands, a drop on her shoe, growing larger and larger as she sat there. No, she was ready for them now.

What did Matt tell them yesterday?

"This way." The woman held the door open and Linda stepped into a room that was half the size of the one she remembered and twice as noisy. Telephones rang, people chattered, computer keyboards clattered away. Five heads looked up, stared at her, and then went back to work.

A sallow man lumbered to the door, patting his face with a damp handkerchief. "Mrs. Crell, I'm Sergeant Morella. I understand you just spent some time with Irene Brandon. Is that right?"

"Is that illegal, Sergeant?" Angry, goddam it. She was angry. Why shouldn't she be able to offer Irene Brandon whatever comfort she could? He looked different, older perhaps or thinner, but she remembered this man; his breath always smelled of chocolate. "I don't have anything to hide from you"—*except the fact that you have my cameo in the evidence room*—"but I still insist on calling my lawyer before I answer any of your questions. I decline to answer anything until I've spoken to her."

His eyes hung closed a moment too long.

A rush of confidence warmed her when she recognized the expression on Morella's face; he understood that she was not going to play victim for him. The man glanced at her hair; she stared into his eyes.

"All right, Mrs. Crell. You can use the phone on the second desk."

Linda reached into her purse, hands steady, and drew out her address book, dialed Mia Honer's office. The secretary's imperious tone changed as soon as Linda said her name; in less than fifteen seconds, Mia was on the line.

"You okay?" Mia sounded tentative.

"I'm fine. They picked me up outside Irene Brandon's house. I told them I wouldn't answer any of their questions until I spoke with you."

Mia chuckled. "You're a tough broad, Linda. I'll be there before you can finish that ugly stuff they call coffee. Meanwhile, mum. What were you doing at the Brandon house, anyway?"

It was a long story. And this wasn't the place to tell it. Morella looked down at his papers but not before Linda saw that he had been staring intently at her face.

"You'll tell me when I get there, right? See you in five." Mia hung up.

Linda looked down at the Styrofoam cup someone had handed her. As in almost everything else, Mia was right about the coffee.

"You mean to say that my client is offering you this information and you're not even going to write down the teachers' names? Morella, don't you see the potential here?" Mia swung her head in disbelief. "I do think the umpire needs glasses."

Grumbling as he crinkled a Hershey bar wrapper, Morella hitched up his pants with his elbows and tossed the paper into the wastebasket. "Honer, how many times do I have to tell you —they all had different teachers. If I was you I'd be more worried that Mrs. Crell here doesn't have proof of where she was when those kids—"

"She doesn't *need* proof," Mia snapped, "unless you're charging her."

Linda's heart pounded. *Charging her*—as though a snorting bull was about to burst from a stall and do its massive best to impale her. Maybe it had been a mistake to tell Mia about the rain jars; when she heard the lawyer make a case for investigating the teachers and the strange lesson, the whole notion sounded like a flimsy fantasy.

"I'm not charging her. Yet." Morella looked at his watch. "Oh, yeah. One more thing."

Only one of Mia's dimples flashed. "All right, Columbo, what is it?" she asked as she motioned to Linda and started gathering her raincoat and briefcase.

Linda grabbed her own raincoat to try to still her trembling fingers.

Morella shuffled through papers, spilling them onto the scratched table as he pushed though the pile. He stood, both hands on a photograph, leaning over it. He picked it up and held it against his chest. "You ever see this before, Miz Crell?"

Lie. Don't tell him the truth. Linda stared at the picture for what she hoped was a proper amount of time and then shook her head.

Morella sighed and stuck the picture back into the folder.

Grandma Donner's cameo has been missing for over a year and a half, she should have said, but she hadn't, and now, for the first time since she'd known Mia, she had a secret from her. Linda slipped her arms through the sleeves of her raincoat as Morella pushed open the interrogation room door. The noise in the Homicide room hadn't really settled into a hush while she was being questioned, it had only seemed that way to her, locked away with the lawyer and the policeman, dropping in on the game both of them played all the time. If she could, she would take her marbles and go home. *Home?*

She followed Mia through the bustle of activity to the hall;

they waited in silence until the elevator rumbled to a stop. The door opened and a knot of people pressed past her into the hall.

It was him.

The man with the Toyota. Almost round-shouldered, with that fluid, graceful way of moving—she'd know him anywhere. Her heart thudded but he walked right by her.

The elevator doors closed. "You know him?" Mia fixed the bright red comb in her hair and snapped the lock on her briefcase.

"Just an old ghost," Linda said.

twenty-eight

If this were a different case, Goldstein might be relieved to have an excuse to work on Thanksgiving. He and his father were expected to engage in trenchant political observations while his mother prepared too much food. Aunt Sheila would rattle on about having her silver service replated, Uncle Morris would fall asleep in the chair, and the three or four stray guests would inevitably include some single woman—"just from New York, very successful"—deemed suitable by Aaron or Rosalie to make a match with their son.

He made a U-turn, took a right at Broadway, and fell in with the easy rhythm of the lights, all the way to the volunteer center. He was sorry that Cruz had to miss the holiday with his family. Come to think of it, Cavessena was the only other person from whom Goldstein had heard no complaint about having to work through the holiday.

He pulled the BMW up to the curb; the volunteer center lights were a strange beacon in the afternoon gloom. Goldstein ducked the raindrops, letting the rain flick at his face. Charlotte Wertz, half hidden under an umbrella, almost knocked him down as she headed for the door. "Pretty long day you put in," he said.

Startled, she stared in the direction of his voice. "I don't need much sleep," she said from under her umbrella. The weariness in her voice might have been fatigue or discouragement or both. The hollows beneath her cheeks deepened as she smiled. "Were you just passing by?"

Even fatigue didn't mar her elegance. What would it take to break her self-control? "Something like that. Can I buy you a cup of coffee?"

Something about her still bothered him—beyond the dance, past the uncertainty of what he wanted from her. Her involvement with this volunteer effort seemed too deep. What was keeping Charlotte Wertz, thirty-one years old and a successful stockbroker, tied to the community attempt to find Marianne Brandon's killer and Cindy Forrest's abductor? Maybe if he pushed her a little . . .

"No decent coffee around here," he said. "If we were in San Francisco, I'd say I'd brew us some Kona at my apartment." Manipulative? Sure, but she was an adult; she'd decide when his interest was official and when it wasn't.

An eyebrow arched and she allowed a remarkable smile to light her face. "We both have to be back here at two, but that's forty minutes from now. If you follow me, Sergeant, *I'll* make *you* coffee."

Her house was two blocks away, an undistinguished stucco with a profusion of flowering plants in terra-cotta containers filling the small front porch. An orange cat scurried into the bushes as Charlotte opened the door. Several blocks away, a bus lumbered toward its destination. Otherwise, quiet lay like a coverlet over the neighborhood.

The living room confirmed Goldstein's first impression of Charlotte Wertz. A huge vase of yellow-and-white chrysanthemums created a visual explosion in the almost austere space. A stack of expensive art books covered a wicker table in one corner; a gleaming baby grand piano graced another corner. Above a simple white sofa hung a large chrome-framed canvas alive with bold strokes of amethyst and sapphire. The lighting was diffuse, the total effect elegant.

"You're not going to tell me that you just want decaf, are you? California gets so boring with all this healthy lifestyle business, sometimes. What's your pleasure?"

If she was aware that her words left room for interpretation she didn't show it. Goldstein declined the banter, hoping that she hadn't intended the double entendre. "Real coffee. And cognac, to take the edge off the chill and damp."

She produced a bottle of Remy Martin, and set about preparing the coffee. How many other women, how many love affairs in the past ten years had begun or ended with a crystal snifter of Remy as witness? Two years ago, Lilla Smith had introduced herself to him and then pulled a bottle of Remy from under her dressing table at a San Francisco nightclub. That relationship hadn't exactly ended the way he'd hoped it would.

"Sergeant Goldstein, we're not here to share a sociable cup of coffee." She kicked off her shoes and pulled her legs under her, settling into the corner of a large, soft-pillowed chair opposite him. "I know it, you know it, and I don't feel like playing that particular game anymore."

Her voice had changed; it was more distant, more removed. Reluctantly, Goldstein stepped back into his official self. People about to unburden themselves often sounded that way; it wasn't yet time to lower his guard with this woman. It might never be time. "You have something to tell me," he said softly.

"I've seen you looking at me and I've recognized the questions in your eyes. It's your job, granted. In a way, I'm pleased that you're not taking anything on face value. But I'm beginning to feel uncomfortable, so I want to tell you some things that you probably don't know."

Goldstein sipped the coffee; it burned going down. "I've been looking at you for a lot of reasons." He turned away from the emerald eyes, from the extraordinary pull of her aloofness.

She picked up her own cup and blew across the steaming

surface. "I have no criminal past. I'm not a former mental patient or anything like that. I'm not a child abuser or an abused child. But I had an abortion when I was sixteen." Her voice rose, as though the effort to get the words out had affected her ability to control the volume. "A little girl. From the second I found out I was pregnant, the thing inside me had an identity. A girl—I just knew it. I couldn't raise a child. My mother drank, my father pretended that both of us didn't exist, and I couldn't bear the responsibility of bringing another human being into such a bleak and confusing world. I was ten weeks into the pregnancy when I had the abortion.

"It took me a month to react. When I finally did, I lost twenty pounds, had to drop out of school. An English teacher who was upset that I'd left school finally got me to see that I had punished myself enough. She was wonderful. If not for her—"

She lifted the cup to her lips, took a sip, and with uncharacteristic gracelessness, wiped her mouth with the back of her hand. "I don't regret it, considering my circumstances then. Still, when Marianne came skipping into my yard two years ago looking for the ball that she'd been playing with, my heart stopped. She was eight years younger than my girl would have been, but without realizing it, I poured all the feelings of love I might have given my own lost little girl into Marianne. After a while I realized what I was doing and I forced myself into therapy. I kept a bit of distance but we'd been bound together, Marianne and me, by my need . . . and by hers, for someone to be with until her mother came home.

"The news of her murder was more than I thought I could bear, Sergeant Goldstein. My first impulse was to hide, but that's not how I get my comfort. I have to make it for myself if I can, or ask for it. And helping to find her killer is my only comfort now." She set the cup on the table and looked directly at him.

If it was difficult for him to understand parenthood, this would never be even remotely accessible to him. What would it be like to be sixteen and to discover that you were carrying a child? A wave of confusion bore down on him; he started to reach for her hand but found that he couldn't move.

"Thank you for listening," she said. "I'm not sure what I thought would come of telling you. I hope this won't make you uncomfortable around me. I was aware of your suspicions and I wanted to explain the reasons—" she swallowed hard "—as I understand them, for my involvement."

He wanted to say that his interest wasn't entirely professional, but this wasn't the time for such an admission. Still, he couldn't walk out without responding to her disclosures. Sometimes, when simple human interaction was practically impossible because of his job, Jay Goldstein wished he had chosen the safe route—philosophy professor at a small but prestigious New England college, editor of an esoteric little journal, anything else.

Her story was too perplexing; it raised too many unsettling questions, and he found himself yearning for a sign. He wanted evidence of nobility, of dignity, but everywhere he looked he saw compensation for guilt or striving for attention. His search for meaning had shifted to a grudging admission that none existed. Goldstein had recognized lately that his personal philosophy had progressed as far as Camus and Sartre and the nothing-is-more-meaningful-than-anything-else school. Was there any coming back from that?

He smiled wryly and pushed away his half-full (half-empty? Today he didn't care.) coffee cup. He rose, startled himself by kissing Charlotte Wertz lightly on the cheek, and let himself out of the house.

. . .

Work—that would help put Charlotte and her story out of his mind. The volunteer center was still a swarm of activity, and after a half hour of trying to focus, the best course seemed to be to gather up the reports he hadn't yet read and take them back to the department.

The piles were growing like fungus on a tree stump, stacks that he and Cruz couldn't quite finish checking each day. If he took them home with him, he'd get more done. A box—he needed something to carry them in. Oblivious to the phones and the jostling, noisy crew of volunteers, he headed for the table beside the file cabinet. He could empty out the yellow legal pads and use that carton. He walked across the room with his eyes on his shoes and his mind years and miles away. The front door opened. Charlotte Wertz stood in the open doorway, her face glistening with rain.

He turned away. A flash of red on the floor caught his attention. The wedge of light from the open door reached across to the file cabinet, pointing to the scarlet glint tucked between the cabinet and the wall.

He knelt, put his face so close to the small red object that he could smell floor wax and the mildewed dampness underneath the building. He'd have to move the file cabinet away to get it out—but he knew what he'd find.

For as long as he could remember, he'd known that the macabre had the potential to connect him to the sublime. He expected it, longed for it when he decided to work in Oakland, against his father's wishes and his own half-examined and then discarded plans to embark on an academic life.

He couldn't take the chance of smashing the thing. His mind raced. This file cabinet had been hauled in two days ago, a donation from Mrs. Silcock's garage. Sweating and grunting, two skinny teenage boys had carried it in, following the direction of Charlotte's outstretched finger to set it down against the wall. Goldstein had watched the scene, amused at the alacrity with which the boys responded to Mrs. Silcock—and their stuttering shyness whenever Charlotte talked to them.

He tugged at a corner of the file cabinet. By now, every one of those papers that had been stacked precariously all over the room had been neatly filed away, adding forty or fifty pounds to the weight of the cabinet itself. Oblivious to the sounds around him, he pulled up on a drawer handle as he shifted his weight and pressed his hip against the cabinet. The cabinet moved a little, nearly enough, but he still couldn't get to the object. He grabbed an envelope from the table, used it to extend his reach. The object skittered out.

He was right.

It was a little red barrette with a floppy-eared rabbit on one end. A fine blond hair was caught in the clasp.

He felt silly, down here on his hands and knees but appearances hardly mattered now. "Rabbits on the barrettes." A volunteer had taken that message on one of the phones in this very room. He curled one envelope into a scoop and pushed it under the barrette. His hand shook as he straightened to a standing position. He held the second envelope open, and then dropped the barrette inside.

He had to get it to the lab.

Across the room, Cruz was talking to Charlotte. Goldstein caught his eye and pointed to the wall clock. Cruz nodded and pulled his windbreaker from the back of the chair, then picked his way past two tables of volunteers. Frowning, he looked over his shoulder at the clock. "You in a hurry? It isn't show time downtown for another two hours, almost."

Goldstein held open the envelope. "Cindy's red rabbit barrette," he said quietly. "We better check with the parents."

His face suddenly pale, Cruz nodded. "We'll have to get something of the girl's. Check for prints and have the hair sampled. If we get a hit . . ." He looked glazed, distracted.

"We'll stop at the lab before we go to the afternoon briefing." Goldstein's mouth was suddenly dry. The pace was about to accelerate. It was no accident that this little object was found in the volunteer center. The only accident was that it was Goldstein who spotted it first and picked it up without obliterating any prints that might remain on the plastic.

"Go ask Charlotte for a list of all the volunteers. Tell her it's important that she doesn't tell anyone you asked for it—and don't tell her why you want it."

Cruz looked like he was about to say something, but instead he walked directly to Charlotte. *I'm lucky,* Goldstein thought, *that he didn't tell me to fuck off for ordering him around.*

Cruz was scowling when he returned. "She says she doesn't have a master list and that she'll try to have something for us by four—if she's not too busy. Come on, man, if I think about this too long, I'm gonna lose it. It's not gonna be a picnic, talking to the parents. Let's get it over with, okay?"

He was right. Goldstein stuffed the envelope in his pocket, tossed his raincoat over his shoulder, and followed Cruz out the door into the light rain.

"I'll drive," Cruz offered. Goldstein was just as happy to sit back and stare at the wet streets. He had to calm down or he'd make mistakes, mess up things that were critical. He visualized a gentle light rising from his feet and his hands to fill his legs, his arms, his trunk. Mr. Yamasake had led him through this meditation so many times; now he could feel the softness suffuse his limbs. The light filled his chest, rose to his neck, flowed into the small bones around his eyes.

"Shit, man, I can't stand it. It's not fair. I fucking can't do this." Cruz was shouting, his voice too loud in the car with its windows rolled up.

The gentle light never made it all the way to Goldstein's brain. He exhaled, then turned to Cruz. "What?"

"Facing these people, Goldstein." Cruz was still shouting; the veins along the side of his neck stood out. "They look at you as though they're sure you're the only one who can do anything to help them. I can't face them again."

They were only half a block from the Forrest house. "I'll go inside. It's okay, Cruz. You wait here."

Cruz pulled to the curb; before either of them could change their minds, Goldstein jumped out. He nodded to the duty cop parked across the street in a nondescript car, then hopped across the rushing stream that churned its way down the hill toward the storm sewer. Lights shone brightly from every window of the neat frame house. Goldstein thought about all the people he'd met in his twelve years as a policeman who had waited for news. They always kept all the lights burning.

He rang the bell.

"Yes?" Ed Forrest's voice was deeper than he'd expected.

"It's Sergeant Goldstein. I'm Carlos Cruz's partner."

The door swung open and Forrest, his back stooped, stood aside to let Goldstein in. His face was seamed with sadness; it was no kindness to keep this big, bewildered man waiting. Goldstein reached into his pocket and pulled out the envelope, opened it, and held it toward Ed Forrest. The man's pudgy fingers shook as he reached out.

"Don't touch it, please. I need you to tell me—Does this look like the one your daughter was wearing?"

Ed Forrest's head jerked forward; his eyes watered and he shook his head. "I don't know. Maybe. Where did you get this? Is she . . . ?" He gagged as he grabbed the collar of Goldstein's raincoat.

"Mr. Forrest, we haven't found Cindy. I don't know what this means yet. We don't even know if it's Cindy's." Ed Forrest's grip slackened; when the man finally let go of his coat, Goldstein stepped back. "Would you look again, try to tell me if it's Cindy's?"

"I'll have to call Margie. She's the one who always—" Forrest choked back the rest of his words, swiped at his eyes, and fled up the stairs.

Feeling like an intruder, Goldstein waited in the entryway. The door to the left had been pulled shut; to the right, the shabby living room blazed with light. Cindy's picture had been removed from the mantel.

"Sergeant Goldstein?" Her arms clasped to her chest, Margie Forrest glided, ghostlike, down the stairs. Shadows ringed her eyes, dark smudges in the pallor of her face.

"I'm sorry to disturb you, Mrs. Forrest. I know this is hard but it may be the break we're looking for."

What right did he have to give her hope? The woman's expression hardly registered a change. Perhaps she'd heard similar words before, if only in her imagination.

"My husband says you found a barrette. Can I see it?" Her voice was flat; he heard neither hope nor despair.

Goldstein held up the envelope again. She didn't reach for it as her husband had, but instead stared at it without speaking or changing expression. "Mrs. Forrest?" he said gently.

"It's Cindy's. She was wearing two, to keep her braids from unraveling. You only found one? Where was it? Oh, God." She leaned into her husband's belly; his arms encircled her and together they stared at Goldstein.

For the second time in a single day, he was at a loss for words. "I wish I could tell you more but I can't. I'm hoping it's going to help us find Cindy."

He explained what would happen next. Quietly, Ed Forrest went upstairs and returned with a plastic bag. Inside, as Goldstein had requested, was Cindy's hairbrush and her bedside clock.

Goldstein thanked the Forrests and left them standing in their brightly lit house while he carried pieces of their daughter's life to the police lab in a shopping bag.

twenty-nine

"Cruz."

McNaughton's voice stopped him as he rushed down the hall toward the Homicide room. Cruz skidded to a stop. "Sorry I'm late for the—"

"Briefing's been postponed until four-thirty," McNaughton said. "I've been with the press, trying to feed them little bits and pieces to shut them up until after the weekend at least."

So McNaughton probably hadn't seen Goldstein, probably didn't know about the barrette. "Mac—"

"Cruz, I've been thinking. Now that we've talked to the Crell woman and her husband, I have more questions about them than I did before. Why don't you go down to Pescadero and check their background—talk to the fellow Crell said he worked for, the grocery store clerk where she shops, that kind of thing. Interviews like that might take a day or two, don't you think?"

McNaughton's offer was generous. Someone from another division could sift through the reports from the volunteer center while Cruz was away, and he could spend nights at least with Elenya and the boys.

Shit, what timing.

A couple of hours ago, he'd have been out of here. Now, if it turned out that the barrette was Cindy's, then he and Goldstein, with their close association with the volunteer center, would become primary resources. Having established relationships—such as they were—with the volunteers, he and Goldstein were in the best position to look close-up at the cast of characters. Which meant that Pescadero and Santa Cruz weren't exactly on the itinerary.

He thanked McNaughton for thinking of him and then told him about the barrette.

Recognition lit McNaughton's eyes; pipe in hand, he finally spoke. "If there's no match, Cruz, then go ahead down there and interview those people. If there is a match, though . . . I'll call down and put the screws to the lab to get the prints run ASAP. While we're waiting, you get a list—names, addresses, phone numbers, occupations, anything pertinent—of everyone, I mean, every single individual including delivery boys and the mailmen, who has been in that center since the damn thing opened."

"Goldstein and I are already working on that, Lieutenant," Cruz said. "We're going back down to the center after the briefing to pick up the list and talk to the woman who's been sort of running things."

McNaughton's pipe clicked against his teeth. "Wouldn't it be something if we wrapped this up by tomorrow? Reporter's dream, you know?"

"That depends," Cruz said, "on the details."

When he thought about it, it was more likely to turn into a nightmare.

McNaughton's eyes narrowed. "We've got a lot of loose ends dangling around here, Cruz. Instead of waiting on our butts for the lab work, we'd better tie up those ends. That ambulance heist—we already cleared the guy who rents the house behind the cottage, but we need to touch base with the owner. And the convertible and our phantom girl with the green Help sign. Pick one, Cruz, and do something about it. Then pick another one. I'll see you at four-thirty." McNaughton marched into the waiting elevator; the doors closed and he disappeared.

Right, Lieutenant, Cruz thought. *A little busywork to keep me out of trouble.* It was only three o'clock—ninety minutes until the briefing. Morella, Quinn, and Cavessena were at their desks; nobody but Morella looked up as Cruz tossed his jacket over the back of his chair. The big man rolled a Snickers wrapper into a ball, dumped it into a paper bag on his desk, and bent his head back to his papers.

Cruz slid into his chair. If McNaughton could get the lab to hurry things, they might have the results in less than an hour —but he already knew how that one would turn out. Having Charlotte Wertz start on that list was going to save a lot of time. Meanwhile, McNaughton was probably right; doing anything would be better than just sitting here. The phone rang and made the decision for him.

"Cruz. Homicide."

"Cruz? Artie Demshin at City Records. You left a message for me to call you?" The voice was curt, almost angry, a perfect ex-New Yorker's camouflage. Demshin was a gentle man, Cruz thought, so he developed this voice to up the odds that he wouldn't be trampled by the bureaucracy.

"Yeah, Artie. I really need that information on who owns that cottage. You get anything yet?"

"Sorry I didn't call you sooner. It's been a bad time for me. I'm being audited. Can you fucking believe it?"

Artie had argued for years that he was glad to pay his taxes because he was proud to be an American, and his money after all went to build roads and bridges and schools and space shuttles. Cruz steered clear of conflict whenever he could, and besides, patriotism was one of those things you could hardly argue with. Still, it was a minor pleasure to think about the tables being turned this way.

"Tough break, man," Cruz said, grinning. "Give me the scoop."

"He said it was medical expenses that popped the flag. I guess it looks strange that two wage earners who make forty-six thousand a year gross had over eight thousand dollars in medical expenses, but what can I do about it? Both my kids needed braces, I broke my leg skiing, and Mary had mono for two months and that cost a lot for—"

"Artie, you don't have to prove anything to me. The property."

"Oh, yeah. Sorry. The address for ABC Properties is a P.O. box in Oakland. A telephone answering service takes calls. I checked with the attorney general's office and found out that ABC is a DBA for one Harvey Kittner. The only listing we got is a residence on Melrose, in Los Angeles."

He had chased so many fizzlers in the past week, so many leads from the foot-high stack of reports, from all over the country, and they had all gone nowhere, as this probably would. The barrette—that was the best bet he'd seen in a week. The balls of the guy, making the cops and the volunteers the butt of a huge, nose-thumbing joke. *Look,* someone was saying, *I'm right in your face and you don't have me.*

Cruz took a deep breath. What were Elenya and the boys doing right this second? He built sketchy fantasies of the book Elenya was reading in front of the fire or the way Julio's boots squished as he tramped to the tide pool or the dreamy expression on Carlito's face as he rubbed a skinny french fry through a sea of ketchup. The pictures blunted his anxiety for a few minutes.

Even if it was useless, he'd call L.A. and try to find this Kittner. At least he'd have something to tell McNaughton.

He dialed the number that Demshin had given him. On the seventh ring, someone answered.

"Yeah?" The voice was female and bored.

"My name is Sergeant Carlos Cruz. I'm with the Oakland Police Department. We're trying to contact someone who can tell us about the property on Opal near Thirty-eighth in Oakland."

"Yeah?"

"Is Mr. Kittner in?"

"Yeah." A wary edge crept into the voice. "He's on another call. Hold on."

Ready for a long wait or an argument, Cruz was surprised when he heard a grunt and a click before he could write Elenya's name for the third time on his pad.

"Kittner."

Was everyone in Los Angeles so stingy with their words? "Mr. Kittner, my name is Cruz. I'm a sergeant with the Oakland Police Department. We're checking some facts for an important case here. I need a list of everyone who rented the cottage over on Opal for the last three years."

"That's easy. I lived in the big house for ten years and used the cottage as my office. Moved out in September. Now I can't get nobody to rent the damn cottage. Maybe I'm asking too much. What do you think—seven hundred for a two-room cottage with a remodeled bathroom and a great garden? Microwave oven, even. That's a pretty good deal, right?"

Cruz didn't want to talk real estate. "No one's lived there for two months and only you lived there for ten years before that?"

"Me and my wife and our three kids. My ex-wife, that is. She lives in this four bedroom beauty in San Diego and thinks I'm made of goddam money just because I own some property. Fucking cottage sitting empty. Not only isn't it bringing in any money, but it costs me—taxes, protection, fucking maintenance."

Must be something in my voice today, Cruz thought. Everyone was treating him like he was a telephone Mr. Fix-it. He was tired of it.

"Thanks for your help, Mr. Kipness."

"Kittner," the man said testily before he hung up.

Sighing, Cruz popped the tab on a Pepsi can and poured the fizzing soda into a Styrofoam cup.

"Thousands of guys with ponytails and knit caps in the nine-county area and their friends are turning them all in." Morella's face drooped. "We're looking for some extra help after the holidays, maybe from Vice, but by then the public's gonna lose interest and things are gonna slow down around here."

McNaughton appeared in the doorway, his normally placid face beaming. "I just spoke to Nelson in the lab. It's a hit. Clear set of prints on the barrette match the ones on the child's clock. Hair test isn't done yet, but so far, so good."

They were going to do it. They were going to find Cindy Forrest. Cruz had a good feeling about this. "What about other prints?"

"One other partial. I sent a guy out to take a set from the mother and father. I'm betting we'll get a positive on the mother. Little girls don't have the dexterity to do braids."

A pulse pounded in Cruz's head. He needed to be calm, to take a deep breath now. It was going to get crazy for a while, what with the holiday coming and people—volunteers, cops, lab technicians—going away. Everything was about to get more complicated, but they were going to nail this guy.

"You and Goldstein are key players now, Cruz. You coordinate checking on the volunteers. Morella, pull in the other teams and have them work with Cruz and Goldstein. We have to cover as much ground as we can today—" McNaughton glanced at his watch "—what's left of it."

Morella nodded, then smacked his forehead and rolled his eyes. "Shit, I know I wrote it down." He pulled scraps of paper from his pocket, tossed them onto the desk, started opening them one by one. He unfolded four torn pieces of paper before his face lit with a wide smile. "Here it is. Some fellow named Margolin called about an hour ago. He said to tell you or Goldstein 'California Association of Science Teachers.' What's that?"

Cruz didn't need explanations. "CAST," he muttered. "Dexter Williams." He remembered the drawings of some part of the human body he'd seen Williams grading the first time he met the man. He knew Williams was a teacher—but they'd checked that connection. None of the girls had the same teacher. And it wasn't just Williams—hadn't Charlotte done something else before she started working at the stock exchange? Wasn't she a teacher first? They'd thought of teachers, of course, but the girls all had different teachers. They'd spoken to all the principals and checked the—

Oh, shit, Cruz thought angrily. *Substitute teacher*—the one way all three girls could have had the same teacher. What kind of position did Dexter Williams hold in the Oakland school district?

"Dexter Williams? Yes, he's on the list. Very reliable. Always shows up when he says he will."

He knew she was going to say something like that. The men sent to cover the Williams apartment had called in twenty minutes earlier with their initial report: No one was home. No one answered the phone or the doorbell.

The principal of Cindy Forrest's school, Emerson Elementary, and the two assistant principals were already gone for the holiday weekend. Three teachers said yes, Dexter Williams had taught at the school—on Friday. One said she didn't like Williams; when pressed for a reason the woman muttered something about leaving dirty coffee cups on the table in the teachers' lounge.

No one from the Hillcrest Elementary school, where Amy

Crell and Marianne Brandon had been students, remembered who had subbed three years earlier. "Records at that level of detail," the principal explained, "are only kept for one school year."

"Did he work there at all in the past two weeks?" Cruz asked. This was going to be the last call today. School personnel were all rushing off for their holiday weekend.

"Oh, sure. He covered for one of the teachers who had jury duty. Tuesday and Wednesday of last week."

Bingo. Marianne Brandon was killed on Thursday. This was a pattern. Work one day, off a student the next. "Mrs. Boldrick, I need to talk to Dexter Williams but he's not home. Do you have any idea where he might be?"

The long silence stretched on; the wall clock's second hand leaped to the next dot and then the next. "His sister. He said his sister sent him a plane ticket. He never said to where though."

"Shit," Cruz hissed through his teeth. A sharp pain traveled from his jaw to his temples. "Sorry. Listen, it's very important. If you remember, call me. Here or at home. Anytime." Cruz gave the woman the telephone numbers and was about to hang up when her voice interrupted.

"He'll be back Monday. At least, I think he will. He's signed on for Mrs. Baum's third-grade class," she said hopefully.

There was no logical next move. Dexter Williams, like half the school people Cruz had tried to reach, appeared to be gone until Monday.

thirty

"What else did you expect? I could have told you the police wouldn't listen. That's why it's more important to keep at it—my way." The hard light in Matt's eyes cut through the gloom in Anton's kitchen, and he licked his lips as though he could taste triumph already.

She shouldn't have told him about her talk with Irene Brandon, but there was no way, once he knew that she'd been questioned by the police, to avoid it. Perhaps, if she examined her heart, she would have to acknowledge that part of her wanted to ride beside Matt into this fray, a subdued Sancho to his almost Quixote.

"Anyway, it's too late now. I—or, I should say, Andrew McCafferty—expect answers soon. I spoke to a couple of people at the Hillcrest and Emerson schools. I have to call back soon."

"The schools are closed for four days. Maybe you won't know anything for a week, Matt. I think we should go home—back to Pescadero, I mean—and let the dust settle. We can take your van and—"

The blare of the telephone brought a wide grin to Matt's face. His eyebrows raised and he nodded at the phone in an I-told-you-so gesture. "McCafferty," he said.

His eyebrows knit together. Was this bad news? no news?

His hand covered the mouthpiece and he held the receiver out to her. "For you."

If it was Mia or Anton, he would have said so. Morella must have seen the dissembling in her face yesterday when she denied knowing about the cameo, was calling to tell her he hadn't believed her.

"Linda, are you going to take this call?"

She took the receiver from him, her gaze still fixed on his face. "Hello?"

"That answers my question," the voice on the other end said with a laugh. "You changed your mind about the trip, but I guess the reservation desk forgot to tell me."

"I didn't know how to reach you or where to leave a message." How was she going to explain Bea to Matt? She didn't have to tell him everything, at least not right away.

"Things going better for you?"

Matt was looking right at her. "Yes, much. Where are you?"

"Still in Pescadero. Had a flat in my driveway as I was pulling out this morning. I figured maybe it was an omen that I should wait for you."

Matt looked confused; maybe what she was seeing was his disappointment that the call hadn't brought the news he was waiting for. He jiggled impatiently but Linda ignored him. She had to be sure. If she cut Bea loose now, her course was defined: she was throwing in with Matt.

If only someone had found her pillbox . . .

"It's an omen that you're a dear, sweet person and a wonderful friend who has an old vehicle with occasional problems. Now, you have a great time. Keep in touch. And you be sure to drive carefully, Bea. I want a chance to win back that money."

Bea snorted. "Or owe me twice as much. Okay, then I'm on my way. Last chance, honey."

No time to think anymore; the decision had been made.

"When you hit the Texas border, you remember to call

everyone 'pardner,' you hear? So long, Bea. God bless." Linda hung up.

"Someone selling light bulbs?"

"I met her on the beach a couple of months ago. She just called to say good-bye. She's going on a trip."

"How did she get this number?"

Here it came—another lie. "I called her yesterday."

Linda expected a barrage of questions, but Matt seemed to do a mental somersault. "I have some phone calls to make. I'm going to do it from upstairs."

She had chosen, and if she was lucky she wouldn't have to think about the road not taken. She *had* to be right about Matt.

"I found him."

Linda wheeled around. Matt stood in the doorway, his jubilant smile fading into sad acceptance. "I know his name. I know where he lives. Poor baby, this has been so hard for you. But it's almost over. Soon," he promised in a whisper.

Linda's knees buckled, her fragile strength almost sucked away, imperiled by the contact with her husband. "Matt, tell the police what you've found out. Let them take care of it. You can't go around playing God."

"God?" His mouth twisted. "I gave up the idea of God three years ago. I'm the only one who can bring this full circle. The cops won't do it, or can't. They proved that after Amy, after they couldn't find the person who . . . It really doesn't make any difference anymore, what they did or didn't do. The fact is that nothing's going to happen unless I make it happen.

"Finding him was simple, really. There I was, chatting up the Hillcrest school secretary, just bullshitting, and we hit on teacher burn-out and from there she got onto the high rate of teacher absences and that led to talking about how hard it is to get decent substitute teachers."

Of course—there *was* a way that the same person could have told all three girls the same story in the same words. Linda was mesmerized by Matt's tale.

"The secretary gave me eight names, five full-time teachers and three subs, who worked there last week in second-grade classes. Six women, two men. Emerson Elementary gave me seven names—all women. None of them matched the Hillcrest list. It almost didn't work, Linda. I almost missed him. I asked who was working Friday and the clerk told me. I almost gave up. And then. Then . . ." He paused, as though he were savoring a fond memory. "And then she remembered that Cindy's class breaks up into reading groups three days a week. And the best readers are taught by a *third*-grade teacher. And a third-grade teacher was absent from Emerson on Friday. The name of the substitute teacher matched with one of the second-grade substitutes from the Hillcrest school. I have to make sure that it's him. Like you've been saying . . . I want to be sure I have the right man."

Linda shuddered. "But none of it proves anything, does it?"

"I don't need to prove anything. I'm neither dumb nor unprincipled, Linda. I'm waiting for information from Sacramento. I called for background on this guy. I told them about the state commission—they didn't even know I was making it up."

"Matt, you're scaring me. Please, let me call Mia. She'll know what to do. You trust Mia, don't you?"

Matt sneered. "Trust? Who is there to trust except yourself? I'm going to finish this—"

The phone rang. Matt twitched and picked up the receiver. "Yes?"

His eyes blazed as he listened, but when he finally spoke he sounded calm and businesslike, the perfect actor. "That's great. Thanks. And what about the anecdotal material?" He sat down on the edge of the chair opposite her and drew curly loops on the message pad.

Evidently, he'd been put on hold. Linda flipped through *Antique Collectors' Journal*, pretending to read. Suddenly, instead of doodling, he was scribbling furiously.

"When was that?" His voice was tight.

She was too far away to see what he was writing, too near to pretend that she wasn't staring at him.

"With a scissor?" His voice was louder now. "Why didn't anyone stop him?"

This was maddening. Who was the *him* and what had he done with a scissor and who should have stopped him?

"A whole second-grade class? Why didn't you people communicate with Sacramento about this? How the hell—" He choked off the rest of his sentence. He listened, shaking his head or nodding at intervals. "I know it's not your fault," he said through his teeth, "but I'm going to have to report this anyway, you understand." His hand dropped to his lap; the receiver banged against his knee but he hardly blinked. "It didn't have to happen."

She held him to her, waiting for his body to relax—but instead of feeling Matt grow calmer, she began to take on his agitation again. She held her breath, then exhaled and let him go.

"He was denied tenure from a full-time teaching job in San Jose. Herded a class of second graders into a storage room and told them that he was going to put spiders in the room with them because they made noise while he was talking. One parent reported that he threatened to cut off her son's penis. Held the scissor in front of his face until the child apologized for asking to go to the bathroom twice in one morning. Eight other incidents, just as crazy, on his record.

"He denied everything. No proof and the allegations alone weren't grounds for yanking his teaching credential. That was

four years ago. According to the Hillcrest school secretary, Oakland was so hard up for substitute teachers then that anyone who came even close to having qualifications was snapped up. References aren't even checked. He taught Amy's class the day before she was murdered and he taught Marianne and Cindy's reading groups. The day before they . . ."

Matt was right: it shouldn't have happened. And it shouldn't be allowed—ever, anywhere—to happen again.

"He just slipped through the damned cracks—"

Maybe now she could convince him to talk to the police. But when she examined his face, she saw too much unfinished business: a need to atone; a terrible compulsion to settle the score.

"Sometimes, a person has to set things right. Most people feel helpless, impotent, and it eats away at them." Matt smiled. "Not me. I laid the foundation, little by little. The structure is solid. And I'm going to close Dexter Williams in it forever."

Dexter Williams.

To give a name to what had been nameless made the breath stop in her chest.

Dexter Williams poured milk on his cornflakes in the morning and scrubbed behind his ears in the shower.

Dexter Williams put gas in his car and paid his telephone bill and decided not to wear his plaid vest with his striped shirt.

And Dexter Williams murdered Amy.

Maybe Dexter Williams murdered Amy, Linda amended.

Roberta Herron had made a similar assumption three years ago. God, how easy it would be to stop here, to lend tacit agreement to Matt's conclusions. It would be so satisfying, so clean to be done with it. But it wasn't right to condemn a man without a trial. This obsession of Matt's wasn't going to go away by itself; the excitement of the chase was keeping his fires stoked too high. Linda dug into her purse and pulled out a piece of paper.

"Here's the number of the police task force." *Pick up the*

phone, she wanted to shout, as she handed him the paper, but she forced herself to wait.

"They don't know what they're doing. Jesus, Linda, haven't they proved that to you already?" The paper drifted out of his fingers to the floor. The cat pounced on it, batted it with his paws, then crouched in front of it, his tail quivering with excitement.

"Matt, what if the Forrest girl is alive? Have you thought that you might jeopardize her safety? Could you live with that?"

Matt smiled another of his ghostly grins. "I'm on the side of the angels this time, Linda. That won't happen. I know what I have to do.

"I've gone this far and I can't let it drop now. I've got his name. I know that he was connected with each of the girls. I know where he lives and that he turned down a substitute teaching job at the Hillcrest school today." His voice was soothing; it wrapped her in its assured sweet tones. "I'm going to call our man."

He reached for the phone and pushed the numbers, fingers hitting the mark straight on. "I'm looking for Dexter Williams."

There was a pause. Matt mumbled something.

"When did he say he'd be back?" Now, he sounded patient, curious; only someone who knew him very well could read in those sharp, precise sounds that he was burning inside. The muscles along his jaw bulged. "Already tried that. Listen, maybe you can think of someone who might know where Dexter is? A friend or someone he knows from school?"

Matt scribbled on the pad and then hung up; his face was dazzling, manic, and he couldn't sit still. "I'm going to find him, Linda. It was a rooming house—lucky I got anyone at all. His landlady said he has a friend who drives him to work a lot. Albert Toller. Maybe Mr. Toller can tell us where Dexter Williams is."

Matt said the name aloud as he ran his finger down the

page of the Oakland telephone directory. "Edna Tokenami. B. Tolland. Albert Toller." He waved his hand in the general direction of Linda's chair and pointed to the address and phone number. "Write this down, Linnie. We're going to see if this friend of our Mr. Williams can tell us something about him."

As she watched him run his finger over Toller's name, questions that she thought already answered crowded in on her again.

Maybe Matt really had been screwing a college girl to shore up his sagging ego the afternoon that Amy was murdered—and maybe the story was a lie. He had been alone, without an alibi, when Marianne Brandon was murdered, and when Cindy Forrest disappeared.

Either her husband was a monster or he had slipped over some critical line, driven by demons he could only exorcise at someone else's expense.

She clung to the lesser anguish: Matt had slipped over the line. Grace under pressure? Not exactly Matt's response this time. It was up to her to supply that.

Daddy, Daddy. Look! The caterpillar is waking up.

—It's going to take a long time, Amy. This is very hard work for that caterpillar.

Will you stay and watch with me, Daddy? It's a little scary.

(Matt grinning into Amy's hair. Amy's earnest face staring at the chrysalis in the jar.)

My husband is no murderer, Linda thought. But he is in danger.

"Wait a minute, Linda." Matt sidled along the wall to the doorway; he snapped off the light and, back pressed against the wall, sidestepped toward the window.

She craned her neck but she was too far away to see anything.

"I'll bet it's the police. They must've put surveillance on me." He peered out the window, flattening himself against the wall.

This was more unsettling, if possible, than his mad determination. "If it is the police, then they'll be watching you all the time. They'll follow you wherever you go."

"I can lose one guy if I need to, but I don't know where I'm going until I talk to this friend of our Mr. Williams."

Matt moved to the telephone and dialed, tapping his foot impatiently. "Mr. Toller? Sorry to bother you. I—" Matt hesitated "—McCafferty. Andrew McCafferty from the Oakland *Tribune*. I'm doing a story on teaching conditions in the Oakland schools."

Another lie sliding so easily from his tongue, another role he was so quick to assume.

Maybe his obsession with finding the killer was the biggest lie of all. How better to cast suspicion away from himself than to convince other people—even her—that he was looking for the killer?

No, she must not let herself think that way. It was disloyal. It was paranoid.

He turned away from her when he noticed that she was staring at him. Now all she saw was his back, shoulders hunched toward the phone.

"No, no. I know you don't teach, but I've been told that you know Dexter Williams. Do you know how I can get in touch with him?"

He shifted his weight from one foot to the other; his head bobbed, and the rise and fall of his shoulders was more exaggerated, as though he were having difficulty catching his breath. "McCafferty, sir." Matt moved toward the open door, dragging the phone cord behind him. Finally, he said, "Why not, Mr. Toller?"

He watched her face, his eyes glittering. "I do understand,

Mr. Toller. I do." He hung up. "Dexter Williams got on a plane at noon today for Providence, Rhode Island. Toller says Williams got a ticket in the mail from a sister. He's going off for Thanksgiving dinner with his family. Seven this morning. Eight hours, Linda. I'm off by eight hours." His jaw tightened. "What am I going to do, Linda? How am I going to find him?"

Linda stroked the side of his face. "Ssh. It's better this way," she said softly. "You're not meant to find him, that's all."

PART SEVEN

Thursday

thirty-one

Cold platinum light fell across the foot of the bed; somewhere among the trees and shrubs of Anton's backyard, a bird trilled a tentative song, then loosed an energetic arpeggio and repeated it over and over. Matt's restlessness kept her awake; when he finally stopped twisting and thrashing, he had begun to mumble, strange, throaty noises that must have been the soundtrack of a disturbing dream.

He rolled over; their eyes met and they both silently admitted that they weren't asleep. "Fifty-seven listings in Providence. I woke up every damn one of them. All I could think was that he'd be staying with someone named Williams. I never even considered that his sister might be married or that he might be with his mother's people. Different name."

Her fingers, laced tightly beneath her head, had gone numb. *The crack in the ceiling seems to have spread since yesterday,* she thought. *The birds are so noisy on this Thanksgiving morning. It must have stopped raining.*

"I'm going to call Toller. I should have thought of it yesterday. Maybe he'll be able to tell me now."

As Matt tossed back the covers and sprang from the warm cocoon in which they'd been wrapped, chill air crept into the bed beside Linda. Longing to touch him, she watched the ripple of his back muscles as he put his arms through the sleeves of his bathrobe. He could make it a real Thanksgiving by saying that he was quitting this insane search for Dexter Williams. Surely he saw that, at least for the holiday weekend, the odds of finding Williams were against him.

Thanksgiving or not, she would call the police. Matt would say she had let him down; she would learn to live with that. She would harden herself against his accusations and against his hurt and confusion. It was the best she could do now.

Some things were more important than Matt's need for her loyalty—Cindy Forrest's life; *Matt's* safety.

Something terrible is going to happen unless I can convince him to stop.

"Matt, you're scaring me. What you're doing—it can only lead to more trouble." Fleetingly, she wondered what he would do if she wandered off into the old craziness again, but she couldn't pretend—it had been too horrible and it was too close, still, to be anything but agony. "Please don't do this. Let the police find him. Please."

"They didn't find him last time. Why do you think they'll do any better now? I don't trust them one bit. But I have this feeling, Linda. Me—I'm going to do it and I couldn't live with myself if I gave up now. She was our daughter, Linnie."

As she stared at the cat, a round ball of fur on the frayed border of the patterned rug beside the bed, the first prick of a new sadness touched Linda's heart. Their lives would never be the same. The best they could hope for now was damage control.

Really, what options did he have?

He could try again to tell his theory to the police and hope that he'd get a sympathetic hearing now that the climate had changed and Roberta Herron's ambitious hype was seen for what it was: a career move.

He could ask Mia to do the talking for him and hope that her credibility would make his hypothesis more palatable to the authorities.

He could write an anonymous letter to a sympathetic reporter.

The longer she lay there, the more possibilities flooded into her brain. What was it that kept Matt from seeing them too? It didn't matter. She was going to step out of the circle he had drawn around them; if she was very lucky, he would follow, but she didn't expect good fortune to be on her side.

She reached for her own bathrobe, pulled the belt tight around her waist.

"I'm going now, Linda." Dressed in his gray corduroy pants and a black sweatshirt, Matt knelt to tie the laces of his running shoes. "I got no answer at Toller's apartment so I called the company where he works. Took me a while to remember the name, but it came back to me. Bay Security. Fellow at the switchboard said Toller's the watchman at some construction site over on Skyline Boulevard. He gave me the number and I called, but there was no answer. He's probably making his rounds. I can't stand waiting, Linda. I'm going to go out there and see if he can help me figure out how to get in touch with Williams. See you later, okay?"

"Not okay, Matt." Linda tightened her grip on the bedpost. "I'm going to call the police and tell them what you found out. If I don't do that, we might be endangering that little girl's life. Can you live with that? I can't."

Frowning, Matt straightened to a standing position. "Why would you call the police, Linda? Please don't do that. They'll only ignore you, or worse, drag me in again and keep me from doing what I have to. Don't do that."

It was as though he had been taken over by a stranger. The face resembled Matt's, but small discrepancies around the mouth and jaw made all the difference. The voice sounded a little like Matt's, but it lacked warmth. The eyes might have been Matt's, but they shone with a hard glitter she didn't recognize.

Maybe she could say things to this other person that she might not have the courage to say to Matt. "I'm sorry, but for the sake of the little—" The words stuck in her throat.

He reached into the pocket of his pants and pulled out a gun. It dangled at his side like a rigid extension of his limp hand.

"Matt!"

She was going to die. If she died now, the last thing in her mind would be the true and terrible knowledge that it had all been a lie. Did he have her pillbox in his pocket? Was he going to leave it someplace?

"Linda, I'm not going to hurt you." Shadows filled his eyes. "I just want you to see that I must make it right. I'm going to talk to Toller and find out as much as I can about Williams. This is the only way, darling, don't you see?"

Linda shook her head, refusing so adamantly to accept his words that the world blurred out of focus.

As Matt approached her, he slipped the gun back into his pocket. With the same hand, he reached out for her, and when she backed away he turned and ran to the door, nearly crashing into Anton, who stood in the doorway.

"Christ, man, this time you've gone over the line. You can't go on with this. Leave it to the authorities. You find the person responsible, then what? And if the police pick you up?" His round face puckered with concern.

"The police aren't going to pick me up. I'm just an honest, hard-working citizen, ordinary guy, out for a ride." Matt shrugged elaborately. "Who knows? Really, who knows what they'll do until the time comes? How many juries do you think would be hard on the father of a murdered child who saw to it that justice was done? At the most, I'd spend four, five years in jail. Then we'd start over. It's worth it to me."

Start over? We'd have nothing to build on except our pain, Linda thought.

"I have to do this. I owe it to Amy. That's all there is to it."
He pushed past Anton.

Linda ran to the window, already feeling a rush of relief.
The police would stop him. One of the men who had been
sitting in the black car and looking up into her window at night
would follow Matt; they'd keep him from harming himself or
anyone else.

The way Matt slid into the front seat of the Honda—
shoulders high, face pinched, his eyes flitting madly from object
to object—anyone could tell something was wrong. Linda
scanned the street. Where was the damn surveillance car?
Surely the Oakland police were still maintaining a watch.

As Matt drove away, she pressed against the bedroom window, straining to peer around the corner. Nothing stirred on
the street.

"Dear God," Anton whispered. His heavy steps echoed
down the hall.

She pulled on slacks and a green sweater, wool socks. She
reached into the closet and grabbed her running shoes, jammed
her left foot inside the left shoe.

The pillbox—it was in her sneaker. Not in Matt's pocket or
beside another innocent child. She shook it out and held it in
her hand; the sparkly little elephant on the lid seemed to wink
and smile at her, but she had no time for him or for the million
questions that cried for answers. She tied her shoes and flew
down the stairs and out the door, nearly tripping over the cat.
Linda stepped into the misty morning and looked up and down
the street for a sign of that damned black car. All she saw was
Hank as he scampered between two hedges.

Seven o'clock on Thanksgiving morning. Mia would understand. Linda ran to the hall, dialed with trembling fingers.

"Yes?" The lawyer sounded as though she'd been up for
hours.

"It's Linda. Matt thinks he knows who killed Amy. He's got a gun, Mia. Help me, please."

The gasp from the other end wasn't what Linda expected. "Okay, wait, hang on and let me get a pencil." Something crashed to the floor and Mia cursed. Papers rustled. "All right, now what's the name of this person Matt's after?"

"Dexter Williams. He's a substitute teacher. Taught all three girls before they were . . . before he . . . Listen, the important thing is you've got to stop Matt."

"Where does Williams live?"

"He's not there, Mia. He went to Rhode Island—Providence—to visit relatives for the holiday, but Matt doesn't know exactly where. He's gone to talk to someone who knows Williams, a friend who he thinks can tell him where Williams is."

"Who, Linda? Where's the friend?"

"I don't know. Wait—his name is Toller. He works for some security company—watchman at a construction site or something. Albert Toller. Matt said something about Skyline Boulevard. That's all I know. What can we do?"

"I'm not sure." In the long silence, Linda could almost see Mia pondering the situation, discarding the useless choices and settling on the most effective and practical solution. "The thing to do is call OPD and lay a tip on them about this Williams person. No, I'll tell them I got a call. Anonymous. Give them everything—the teaching, that he's visiting relatives. Even if they suspect Matt's involved, they won't be able to prove it. I'll convince my friend Quinn that they have to do a real heavy-duty search for the guy. That accomplishes two things." Mia was breathing fast and her words tumbled out. "Gets Williams off the streets and keeps Matt from jumping hip-deep into trouble. I'll call my friend Josiah in San Francisco and see if he can find Matt and persuade him—physically, if necessary—to go home. What's he driving?"

"The Honda. White Civic. License XGP341. He's so close to the edge. I'm afraid."

"Don't worry. Josiah'll take care of him. You sit tight. I've got to get off now and make those calls." Mia hung up.

What if this Josiah, whoever he is, surprised Matt and Matt's reaction was to pull the gun on him? And what if this Josiah, in response to that . . .

While Mia was setting her machinery in motion Linda couldn't simply hang in, sit tight, hold on—all those words that indicated using sheer willpower to keep together what wanted to fly apart.

She had to get out of here. Her purse, her car keys—she needed them. She raced to the kitchen. Her purse was on the table, but her car keys weren't in it.

"Anton." She shouted his name from the bottom of the stairs, counted to ten and shouted again. "Anton, I'm going to borrow your car for a while." She grabbed his keys from the peg and ran to his Thunderbird, started it up, and drove off.

The streets were still wet but a pale Thanksgiving sun was beginning to poke through the clouds. A pickup truck swerved to avoid her, and the driver stuck his head out the window and let loose a string of Spanish curses. She slowed and pulled back to the curb.

She had to find that construction site. An umbrella bounced down the middle of the street; a woman chased after it.

I can't lose you, too, Matt.

The burning in her gut had lasted for weeks, the tearing and ripping, everything colored red and black. When she'd tried to sleep, the colors had grown more and more intense. At first she thought that she was dying and she'd been glad. But it had been her body's recognition of the pain that Amy had suffered, Linda's way of being closer to her child, and she had borne it gladly until it went away.

She couldn't go through that again. How long had she been sitting here with the motor running? It didn't matter. She was calmer now, and she looked over her shoulder before she backed up, then turned the wheel and pulled out onto the street again.

She drove east; in about a mile, Broadway Terrace would become Skyline and veer off to the south. *Save Matt,* she thought with determination. *You couldn't save Amy but you can save Matt.* She drove on.

She deserved to find him. She had been so good. She had survived the long ordeal; faced with this new crisis, she was sure she had earned the right to find him. Adrenaline made her heart thrum; her head was light and she felt like she was floating.

Concentrate—she had to concentrate and get the job done.

She wouldn't fall apart. She couldn't allow that to happen; it was clear from his behavior that Matt needed to be saved from himself. And she wanted desperately to do it.

He was all she had left.

Except for herself.

That was true, wasn't it? Somehow, in the midst of all this chasing and hiding and running to and from things, she had discovered herself again. And it felt strong and good.

thirty-two

Cruz untangled his feet from the covers and stretched out, reaching for Elenya as he always did and feeling nothing but cold sheets, as he had since Saturday. Through his half-open eyes, he realized that light was just beginning to show outside. The rain had stopped. He was glad for the people who had to drive to family dinners, for the women worried about guests tracking mud across their newly polished floors.

Drifting, drifting, he thought about all the chances he'd missed this week: searching the tide pool for abalone shells and starfish with Julio; building a plastic riverboat model from start to finish with Carlito while they talked about life; sitting wordlessly beside Elenya in front of the fire. Those moments were lost forever. Dinner this afternoon was likely to be stiff and awkward unless he could put aside his resentments and his preoccupations with the case.

What would Cindy Forrest's parents do? Would they pretend that everything was fine and make all the holiday preparations in the awful hope their daughter would come home today? Did they do that every day, to keep their hope alive? Or would they sit in silence, already grieving for their child?

He couldn't let himself think about it. It would stop him cold.

Someone who had been inside the volunteer center was

responsible for bringing that little barrette inside. Whether it was intentional or accidental didn't really matter.

And Dexter Williams . . . Did that CAST pin found near Marianne Brandon's body belong to him? Williams wasn't home and no one they'd spoken to had any idea where he was.

A substitute teacher.

How could they have missed that?

The holiday was making things sticky; yesterday, even Charlotte Wertz had acted the bitch, making noises like this was her turf and why should she give them a complete list of volunteers if they weren't going to tell her how they planned to use the information. As soon as Goldstein reminded her that a child's life was the real issue here, she'd blushed and gotten started on it. How strange, Cruz had thought then, for their work to be concerned with people who were—who *might be*— alive. Strange, but wonderful for a change. Hopeful.

By the time Charlotte gave them her list, she was really into it, writing down stuff about the mailman, delivery people, one of Mrs. Silcock's grandchildren who came to pick her up.

He and Goldstein and the rest of the Homicide division had split the list. By eleven o'clock last night, they'd worked their way through to the end of the Rs.

Today they'd start with S. Schwartau, Sendyck, Swann. Then on to T. Tennyson. Tintorini. Toller.

Cruz sat up, clutching the blanket to his bare chest. It was silly, only a small chance that it meant anything. But yesterday, hadn't Harvey Kittner complained that he had to shell out money for *protection* for the cottage?

That meant he'd hired a security company to watch the place. Albert Toller worked for a security company.

Why did it have to be Williams?

He had to keep an open mind. This could be the connection, the fragile link, the kind that he'd always known would be the way this case was broken.

Toller.

He'd been so eager, right from the start, to help. Installing telephones, running off copies of new forms, briefing other volunteers on how to get information. And the man and the little girl in the convertible. The hours spent on the sketch.

Fixing things.

Helping.

Making everything come out okay, just as Goldstein's shrink friend had said.

Too many missing pieces, though. Why *these* little girls? Was it just luck that they were all in second grade? They were in different schools and Dexter Williams was—

Slow down. It was important to do this right; he couldn't blow it just because he wanted to eat a dumb turkey dinner with his family. He couldn't afford, for the sake of the little girl, for the sake of living with himself for the rest of his life, to screw up. He'd call Kittner first and find out the name of the security company keeping tabs on the cottage.

The telephone number was still on the crumpled paper in his jacket pocket. His stomach churned as he dialed the numbers.

Harvey Kittner growled when he answered the phone. "Yeah?"

"Kittner, this is Cruz from the Oakland Police."

"It's fucking seven oh five in the morning. It's fucking Thanksgiving, for Chrissake. What's the matter with you? Call back Monday, Cruz." He slammed the phone. A dial tone buzzed.

Cruz dialed again. *Answer the phone, man.* It rang twelve, thirteen times. I'll just sit on it, Cruz thought angrily. He'll have to pick up. Unless he's unplugged it and gone back to sleep. LAPD wouldn't like it but they'd help, he was sure. He was just about to break the connection when Kittner answered the phone.

"Will you fucking stop harassing me on fucking Thanksgiving morning?"

"A child's life is at stake," Cruz insisted. "I want to know what security company patrols the cottage."

"Bay Security. You woke me at seven in the fucking morning to ask me about a fucking—"

This time it was Cruz who hung up. This was it. He was going to do it. The air grew brighter. *Thank you,* he thought, *for letting me be a part of this.*

He dialed Goldstein's San Francisco apartment and was surprised at how neat the whole thing sounded and how quickly he was able to lay out the key points to his partner.

"First thing," Goldstein said, his voice not at all sleepy, "is I'll call Bay Security and find out Toller's work schedule. He may even be on the job right now. Then I'll call you right back. If he's working, we'll go there. If he's not, I'll meet you at his apartment."

Cruz hurried into the bathroom and splashed cold water on his face, then rushed back to the bedroom and grabbed the clothes that he'd tossed on the chair last night. He was tucking his shirt into his pants when the phone rang.

"The Tri-Valley construction site, over on Skyline, half a mile past Broadway Terrace. Toller had midnight to eight. He called in about forty minutes ago like he was supposed to. The dispatcher said that someone else called asking about Toller. Fifteen minutes ago. What do you think?"

"I think we better get going."

"Meet you there in twenty minutes."

They hung up.

Before he could get to the construction site, Goldstein had to go from the Marina District through North Beach so that he could cross the Bay Bridge to Oakland. No regular traffic today, so he might make it in twenty minutes. But Carlos Cruz lived twelve minutes from Skyline Boulevard.

He scribbled a note to Elenya, in case he was delayed, and headed out into the brilliant November morning.

thirty-three

Three half-finished two-story buildings formed a broken U around a huge mound of dirt and debris. No doors, no windows, not even any sidewalks yet—work must have been halted by the rains. Along the heavily rutted road that ran in a choppy circle around the three buildings, massive earth-moving equipment stood, silent and mud-spattered.

Linda pointed the car past bright yellow bulldozers and backhoes and came to a skidding stop in front of a small trailer perched in the mud at the base of the U. Matt's Honda was parked next to an unfamiliar blue Ford, just to the left of the trailer.

Thank God—she had found him before he could do anything about Dexter Williams. She would tell him that Mia was taking care of everything; he would be angry but he'd get over it.

Or maybe he'd never forgive her for taking away his chance at revenge. She didn't want that to happen, but if it came to that, she would go it alone.

Now that she knew that Matt was here, she could go a little slower. After all, Dexter Williams was in Rhode Island. Matt would certainly be calmer now . . . and Mia's friend was bound to arrive soon.

Her sneakers sank into the slippery mud as she got out of the car; she picked her way to the trailer, stopping to scrape mud from her shoes.

The watchman Matt wanted to see probably spent some of his shift in the trailer. Maybe they were inside, talking.

Linda squished her way across the moat of mud to the trailer door, then paused. If people were inside, they weren't making any noise. She knocked on the door. No answer. On tiptoes, she looked into the front windows. Yellow light leaked around the edges of the venetian blinds.

She pushed at the door. A musty smell—wet paper and dust and hot coils from an electric heater—blew toward her. Empty. The trailer was empty. On a battered desk, a thermos, lid unscrewed and stopper removed, sat atop an open newspaper. The coffee in the red plastic cup was still warm. Another desk was piled high with papers, an old-fashioned adding machine, a telephone.

Matt and Toller must be in one of the buildings.

The building on the right and the one that formed the base of the U appeared to be rough-finished. The third building, on the left, was only a concrete foundation and skeletal uprights— no walls, no doors, no roof. No one there.

She skirted a large puddle and picked her way around piles of lumber covered with plastic, stacks of girders, two large dumpsters filled with trash until she reached the wooden walkway in front of the middle building.

Better to be out of the mud. Easier now, to hurry to each doorway. But the doors and windows were all covered with thick, opaque plastic sheeting, and she couldn't see inside.

At the bottom of the third doorway of the middle building, the plastic covering was torn. Linda knelt and pulled at the slit with both hands until she could stick her head inside. Support struts marched the entire length of the building. Otherwise, it was empty.

That left the building that formed the right side of the U. Unless Matt and Albert Toller had gone off somewhere, out among the massive machinery. No, Matt had to be in that building.

The sky glistened, a sharp, bright blue. A cloud of steam rose from the planks in front of her as the sun evaporated the water that had soaked into the boards. A little like walking into hell, she thought, except that here the resinous mist was fragrant.

She glanced again at the trailer. A gust kicked up, tossing papers about. The trailer door caught on the wind and slammed shut with a sharp crack. Linda sucked in a breath, then cantered toward the last building.

More plastic, stapled over the first doorway. The middle door was unprotected, set a foot and a half above the plank. No steps yet—Linda grabbed the door frame and hoisted herself up.

Voices.

Two men, one in shadow, sixty feet away.

He's here, she thought. I've found him—it's not too late. She could make out the unmistakable breadth of Matt's shoulders and even the two points where his hair was receding at his temples. One hand gestured at something she couldn't see.

A latticework of beams crisscrossed a three-foot-deep pit. If only the subflooring had been laid . . . She stepped onto a beam, placed one foot precisely in front of the other. The black hole below seemed to reach up for her. She stopped, wiped the cold sweat from her palms. *You've been at construction sites before. You know how to walk on beams.*

She found her balance, saw that if she zigzagged between uprights, she'd have to take only two unsupported steps in between.

One, two, then grab the upright. She repeated the pattern, forcing herself to look straight ahead and not down into the hole.

"I'm calling the shots, Toller." Matt spat out the words.

Everything swayed, tilted.

Matt's voice rang through the empty structure again. "I've got the girl," he said.

Linda teetered on the board, dizzy and disoriented. The hole below was dark, inviting her to relinquish everything to the pull of gravity. Give up. Let go. Stop trying to balance the impossible . . . Just in time, she grabbed the joist.

I've got the girl.

She lowered herself and crawled to the next upright, leaned back. A coppery taste coated her tongue. She pushed up from her hands and knees, looked down the length of the building.

Matt waved his arm wildly. The other man—tall, thin, dressed in blue—stood on a piece of plywood, facing Matt. Behind him, the open doorway gaped, its plastic covering torn and hanging down like flayed, split skin.

Matt edged along a beam toward the rear wall. With his left hand, he guided a child who until now had been hidden from Linda's sight. She was blond, her long hair matted and tangled; it was difficult to tell what color her clothes were, covered as they now were with mud.

—Amy, Amy, where did you get those beautiful purple eyes?

Oh, Daddy, you're so silly. My eyes aren't purple. Come close, Daddy. Look.

—Purple. Absolutely purple.

Well, then yours are orange.

(Followed by fits of uncontrollable giggling. Hugs. Tosses in the air.)

"You should have left things alone, Crell. Whatever happens, you're responsible." Toller's voice was steady, deliberate. This was a trick. Toller had to be wrong. Appearances could be deceiving. Matt *couldn't* be responsible. He had made mistakes, sure. But the same person who was so tender a lover to her and so gentle a father to Amy wouldn't kill anyone.

Linda turned, a half-step at a time, retraced her steps to the doorway. She jumped back down to the wooden walk. A weapon—she needed something to use against the child's captor. Piles of rocks. Sharp long sticks. Iron beams and wooden boards. Bags of nails. How would these help?

"You gonna let go of her or what?" Again, the same quiet voice.

She grabbed a handful of rocks from the pile, the jagged points biting into her palms as she made her way to the third door, stopping every couple of steps to listen.

Matt's voice rang loud through the doorway. "Toller, just give me the satisfaction. What's in it for you?"

She inched her way along the outer wall. Her fist tightened around the rocks; the pain kept her moving forward.

"You ever have a dream, Crell?"

A dream of family. Linda clutched the rocks tighter.

"Starting when I was three, four years old, for as long as I can remember, all I wanted was to be a cop. Sergeant Toller. *Lieutenant* Toller. I'd get rid of the creeps and parasites, one by one, and my small part of the world would be a little safer. But they wouldn't take me because of my goddam hearing. One side —I'm deaf in one ear and no police force would have me. You know how bad that feels? Why am I telling you this? You've got twenty seconds to let the girl go."

Toller. Not Dexter Williams. Not Matt. It was Toller who had done these terrible things.

"It should have happened differently. I was just going to hide the first one, then help them find her. She made so much noise I had to—"

You sick bastard, that was my daughter, Linda thought as she bit her lip to keep from screaming. She licked at the warm blood and formed a very clear mental image of Cindy Forrest.

"—and they didn't have a clue after the mother was acquitted. It was pretty discouraging, but then I got this job."

The mother: Linda choked back her rage. *The mother* was about to help Toller skewer himself. She set the handful of rocks on the ground. Sharp flecks of grit stuck to the fleshy mound below her thumb.

"—no action. At least I got to wear a uniform. But after a while I realized how goddam boring this job really is. Safe and boring."

She had to get the girl out of there. And she had to do it quickly, with whatever was available. A little knowledge, dangerous or not, was all she had to work with.

Toller wanted to be a policeman all his life.

He was hard of hearing. On which side? Was he wearing a hearing aid?

His back to her, Toller loomed, a dark shape in the doorway. Beyond him, the little girl and Matt stood, clutching each other; they saw her at the same time.

Matt covered his surprise quickly. His eyes darted to Toller and then away. The little girl opened her mouth; Matt's grip tightened on her arm and he bent and whispered to her.

No eyeglasses. Toller probably wasn't wearing a hearing aid. Every time Matt said something, Toller tilted his head, offering his right ear to the sound. His bad ear must be on the left side.

She tossed a single stone to the ground, to the left of where Toller stood.

He didn't look around. Maybe she couldn't overpower him but she'd make sure he was caught in a trap of his own making.

"Keep your hands away from your pockets, Crell. I know you've got a gun."

Matt offered a palms-up apology and Toller's fingers twitched. Linda moved toward the doorway, a glimmer of a plan forming.

"You really messed things up, Crell. After I got the insulin and everything, too. This would have been a good one. A call to the volunteer center on Thanksgiving morning from a psychic who tells the cops where to find the kid. Beautiful, right? Rain and all, the construction crew wasn't here so she was safe in the toolshed. Of course, I had to keep her blindfolded the whole time. You screwed it up for her, Crell."

Linda choked on the sour taste that rose in her throat. If only she could tear at his eyes and rip him apart, rend his muscles and snap his bones. But Cindy was more important than personal satisfaction.

Circling behind Toller's back, Linda came around the open doorway. "Don't look at me," she whispered to Matt. "When I say 'Amy,' you give me the girl and then go for Toller."

Matt's nod was so slight that Toller didn't miss a beat.

"It was perfect. Every time I drove Dexter to work, I asked him what he was teaching. I decided on this pattern, see. He teaches about the rain, next day something happens."

Linda circled behind Toller again; she had to come up from his good side so that he would hear her coming.

"I even dropped his pin, that teacher's club thing, next to the second one. You'd think somebody, some cop or a reporter, would see the pattern," Toller continued, "but I never guessed it'd be you. Dexter was so scared of being fired that he never said anything about the kids being in his classes. He was sick, you know? Somebody had to protect those kids from him. He threatened them, pointed scissors in their faces. He needed to be punished for what he did."

And you were the self-appointed minister of justice, Linda thought. She would use it all—every shred he had revealed. His needs, his weaknesses would become her weapons.

"He gets nailed, I get to lead the cops to this object of their big manhunt. That's something the world would notice. But you had to go fuck it up, Crell."

There it was, the final piece she'd use to nail him to his self-made pillory. He'd get the attention he'd been seeking, all right.

"What about my wife's cameo?" Matt's face was pale.

Let my notebook and a pencil be in my purse, Linda prayed as the details of her plan grew clearer in her mind. She rummaged in the bottom of her purse. There—a pencil. And the pad. It was small, but if she held it just right, he might not notice.

"After I saw that the first one didn't work the way I thought it would, I figured I needed insurance. If they didn't pick up on Dexter the next time, then maybe I'd set them looking for *her.* The mother. After they let her go, I walked into your bedroom and took it. Just about two years ago. You learned yet not to leave downstairs windows unlocked when no one's home? You never know who's gonna pay you a visit. Stupid kids —they ruined her prints handling the damn thing too much."

How could she have thought that Matt . . . Later. She'd ask all those questions later. The girl began to whimper. Toller rambled on. "You were the only one, Crell, the only person to catch on to the Dexter Williams connection. I have to give you credit. I was real careful setting that up."

Would he recognize her? Maybe he had stared for so long at her pictures in the newspaper, before and during her trial, annoyed that she had gotten so much of the attention that should have been rightfully his, that even without her hair he would know her.

"Cops never did figure out that I'd driven him home from school the day before each of the, um, incidents. He led all his last period classes outside at dismissal time. Always did that, and I always had a chance to see them, to pick out the prettiest little things. . . . Maybe I should have figured out a way to get Dexter's fingerprints on the barrette. Whaddaya think, Crell?"

Now. Linda squared her shoulders. Half-jogging, panting as though she'd been running, Linda approached the doorway. "Tracy Smith," she gasped. "Oakland *Tribune.*" *Keep talking. Don't get spooked by his eyes, by the hands that were the last things to touch Amy.* She pulled herself up into the doorway, stepped away from Toller. "Congratulations. You found Crell and the girl. How did you do it?" She held the pencil above the pad in her hand. Tilted her face and looked at him with enthusiasm. Opened her eyes wide with wonder. Like all the reporters who had hounded her, hungry for the details of a tragedy.

Toller's face paled with shock, but after half a heartbeat he seemed to get taller, straighter. The set of his mouth grew more determined and he hooked his thumbs into his belt loops. The fingers of his right hand dangled above the butt of his holstered gun. "What are you doing here? This man is dangerous, Miss Smith." His gaze flickered between Matt and Linda.

"I'm not worried about him, Mr. . . . What did you say your name is?" *Keep him busy until Mia's friend arrives. That's all you have to do.* Linda let his face blur as she stared at him; looking into his eyes would be impossible.

"Albert Toller. That's T-o-l-l-e-r." He beamed, then drew the corners of his mouth down. "He's crafty, Miss Smith. He's got a gun. He hasn't used it yet but you never know with these desperate psychopaths."

"I, uh, I see you're wearing a uniform. Are you from an OPD special forces group, Mr. Toller?" Linda pretended to scribble on the pad. She stole a glance at the parking area. No approaching cars, no police cruisers. "You have previous experiences with hostage situations?" How much longer would she have to look at this man, think of how his face twisted when he

. . . Her legs buckled; she swayed and caught herself on an upright beam.

"Don't be frightened, Miss Smith. I've got the situation under control. How did *you* find him?" Toller pursed his lips, his eyes squinting like a man who didn't trust what he saw.

Linda looked at Matt for one last boost of courage. "I recognized his picture from the paper. Spotted him in his car and followed him here."

Toller might decide to kill them all; he would claim self-defense and be the hero. *KEEP TALKING.*

"So, Mr. Toller, I'll need some background on you. I'm going to write your story—" The little girl was shaking now, a noiseless terror issuing from her half-open mouth. She was so thin, so exposed. Linda moved closer. "—and everyone in the Bay Area is going to read it, so I want to get the facts right."

His brows knitted; he canted his head toward her. She stepped onto the plywood, so close she could hear the child's ragged breath. Pay attention to *him,* she reminded herself.

"Tell me how you found them, Mr. Toller." She took another step. Toller's eyes narrowed as she moved closer. She stopped, looked at him, held the pencil poised above the notepad in her hand. "Mr. Toller?"

His chest expanded and he glared at Matt. "I've been with Bay Security for six years. It's a very responsible position, you know, and today, as I was making my rounds . . ." He frowned and stared at her. A muscle below his right eye twitched.

He was on to her. Linda felt as though her heart would burst through her chest.

"Go on, Mr. Toller. I need all the details, so that I can tell your story to—"

"You got your press ID, Miss Smith?" Toller's fingers slid to the handle of his gun.

It was time to improvise.

"Now, Matt!" Linda shouted.

Matt pushed the little girl toward Linda and then whirled toward Toller. "Run, Linda! Get her out of here!"

Moving without thinking, Linda grabbed up the child and jumped down to the wooden walk. Burning pain shot through her leg as her ankle hit the edge of the plank.

thirty-four

Cruz careened through the streets, red light flashing on the top of his Toyota. Could he have known? There must have been something about Toller, some signal to look more closely.

When Cruz met him, Toller was already wearing a label: Concerned Citizen. Maybe that was the first mistake—lumping all the people in the volunteer center into the same category. Mistakes like that got people killed.

Toller practically strutted when he was wearing his uniform; he'd described his job with the same intensity that he brought to his tasks at the center. What was pathological about that? Enthusiasm didn't equal probable cause.

And when he came down to headquarters and worked so hard with Shirley Johnson on the composite drawing, so awed by everything—should that have been a sign?

Cruz shot past a slow-moving station wagon, angry that he was getting hung up in theories. He had to take Toller without endangering the child. If the child was still alive. If the child was with Toller. If Toller was at the construction site.

If.

If.

It wasn't his job to figure out *why*. Goldstein's friend, the shrink, would do that better. Lois Edelberg had gotten part of it right.

It was his responsibility to figure out how.

Cruz spotted the Tri-Valley sign and turned in at the open gate, his rear fishtailing for a hundred feet. Ahead, he spotted the parking area, full of cars. The white Honda from Pescadero. A Thunderbird. A Ford. What the hell were all these vehicles doing here?

Maybe it *was* Linda Crell who had killed the children. Or the husband—he had no alibi for the time of Cindy's disappearance, no verification of where he was when Marianne was killed. *Shit,* Cruz thought angrily, *no more fucking theories. Just find the kid.*

He stepped hard on the brakes and almost slid into the Honda. A gust of wind pulled at the trailer door; it banged shut, then flew open again. No one inside—they had to be nearby.

The kid—I have to protect the kid, Cruz thought, his eyes blinking back cold sweat. Where was Goldstein? Two of them, ten of them even, could do this better. He called in his location on the radio, then stepped out of the car. He drew his gun and approached the nearest building.

Let her be unharmed, he prayed. *Let me not blow a hole through this guy's face, right in his eyes or his mouth and watch his brains splatter out of the back of his head. Let me not grind my heel in his stomach or smash his balls with the tip of my shoe. And please, God, keep Julio and Carlito from ever knowing what I'm thinking right now.*

He stopped every ten feet, listening, checking for movement. A piece of brown paper fluttered along a wooden walkway, rolling lazily into the mud. Cruz continued toward the middle building.

A woman was crouched below the open doorway of the building to his right. She was cradling something large and round in her arms.

Madre de Dios, it was the child.

He ran toward her, trying not to make noise. Cruz heard voices, shouts, saw the woman stand up with the child in her arms. He ran as fast as he could, slipping once on the slimy edge of a puddle. *Fucking mud.* He stopped, frozen as voices burst from the open doorway at the far end of the building.

"You killed my daughter, Toller. And Marianne Brandon. But you're not going to do it again."

Matthew Crell. The voice he and Goldstein had heard in the interrogation room.

"I made sure they didn't suffer, Crell. I'll do the same for you."

Toller.

He had been right: the Crells were innocent. Albert Toller was his man.

God help him if he was wrong.

thirty-five

Her hair smelled sour.

It was tangled, matted with burrs and pieces of straw. Her body smelled of urine, long dried. The child's face was expressionless; mud had formed a cracked skin on her face and neck. From her filthy hand hung a doll. Mud-stained, limp. A crude X slashed through its chest.

Linda pressed her cheek to the little girl's face. She had to get her cleaned up. They'd be coming to take her picture and she didn't want the child looking like this. They had to get someplace where she could give the child a warm bath, make her feel smooth and soft again. A little girl should have shiny hair; it would take lots of shampoo, and maybe she'd even have to have it cut. And after the bath and the haircut, she would put on the little plaid skirt and the matching sweater. Just right for Thanksgiving.

The child in her arms began to sob.

The sobs turned into choking, then became a keening wail. Linda shuddered, held on to the child's shaking body, stroked the dirty cheek. She tried to stand, tested her ankle, winced at the pain.

It was hard to judge distances in the open spaces of the construction site; the car seemed a universe away. She picked up the little girl, cradling her like a baby.

Linda hobbled toward the car. Midway between buildings,

she stopped, her breath short and her shoulders aching from the pull of the weight. She stumbled forward again, looking back over her shoulder and then down at the little girl. The child's fingers clung to her neck.

Angry shouts carried on the wind from the skeletal building behind her. Maybe she should go back there, do something to help Matt.

No, it was Cindy she had to help, Cindy she had to keep safe and alive.

She missed her step on the board, slipped on a muddy place, faltered. The child in her arms clung even more tightly. Linda went down with a thud. She landed on her bottom, the wind knocked out of her.

As she tried to push up again, she heard a third voice.

"Police! Toss your guns out the door! Both of you!"

Thanksgiving—now she did have things to be thankful for. Cindy, safe. Matt would be, too, in a second.

The past is behind me, she thought, *finally.*

She whirled around as a white BMW and a green Volkswagen squealed to a stop; a dark-haired woman jumped out of the Volkswagen and took off toward the building. The BMW driver followed, his long legs flying.

Linda ran faster.

The first noise stunned her. It sounded like a sharp clap of thunder or a huge branch snapping in two, louder than anything she'd ever heard.

When the second explosion came, she knew she was hearing gunshots. The third and the fourth followed quickly. The tall blond man sprinted toward the shots, his own gun extended. The woman had disappeared. The little girl's eyes, no longer blank, stared up at her in terror.

Linda raised her face to the sky. *Matt must survive.*

thirty-six

The mud was everywhere, slippery, greedy to suck him down into it. Jay Goldstein's first sweeping glance as he drove onto the construction site took in the cars, the trailer, the woman with the child in her arms. But no Toller. No Matthew Crell. And, goddam it, no Cruz.

Cavessena pulled up beside him and signaled that she was going around the side. He nodded his assent; it would all be over soon.

He was twenty feet from the right-hand building when the shots exploded.

The first came when he was two doors away. On solid ground instead of an ocean of mud, he would have been there before the second and third and fourth shots.

By the time he reached the doorway, smoke mingled with the silence that hung over the unfinished structure.

He pulled himself up to the doorway and stood with his back to the morning sun.

Sprawled on the plywood floor in his Bay Security jacket, gun in hand, Toller lay beside an upright beam, legs twitching. Blood spurted from between fingers that clutched at his neck. As Goldstein watched, the twitching stopped.

In a pose of bizarre intimacy, Matthew Crell lay with one leg dangling over Toller's. He grabbed his shoulder, mumbled, shivered. *Alive,* Goldstein thought. *He's still alive.*

Where the fuck was Cruz?

Goldstein hopscotched to the rear doorway.

Cruz lay sprawled on his back. A dark stain spread across the front of his shirt. Goldstein leaped down to the wet ground, skidding and sliding. He knelt in the cold mud and pressed his ear to Cruz's chest; the heartbeat was weak, his breath shallow.

Live, he commanded. *Live for Elenya, and for Julio and Carlito. Live so that you can complain about your feet hurting, live so that Cavessena can smile at you. Live,* he pleaded, *so we can fight about the next case.*

Goldstein folded his jacket and lifted his partner's head onto the soft, dry pillow.

"Tell her . . ." Cruz licked his lips; his voice faded.

He would need all his strength just to stay alive. Goldstein pushed back a shock of damp hair from Cruz's ashen face. "I'll see Elenya. I'll tell her—"

"Linda Crell—tell her Toller . . . shot . . . first." Cruz's chest rose and fell; his eyes closed and his mouth hung open.

Breathe, damn you. "She might not believe me, Cruz. I wasn't there. I'll have her give you a call tomorrow, the next day."

A trickle of saliva leaked out of the corner of Cruz's mouth. Goldstein dabbed at it with the corner of his shirt. *Don't give up.* "Okay, okay. I get it now. You just don't want to write this report. Okay, Cruz. I'll write it up." The low moan of a siren sounded in the distance.

A half-smile lifted Cruz's bloodless lips.

"I called for an ambulance." Cavessena knelt on the other side of Cruz. "The little girl's all right, Cruz. She could use a bath but she's fine." She leaned over and brushed his forehead with her lips. When she straightened, a slash of mud smeared her cheek. "You're a goddam hero, you know?" Her eyes were bright with tears.

"Just keep breathing, *amigo,* until the ambulance comes."

Goldstein held onto Cruz's fingers, watched the fluttering eyelids. "You got it mixed up, Cruz. I'm the one who needs an excuse to avoid Thanksgiving dinner, not you."

Cruz licked his lips. "Stuffing," he rasped. "Save me—" he smiled and coughed weakly "—some stuffing."